SO MUCH BULL

A PENNY POST MYTH AGENT NOVEL

ALEX A. KING

er than my flesh and snot

puberty roared into my life.
and slammed the gas pedal,
and into the cosmetics aisle
est friend Lena and I started
eup, and squeezing pimples,
ke put me on his ignore list.
ıp for whatever it was he was
harm, Lena decided.
e were friends and now he
e honest."
ıid like she knew. "Ten bucks

ıount of excitement coursed
them!"
o somebody sooner or later.

flaw in her twelve-year-old
Saint John the Baptist, the
on Easter Saturday, minutes
as in a foul mood because he
ısting on his new go-to outfit,
ıke won that battle, but only
ıo be late for the service. The
when she was sure she could
ıeel.)
me, as if the flouncy, childish
my arm into wearing burned

idiculous, I'd unbuttoned my
ır on my only bra that opened

This book is for all of you who return your shopping carts to the corral.

Remis was a better big

sibling, John.

Everything changed

Boobs and BO seized the

spinning me out of Toys '

at Dollar Tree. Overnight,

obsessing about things lik

and boys. At the same tin

Rumor had it girls were li

handing out. His penis and

"He hates me," I said

totally hates me. Is it the zi

"More like the tits," Le

says he wants to see them."

Panic and a disturbing

through me. "Well, he can't

"You have to show the

Why not Luke Remis?"

Because I couldn't fin

logic, I cornered Luke bel

local Greek Orthodox chu

before midnight. His mothe

had refused to wear a suit,

jeans and a leather jacket.

because his mom didn't wa

war would recommence lat

crush him under her sensibl

Luke's gaze slid away fro

blouse and skirt Mom twist

his eyeballs.

"S'up?"

"This." Feeling bold and

blouse and popped the faste

at the front: a sports bra that flattened my new breasts to pancakes.

Luke ... *stared*.

Five endless seconds later, his survival instincts kicked in. "Jesus Christ, Penny!" He shrugged out of his leather jacket and threw it over my head.

My shame and I went to find Lena. "He definitely likes you," she said. "Do you seriously think he would cover up any other girl?"

"Yes?"

"No! And you know why? Because he doesn't respect other girls."

"Isn't that bad?"

She shrugged, one-shouldered. "For them."

The day I turned eighteen, Luke Remis rang my doorbell. Over the past six years he'd gained a whole lot of muscle and enough height—6'1" in his final form—to wear it dangerously. He leaned against the porch railing looking like same-old Luke Remis with a brand new streak of bad.

"Can I get a do-over?"

That night at the church came flooding back. The embarrassment. Lena's assurances that he respected me more than every other girl.

I shrugged. "Okay."

Luke got his do-over, my virginity, and access to my mom's cookie jar. Our families started eyeballing china designs when they thought we weren't looking.

After he flew to Greece to perform his mandatory national service—a must for all Greek men who lived in or out of the homeland—the Luke Remis who returned was flakier than the average box of cereal.

We fought and bonked and fought.

Then he vanished.

And now here was Luke again, his mouth overflowing with what I was positive was bullshit.

"I can explain," he said.

"This better be good—and true."

"I was chained to a rock. There were birds. Well, one big bird. It ate my liver."

"For six months?"

"I know how it sounds ..."

"Like bullshit?"

"Penny ..."

"You were chained to a rock for six months, and there was a bird? And now suddenly there's no rock, no bird, and you've got a spectacular tan? You should get checked for skin cancer, by the way."

He hoisted up his shirt, revealing a tattoo of a snake, coiled around his six-pack. "And this."

"*And* a tattoo?"

He opened his mouth. Before he could speak, I thrust my hand in front of his face. The world's tiniest diamond winked in the sunlight.

"Zip it, Remis. I'm getting married."

The very last time I saw Luke Remis was on my wedding day. He hobbled out of the room, smothered in cake, in dire need of an icepack.

It was my big day, but he got the better deal.

———

Five years later ...

All summer long, Betty Sue Bentley swept into Salome's Salon bi-weekly for the blowouts she'd wear to fundraising lunches and other assorted events for the high maintenance set with deep, dubious pockets. Every time it was the same thing: wash, blow dry, style into a helmet that could stand up to blowhards and other Oregonians.

Summers—and Betty Sue Bentleys—in Oregon were unforgiving. They weren't the summers I remembered from my childhood. The dry season used to be a gentle thing. Now every year it was a raging, hormonal she-dog, until around mid-September when the switch flipped and the weather wept and howled until April became May.

I had ten minutes left until lunch—ten minutes of Betty Sue nattering about the most effective methods of squeezing money out of donors—then, I'd get to drive the two blocks to where my mother would be hauling lunch out of the oven. (My family doesn't do light lunches. Given that one whole half is Greek—Mom's side —we go all in and get the main meal of the day under our belts before the afternoon heat sucks the life out of our bodies. Of course, the rest of my family gets to sleep.)

I wasn't qualified to cut, but I was a wizard with a styling brush and hot air. My own hair had persuaded many a client to take a chance on my skills. Thanks to my Greek heritage, my thick, dark hair skimmed the bottom of my shoulder blades and gripped a curl or wave like it would die if it let go. Salome's Salon was my longest lasting job. I'd been gainfully here a whopping six months, since my divorce was finalized and I could finally afford to knock three jobs down to one.

Betty Sue was wriggling in her seat.

"Hold still," I told her.

"I'm gonna lose my shit if I don't get a cigarette soon," she muttered. She reached for her bag—expensive and definitely not a knock-off—and hoisted the whole thing onto her lap.

"No—no cigarettes in here."

"The whole fucking world has lost its mind over this whole 'no smoking thing.' I remember when you could light up in a hospital room. Nobody cared. Nobody died."

I was pretty sure that wasn't true. The way I heard it, smoking around oxygen was a big no-no, even in the old days. How many people had exploded before someone figured out the correlation, that's what I wanted to know.

"Well, you can't smoke in here. Salome has a sign." I pointed to the sign with my styling brush.

Betty Sue laughed. Her hand was busy in her bag. Hunting for her purse, hopefully. "What are you going to do? Throw me out?"

I set down the brush and reached for the spray. Extra-heavy hold. Betty Sue didn't want her hair to budge while she was writing checks and slamming wine spritzers.

"My arms are way too noodley for throwing people."

Several things happened in the same moment. Individually they were benign. Together, they spelled catastrophe.

My client brushed off my warning and pointing. In my haste to get her out of here so she could get that cigarette, I ignored her fumbling hands and depressed the button on the hairspray. As a person who didn't follow things like rules —they were for "other people"—she flicked her lighter. I glimpsed the tiny dancing flame a split-second before Betty Sue's head went WHOOSH.

My instincts screeched, "RUN."

I didn't listen.

Instead of hauling ass out of the hair salon, I threw a towel over Betty Sue's head and shoved her toward the basins.

"AHHHHH," she screamed.

She dropped her cigarette, now lit thanks to her flaming hair.

Things that happened next, in somewhat chronological order:

The salon went *WHOMPH.*

Everyone managed to get out. Some carrying their favorite scissors and styling tools.

An ambulance arrived with the fire department. They wheeled Bettie Sue away. She didn't tip me; probably because I didn't warn her hard enough not to light a cigarette.

Salome—not her real name, which was a less exotic but more glamorous Marilyn—barked at me to go home. Something told me I was on the verge of losing the most stable job I'd had in years.

"But—"

"Go," she barked.

"If you'll just—"

"Which part of 'go' didn't you understand?"

"The g and the o, mostly. At least not in that order. I'm sorry—" I started to say, but she turned her back on me and stalked over to the firefighters. I heard her demand to speak to their manager. The fire wasn't dying fast enough for her liking. Which I totally got. Nobody likes a fast-moving fire. But what did she expect when the air and surfaces in her salon were smothered in flammables?

I waved at her back, told her to call me later, and crossed my fingers that I wouldn't have to look for a new job. I'd already done all the minimum wage jobs that required clothes.

The only things left were poles and street corners, and I didn't have the underwear for those.

I pulled into the driveway in front of my parents' house, a triple-level threat to good taste. In a sedate neighborhood of craftsman and ranch homes, my parents had built a tribute to my mom's cultural heritage. The stone and stucco house was white with random columns holding up the gables. Two lions—more stone—glared at anyone trotting along the sidewalk. Mom had wanted to dig up the lawn and concrete the whole thing, but Dad put his foot down. Like most neighborhoods, theirs could only handle change in small doses. An absence of lawn would freak out the neighbors.

My family was assembled on the driveway, using their hands as visors. "Would you look at that," my mother said to nobody in particular.

A discerning person—anyone with semi-functioning eyes, or better—would instantly notice I was a Frankenstein's monster made up of my family's DNA. Mom, a Greek expat since childhood, was all hips and boobs and butt. She passed down the hips and butt, and kept the boobs, fiery temper and platinum blond hair—probably because the last one came out of a bottle. We were the same height—5'3" —which was only a problem at the supermarket. At 28, I was sure my growing upwards days were over. Dad, who hovered around 6', hadn't donated any of his height to my physical makeup, but he had contributed my cheekbones and my skin's ability to burn. Sometimes I questioned whether we were part vampire. One ray of natural sunlight and my skin would throw up its metaphorical hands and yell, "Take me, I'm yours!" My brother, who wasn't on the driveway, had Dad's build and Mom's face.

"Somebody made fire," my grandmother said. Yiayia (Greek for grandmother) was my mother's mother, a tiny raisin of a woman with skinny legs and a pot belly. A life-time of shunning good foundation undergarments meant everything swung to and fro. Probably she could tie her boobs in a neat decorative bow and throw them over one shoulder—or both, simultaneously. She was the reason I invested heavily in good bras, no matter how hard my bank account cried

"Somebody made fire," Grandpa said in a mocking voice. "Ain't nobody around here says somebody *made* fire. Fire is a thing you set. You ever gonna learn English?"

Grandpa is Dad's Dad. He loves beer and guns, and guns and beer, and his favorite color is mossy oak camouflage. Physically he's a bigger version of Yiayia—minus the dangling bosoms—but nobody mentions the resemblance because they're afraid he'll cut them out when he makes homemade jerky. Grandpa moved into my parents' converted garage after Grandma (Dad's mother) was crushed in a Black Friday sale at 7-Eleven. She'd really wanted those half-price air fresheners, and so had everyone else. The move was supposed to be temporary, but after fifteen years I figured he wasn't going anywhere.

Yiayia stabbed his face with a look sharp enough to shatter rock. "That how we say it in Greece."

"Would you look at that," Mom repeated. This time she was talking to me. "Christos and the Virgin Mary! I hope it doesn't spread here. Maybe I should pack a bag."

"I don't need to look at it." I slouched past them. "It's my fire. I did it. Sort of."

Mom followed me into the house. "You're an arsonist? *Po-po-po*, my own daughter. What am I going to tell people at church?"

"It was an accident! A stupid hair accident. Betty Sue Bentley will be fine, and they even think her hair might grow back. In my defense, it wasn't my fault she lit up while I was spraying her hair. I warned her—twice! It says on the can that hairspray is highly flammable. Who doesn't make it to adulthood without knowing that? It's like how everyone knows not to shower with the toaster!"

The Post family home is as Greek on the inside as it is on the outside. Lots of froufrou. Frilly curtains. An overabundance of doilies. Pictures of Jesus and his family and friends tacked to walls all over the house. Like all Good Greek Women, Mom has a room reserved solely for special guests. In there, the furniture wears plastic and the table is covered in photographs of her beloved family. Every embarrassing pre-cell phone picture that exists of me can be found in that room. When I can, I sneak in and hide myself behind the family wedding photos. Because she misses nothing, Mom always moves me back to where I can be silently mocked by her guests.

Without stopping to sit my bag on the foyer table, I headed toward the kitchen, the one place I could reliably get a temporary sugar fix for my anxiety. Today, the kitchen was bare. Not a single baked good under the cake stand's dome. The plastic containers that always held Greek sweets were empty. Even Dad's cookie jar, the one that contained his store-bought American cookies was empty. What madness was this?

"No cake?"

"I threw it to the birds," Mom said.

"You threw the cake to the birds?"

"I'm trying to watch my figure," Mom said. "Your grandmother said I was getting big enough to mount on a spit."

"Grandma has a hump and brittle bones from starving when the generals did their coup in Greece fifty years ago.

Don't take advice from her!" I slumped down at the kitchen table. "Today sucks. Fire. No cake. What's next?"

Mom snatched up her wooden spoon and gave the spaghetti sauce a poke. "Think positive. You dwell on the bad, the bad bring friends."

My cellphone rang. Hopefully not work calling to fire me.

Ah, crap. Caller ID flashed a picture of a poop emoji. Chaz, my ex-husband.

"What, Chaz?" I said with utter resignation. "What now?"

His high-pitched voice had teeth in it. "Your child support check is late again."

My butt clenched. My gut spasmed. We didn't have a child. What we shared was custody of our cat. Prince Charleston—Chunky for short—was mine on weekends, when Chaz would allow it. Prince Charleston's horrendous moniker was my former mother-in-law's fault. She'd named our cat for us, claiming Chaz was her little prince and she wanted to give his cat the same name.

"You'll get your money."

"You always say that."

"And you always get your money."

He inhaled hard. I recognized the sound of him winding up to deliver an insult. "You're a loser, Penny."

"Well, you're the loser mommy's boy that married me."

"I told you up front that Mommy and I are close! You don't get to complain—"

I stabbed the red button before he could wedge another word in and face-planted on the table.

"What are you doing?" Yiayia wanted to know. The rest of the family trickled into the dining room.

"Trying to slump down deeper into the table, but the

wood won't let me. We should get a different table. Something softer. A repurposed mattress, maybe."

"What's wrong with the table?" Grandpa said. "I made this table.

Yiayia leaned over. "What is that *malakas* saying?"

Given that she had lived in Oregon for forty years, Yiayia understood and spoke better English than the average person on the street. But she frequently got her kicks faking ignorance, mostly to get under my grandfather's skin.

"He said he made this table," I said, playing along.

"Tell him it looks like it," she said in English.

"I'm not telling him that."

"I can hear you," Grandpa said.

"Funny, because he cannot hear his own *klasimo*."

"This here is America." Like a microwaved marshmallow, Grandpa puffed up. It was all an act. This twisted game was what my grandparents did for entertainment instead of bingo. "Speak English."

Yiayia hurled the translation at him. "Fart!"

I slid out of the chair and waited while Mom finished the salad. When she was done, I ferried the bowl to the table then went back for our plates.

"Foreign food," Grandpa muttered. That didn't slow him down any. He slumped down behind his phone screen and began forking food into his mouth.

"This is almost as good as mine," Yiayia said.

Mom's eye twitched. She picked at her own pasta.

I gave Dad a pointed look. He slid down behind his newspaper, perched on his uncomfortable fence. No matter whose side he took, things wouldn't go well for him. Dad left his office and came home for lunch every day, mostly to make Mom happy—and because he enjoyed naps. His office was conveniently located in the spare bedroom. Dad was in the design arm of construction.

"You know what I think of this?" Grandpa said.

Nobody answered. He didn't care. He raised his cheek off the chair and farted.

"That is your father's father," Yiayia said.

My mother jumped up out of her chair. "I can't take this," she muttered. "I need cake, brownies, cookies, anything."

Now that was a can-do attitude I could get behind.

My phone rang again.

"*Ah-pah-pah*! Young people today, always on their phones," Yiayia said like she wasn't addicted to social media. "In my village we had one phone at the post office and my mother's mouth."

"In America everyone's got a phone," Grandpa said. "It's in the Constitution."

I was pretty sure that wasn't true, given that cell phones weren't a thing when Congress tacked on the Twenty-Seventh Amendment in 1992.

This time it was my boss. Salome/Marilyn didn't waste time asking how I was doing after I almost went up in flames.

"We have to let you go."

"You're not talking about a business trip, are you?"

"Fired. F-i-r-e-d."

"But it wasn't my fault Betty Sue lit a cigarette! You're not even supposed to smoke indoors. There are laws about that. There was a whole campaign. Secondhand smoke and all that. You had a sign up!"

"This isn't about the fire. You suck at doing hair."

"That's not true, and it's just mean."

"It's not mean if it's the truth." She ended the call.

I shoved my plate away. Mom's delicious pasta looked as appetizing as chickpeas now.

"I need cake," I said to nobody in particular.

"On it," Mom called out. "Brownies okay?"

"Brownies are great."

"Nuts?"

"I don't think they want any brownies," I said.

There was a snuffling sound from the kitchen as Mom stifled a laugh.

Yiayia blew out her cheeks.

"Someone wants to die," Dad said.

She narrowed her eyes at him. "What did you say?"

He raised his paper to cover his face. "Nothing."

"I lost my job," I announced. "So the good news is that there's no good news."

Everyone looked at me.

Yiayia clutched her chest. "You were fired? Again?"

"It's only the second time," I said, mustering at least half of my indignation. "This year." Keeping a job hadn't been easy while I was married to Chaz. At any given time, I'd juggled three while attending to his constant needs.

"No problem," Yiayia said. "Go see Androniki Remi. Her grandson Loukas works for a company that has an opening right now. You remember Loukas, yes?" A cunning light appeared in my grandmother's eye. "She told me this morning when we were stringing beans."

Androniki Remi. Luke's *yiayia*.

The bottom fell out of my stomach. Of all the people in the world I didn't want to work with, Luke Remis was at the top of the list. Well, second from the top below my ex-husband.

"I can find something on my own."

"*Malakies*! I will call." Before I could beg, plead, and fake my own death, Yiayia had her phone out, holding it out a mile from her face so she could see the numbers. "Androniki? It is me, Penelopi. My granddaughter was fired from her job because she burned the building down. She needs work, otherwise she will be moping around the house, sad, getting chubby like her mother."

Hey now, that wasn't precisely how it happened. There were circumstances. Betty Sue and her cigarette and lighter took all the blame, from where I was sitting.

She listened for a moment. "Okay, I will send her." Yiayia dropped the phone in her apron. "As soon as you finish eating, go see Androniki."

"Do I have to? She hates me."

Yiayia patted me on the cheek. "Oh, my love. She hates everyone." She rooted around in her apron and pressed something into my palm: a crumpled one-dollar bill. "Take this. For chocolate."

The concept of the pecking order was originally observed in chickens. The biggest, strongest, bossiest hens literally stab and jab their way to the top by flaunting their pecking prowess.

Androniki Remi, Luke's grandmother, possessed the local Greek community's largest, sharpest beak. Can opener nose. Hide-piercing tongue. Bodies of countless opponents littering her past. Sticks and stones could break bones, but Luke's grandmother could shred a human soul with a few well-placed words. If given the choice, I'd rather shove my arm in the wrong end of a crocodile than ring the doorbell of her colonial-style home. Sadly, crocodiles didn't prowl the streets of Salem, so I was left with the more terrifying option.

Thoughts paraded through my head as I parked at the curb and slunk up to the house. Mostly it was me wondering if I should have made a will. I didn't want Mrs. Remi to tear off my head before Chunky bit me one last time. Chunky was the only reason I was braving the gauntlet. I didn't want him to go without.

Before I'd left the house, I'd showered the smoke and failure away. I swapped my work clothes for a simple dress that even Luke's grandmother couldn't find fault with. If you ask me, by the time I pushed her doorbell and the Greek anthem rang out, I looked downright prim and proper.

She opened the door with a wooden spoon in one hand.

So it was true, then. I'd heard rumors she kept the spoon by the door to hit solicitors and other unsavories. I held my ground. No way would I flee while piddling like a terrified puppy.

Mrs. Remi scraped her black gaze over me. Luke's grandmother had eyes like coal pressed into a leather pillow that had been dumped on the roadside near Athens seventy years ago, and left to fend for itself in the elements. She was approximately the same size and shape as Yiayia, and they shopped at the same places: anywhere that sold cheap black clothes with stretchy waistbands.

"You better come in before someone sees you dressed like that. Are you not cold?"

My confidence plummeted. "It's July."

"Did I ask what month it is? I know the months. I have bones that tell me the weather. Today is going to rain. I feel it in my hip."

Spoiler alert: It wasn't going to rain until September, probably. But who was I to argue with her hip?

She ushered me into the house with her spoon. Like Mom and Dad's house—and Yiayia's second-level abode— Mrs. Remi decorated with Jesus and Pals and their band of crocheted doilies. Her furniture was covered in plastic, except for a threadbare glider in the living room.

I wasn't worthy of the Good Room, but she did offer coffee and sweets because a Greek woman's reputation as a hostess is constantly at stake. Because even a half-Greek woman's reputation as a guest is also always being judged, I accepted.

While I hovered in the living room, trying to avoid eye contact with the religious icons, she prepared a tray and placed it on the coffee table.

"How is your family?" I asked politely.

"Terrible." She slapped the air in a downward motion. "They never come to see me. One of these days I will be dead and they will be sorry. Come. Sit."

I perched on the offered chair's uncomfortable edge. The moment my backside hit the seat, the old woman's slipper came off and she swung her foot up into my lap.

"Rub it. *Po-po*, my feet hurt."

"Have you considered a podiatrist?"

She cupped her hand to her ear. "Eh?"

"A podiatrist. A foot doctor."

"A foot doctor cannot help me. They want to do the surgery. My cousin had the foot surgery, and do you know what happened? She went in with two feet and left with no feet and an extra hand."

"That seems ... not entirely true."

"Are you calling me a liar?"

Panic swept over me. "No, Mrs. Remi."

Her eyes tightened. The lumps of coal turned to hard, brittle beads. "Your grandmother says you were fired."

"Only because the shop burned down."

"You know what I hear from other people? That you made the fire, and a woman died."

"What? No! Her hair burned, yes, but she's still alive. It was her fault! I told her not to light a cigarette while I was spraying her hair, but she didn't listen!"

"Victim shaming, *po-po-po* ..."

My nervous system was desperately clawing at my muscles, trying to force me into fleeing. But my muscles were locked in place, held in bondage by fear. Coming here was a massive mistake. I'd be better off remaining unemployed forever, or joining a circus.

Mrs. Remi swapped one foot for the other. "Penelopi tells me you need a job. Today is your lucky day because my Loukaki and Nikoula's workplace is hiring a new janitor. Nikki called me this morning to tell me that her boss told her to look for someone." Nikki Remis is Luke's cousin. I'd forgotten that they worked for the same organization.

"I was kind of hoping for something more than a janitor."

"Are you too good to clean? It is respectable work."

Not only was I not too good to clean, but I'd done it professionally in the past, back when I was married to Chaz. Someone had to pay the bills.

"No, Mrs. Remi. Cleaning is ... fun."

"Besides, what else can you do? With those hips it is cleaning or raising children, and I do not see any children. What are you now? Forty?"

Yikes! "Twenty-eight."

Her beady eyes inspected me. "Hmm ..."

"I'll go apply for the job," I whispered.

"Good. Probably they will give it to you. I will tell my

grandson to tell them you are Greek and you know our family."

"No! It's fine. Don't say anything to Luke."

"Why not?"

I calculated quickly. "Because I want to get the job on my own merit?"

She laughed. "You are very funny. What merit? Go. I will give you the address."

———

The Labyrinth Agency, whatever that was, occupied space in a Northeast Salem strip mall. Its neighbors were a martial arts studio and a restaurant that sold Thai cuisine. Next week it would be a Mexican joint. The week after that, who knew? This was one of those locations where eateries went to die.

The gap between the two businesses was empty. No sign. No nothing except a big window and one door—also glass. Definitely no business that was hiring.

Maybe Mrs. Remi had the address wrong. I was too scared to call her to double check. She would twist the story like a pretzel, until I was a monster, accusing an old woman of lying.

Greek DNA comes imbued with an extra serving of curiosity. The Greek half of my genetic makeup grabbed my shoulder bag and propelled me out of my car to take a closer look. It wanted to be sure nothing gossip-worthy was happening here.

Gripping my bag like a security blanket, I pressed my nose up against the storefront window.

Empty. Nothing inside except the building's bare bones.

Nobody was hiring. By the looks of things they weren't even close to a grand opening.

The door swung open.

"You, girly. Get in here," a male voice said.

Unlike most voices, this one didn't come with a body.

Oh heck, was this a ventriloquist situation? Nobody warned me about ventriloquists. Mind you, dummies and puppets were a step up from mimes and other clowns, so that was something.

"Are you Oz the Great and Terrible?"

"Who?"

Okay, so he wasn't a reader or a movie buff, and he'd avoided pop culture for more than eighty years.

"Do you know Androniki Remi?" I clutched my bag tighter, hoping I wouldn't have to use it as a shield. "She told me you have a job opening. Her grandchildren allegedly work here."

He made a shuddering sound. "Can you not say that name too loud? I don't want to invoke her. That woman scares me."

"She scares everyone. That's kind of her thing."

"Come inside before she hears her name being used in vain."

Normally I'd run. Today I felt vulnerable. I'd been fired, blamed for a fire, called a loser by my ex-husband, and forced to massage Mrs. Remi's cracked and calloused feet. Because I couldn't see any red balloons hovering over a grate—a dead giveaway that murder and horror were afoot —I eased inside.

The door closed behind me.

I gave it a small push, half expecting it to be locked. It opened easily.

"I'm not trying to trick you." The voice was coming from

inside the empty store now. "The door is unlocked and you can leave at any time. You know the Remis family, then?"

"I know them."

That got some enthusiasm out of him. "Great! Run along and find Luke for me, would you?"

"What?"

"I'll give you some money for your trouble."

My brain was already struggling, and now he'd thrown Luke Remis into the mix?

"You want *Luke*? Luke Remis? Doesn't he work for you? What do you need me for? You should have his number and address on file ..."

"Ah, yes. Bit of a problem there. We seem to have misplaced the Remis boy. Be a shame if we don't find him. He's one of the agency's best agents."

I turned in a small circle, checking out the bare walls, the naked pipes, the dusty concrete floor. "What is it you do here?"

"Consulting," the voice said.

"And you consult ..."

"Companies, businesses, people that require consultants."

"And what do your agents, like Luke, do?"

"They consult," he said, his patience blatantly threadbare.

"Then why call them agents instead of consultants?"

"Has anyone ever told you you're pedantic?"

"Why do you want me?"

"It doesn't have to be you, per se. You're not special. I just need someone who knows Remis, with some insight as to where he might be hiding out."

"Why? Did he do something bad?" I liked that idea. "Is he in trouble?" I liked that even more.

"Moving on," he said quickly. "Can you find him?"

"Maybe."

"Then it's a deal. You find Luke, I give you money. Or rather, I'll have the girl give you money. That's what she does. Hands out money and mocks me. Be here tomorrow at 8:00 A.M. and the girl will give you what you need."

"So this isn't a janitorial position?"

"Does this place look like it needs cleaning?"

"Maybe a good sweeping ..."

He blew out a sigh. "Just locate Luke Remis and you can sweep it all you like."

"What do I do with him if—"

"When."

"—I find him?"

"Whatever you want, as long as you make sure he's alive. I'll never hear the end of it if he doesn't make it to his grandmother's place for lunch Sunday. She'll show up waving her wooden spoon. Do you know how much damage an old Greek woman can do with a wooden spoon?"

I could think of a lot of things I wanted to do to Luke Remis. Wringing his neck was high on the list. Ditto slapping the snot out of him.

"Can I crush his balls with my heel?"

"That's between you two."

One more question. Probably the most important. I wasn't born yesterday; the pay was high for a reason. "Is it dangerous?"

"On a scale of one to ten, it's like trying to beat three elderly Greek widows onto a city bus."

CHAPTER 2

A PANG of longing struck me as I peered through the window at the empty tables in the Thai restaurant. Once I had a paycheck again, I'd swing in and order a thirty-gallon drum of *tom kha gai* and a bucket of *pad thai*. If they stayed in business that long.

I drove home wondering what had just happened. The whole thing had the feel of a fever dream. Maybe it was a dream. In the morning I'd wake up to discover the hair salon resurrected from the ashes and my employment secure. Why, then, was I experiencing stabs of disappointment? The salon was a good job. Okay, good was an exaggeration. Styling hair on my feet all day long wasn't ideal, but it didn't suck nearly as much as some of my previous jobs.

Luke Remis. I hadn't laid eyes on Luke in years. Married to Chaz, it had been easy to avoid the old Greek crowd. Lena was my only lifeline and gossip delivery system outside of the family. But now Luke had apparently vanished, and it was maybe somehow related to his mystery job as an agent-slash-consultant. Curiosity had me by the mustache I regularly waxed.

Yiayia and Grandpa were on the porch when I pulled into the driveway. My grandmother's fingers were using a crochet hook to whip up something flowery with black yarn.

I leaned against the railing. "What is it?"

"This one's death shroud," she said in Greek. "I want to finish it before he dies."

Grandpa made a face. "How many times do I got to tell her to speak-a the English?"

"Kiss-a my ass-a," Yiayia said in perfectly good American lingo.

"Alrighty then." Grandpa rocketed up and out of his chair, preparing to bend over.

"I got the job," I said before war and nudity broke out. My grandmother dropped her crochet in her lap and erupted in a joyful hand-waving chorus of *kou-pe-pe*. (*Kou-pe-pe* is a Greek song sung to small, defenseless children, who lack the coordination required to pierce their eardrums with a knitting needle.)

From the look on Grandpa's face, I could tell he was measuring her for a padded jacket. "What sort of job did they give you, then?"

"It's a consulting firm, I think. They consult when businesses need a consultant."

He peered down his nose at me. "What's that when it's at home?"

I took another stab at answering. "A consultant is an expert who gives advice."

"Sounds like a professional know-it-all to me. You sure this is a real job?"

I shoved away from the railing. "They're paying me, so it must be."

"What will you be doing?" Yiayia asked.

"I don't know, exactly, but I'm sure they'll tell me."

Mom was in the kitchen preparing dinner. Because she had two parents from completely different cultures to appease, she was stuck fixing big lunches and evening meals. Grandpa refused to eat his main meal at noon, so he ate a huge meal at noon and an equal amount at dinner time. Tonight's meal was a pile of Hot Pockets that he enjoyed dipping in queso, for an extra kick of salt and cheese.

"One of these days," she was mumbling. "One of these days."

"I got a new job."

She looked up. "Can't one of them die already? I don't care which one. Do you think I should poison one of your grandparents? I could do eenie meanie miney mo. Or a blind thing where I poison one dish but don't know which one. Mix them up like a shell game. It'll be a surprise when one of them collapses."

"Are you okay?"

"It's just a sugar drop," she said. "I ate that whole pan of brownies. Your grandparents drove me to it."

"I might be able to move out soon. I got a new job."

"Stay with us forever." She kissed me on the forehead. "But if you leave, can you take them with you? Wait—it's a job where you keep your clothes on, yes?"

"Sex work is real work, Mom."

She stared down her nose at me.

"Relax, it's a consulting job. As far as I know, there's no nudity involved. Probably. Luke Remis works there, and his cousin Nikki."

Not that I'd seen Nikki there.

"That's not so bad. They're decent people," Mom said.

"Well, Nikki is decent. Luke is ... is ..."

I trailed off. Luke was a whole bunch of adjectives,

starting with trouble and ending with delicious and bad-for-my-health.

"I like Luke. Nice kid. Good-looking. Always respectful. A Good Greek Boy, if you know what I'm saying, and I think you do."

Yeah, that's because she didn't know about me flashing him behind the church on Easter or the lies he told me. He got chained to a rock? For six months? Please. What a crock of crap. How stupid did he think I was? Then he showed up at my wedding and had the audacity to slip the tongue in. Yes, okay, in a moment of weakness I allowed him to get close enough to touch me. But only because I was feeling emotional and scared of the whole impending ceremony.

"I'm not going to marry him, Mom. Not now. Not ever."

She wiped the counter. "Never say never."

"You going eat one of those Hot Pockets?"

"Not while I'm still breathing."

"Never say never."

She swatted me with the cloth. "Terrible child." She offered me the tray of oozing pastries. "Here, take one. Grandpa won't miss it."

I helped myself to an egg, bacon, and cheese and went home. Because I currently live on the third floor of my parents' house, I didn't have far to go. I exited the main house, walked around the side, and climbed the stairs to my third floor apartment, directly above Yiayia's level. Originally intended to be my brother's place, the two-bedroom, one-point-five bathroom apartment was mine now, for as long as I wanted it. John whizzed on our parents's love and generosity by accepting an out of state job, which meant the place was languishing fully furnished when I finally snapped and left Chaz. If Mom got her way, I'd be there until I tossed Charon a coin for the cruise to Hades.

While Mom and Dad's house and Yiayia's place were shrines to the Greek culture, my place was mine: sedate colors; no plastic suffocating the furniture; no religious icons, except for the small crucifix over my bed. Mom insisted on Jesus watching over me while I slept. I left it there to make her happy. At the back of the apartment, facing the backyard, I had my own private balcony. On the inside of the sliding door, there was a massive cat tree that I'd bought for Chunky so he could watch the outside channel on the rare weekend Chaz allowed me visitation. From his high perches, Chunky got a perfect view of Dad's bird feeders. My sweet fuzzy wumpkins was desperate for his own pet squirrel.

I flopped down on my couch and stuffed the Hot Pocket into my face. When that vanished, I chased my shame with a tortilla slathered with peanut butter and blueberry jelly. By that point I was feeling about as low as a subbasement, until I reminded myself that the peanut butter was the natural variety. At least I had that going for me. Okay, yes, I also had a new job. But the nagging voice in the back of my mind said this was probably bound to end up like the last Christmas at Chaz's mother's house. My former mother-in-law went all out for the holidays (every holiday, except Father's Day; she liked to pretend Chaz had been delivered by an angelic stork, without a single drop of semen involved), so Christmas was an overblown ornate affair where the whole yard and house were lit up with inflatable Santas and an Elf on the Shelf in every room. (If that little dweeb wasn't CIA or NSA, I'd eat my favorite hat.) Under the tree, a mountain range of presents waited to be opened. Everything was labeled with Chaz's name or Prince Charleston's. One single gift was for me. Chaz's mother delivered it into my arms and announced that it was "So you can do that thing my baby boy likes." I'd frozen in terror, a proverbial deer glued to the center lane, unable to move, despite the oncoming big rig.

Chaz tore it out of my arms, ripped the paper, and lit up like the angel at the top of the tree with a twig up her butt and a lop-sided halo. "Fuck yes, a Hitachi!"

My eye had started to twitch, probably because my brain was slowly imploding, the neurons committing rapid, spontaneous suicide just to get out of this festive red-and-green hellscape.

"Is that ... don't you ..." Words. I couldn't ... *words*.

"It's a MASSAGER," Chaz's mother declared. "You can use it on my furry little baby, too. You love Grandma's back massager, don't you, Prince Charleston?"

(Chunky, to his credit, ignored her. He was too busy shredding garlands.)

Fast forward to now, where I was at least ninety percent convinced this new job was bound to involve drudgery, obligation, disappointment, and horror. If I was lucky I'd get a personal massager out of it. But given that Luke Remis was involved, the only thing I was confident I'd get was screwed —and not in a good way.

It was the next day. Several minutes after eight o'clock. I'd had my wake-up coffee and picked up my booster shot on the way to the Labyrinth Agency's Northeast Salem slot in the strip mall. Nikki Remis had just handed me a pile of gibberish.

"What. Is. This?"

Tiny rewind. Back, say, about five minutes.

At precisely 8:00 A.M. I'd pushed through the Labyrinth Agency's glass door for the second time in two days. A bell over the door tinkled.

That wasn't there yesterday.

None of this was here yesterday.

Not twenty-four hours ago, this space was a lifeless husk. Today it had transformed into a generic office. One desk and office chair, occupied by one receptionist. A filing cabinet with a doily thrown over the top. A small beige sofa, two chairs, a coffee table, and a water cooler that looked like it was filled with lemonade.

"EPSA, direct from Greece," the receptionist told me when she noticed me gawking.

She had me at EPSA lemonade. No other lemonade came close. Every so often, Yiayia used her pension money to buy a crate from a supplier on the East Coat.

"You can buy it by the water cooler?"

"The boss can do anything. He's weird but he has connections." She jumped up from behind the desk, kissed me on both cheeks, then squeezed me tight. "Penny Post, where have you *been*? I haven't seen you in forever. You never come to church anymore."

Nikki Remis is one of life's huggers, something that doesn't come naturally to me. Dad's more reserved genes had elbowed aside Mom's huggers when they were divvying up traits. I was immediately swallowed by a cloud of perfume. Vanilla with a bucket of sugar. Nikki favors the more-is-more philosophy. Layers of makeup. Contouring that shifts her face from sweet to lethal. Her look is business professional—if the profession is administrative assistant at a high fashion magazine. In school, she had a five-year head start on me. She was leaving elementary school with new body odor while I was learning to read.

"You sound like my grandmother."

She laughed. "And mine."

I shuddered at the thought of her grandmother. "Busy working, mostly." And avoiding Luke. "That's why I'm here, actually."

"You're the new agent! I love it!"

That's when she handed me the gibberish.

"What. Is This?"

It looked like a file, it felt like a file, but everything between the pages of the manila file were what my mother and Yiayia called *malakies*. This was nonsense. Fiction. So much ... *bullshit*.

"Case file," Nikki said. "Everything Luke put together before he vanished."

"These are ... Greek myths. What am I supposed to do with these? Visit the library? Did he fall into a Rick Riordan book?"

"We think Rick has a source," Nikki muttered.

"What?"

"Nothing!" she said cheerfully. "Luke was on the trail of Subject M when he vanished. You'll find a picture on the first page. See?" She stabbed the page with her long gel tips. "There."

Subject M was a guy in cosplay. The man or someone close to him had serious design talent. His Minotaur suit was flawless. I wondered if he was a theater kid.

"I don't know who that is, but that's a sweet Minotaur costume."

"Not a costume."

"You're telling me that's a real Minotaur?"

"Uh-huh.

"A half-man, half-bull?"

"Uh-huh."

"Come on, tell me. Is it makeup? Prosthetics?"

"Nope."

"Special effects?"

"A hundred percent Minoan Minotaur, born and raised."

"Am I having that dream again?"

"No."

"You seem calm," I said to Nikki. "Why are you so calm?"

"Because this is how every new myth agent reacts. Nobody believes, right up until they do. You'll be fine."

My head swam. I didn't have enough coffee to deal with this. "Myth agent," I said in a weak voice.

"Send her downstairs," the disembodied voice from yesterday said. "Have her take the shock tour."

My brain edited out the bit about shock. I perked up. "Tour? There's a tour? You should have led with that."

Nikki reached back and slid the desk drawer open. She conjured up a sheet of paper and handed it to me. "Through the door, then the door directly at the end of the hall, and follow the directions. Don't deviate, no matter how much you're tempted."

"Are you coming, too?"

"I just hand out assignments and answer the phone." The phone rang. "Oops, there's a phone call now." She wiggled her fingers at me and popped her headset back on without messing up her perfectly styled bun.

Well, okay. I could do this. How bad could it be? Probably I'd go through the door, follow the map, and find Luke and his grandmother and whoever was on the other end of that weird bodiless voice cackling their heads off at my expense. Why, I don't know. I wasn't exactly in my most rational frame of mind. Maybe some kind of retribution for rebuffing Luke at my wedding, or for ignoring him after his crazy excuse. Or for kicks. His grandmother was the kind of person who enjoyed watching people squirm. Other folks' discomfort refilled Mrs. Remi's well.

I adjusted my pencil skirt and fitted black t-shirt, tucked my aviator sunglasses away in my shoulder bag. I'd worn what I hoped was an appropriate outfit for whatever duties an agent-slash-consultant at the Labyrinth Agency was supposed to fulfill. My hair was slicked back in a low, professional ponytail. Someone—me—had definitely sunk too many hours into watching *Men in Black* and its sequels.

Yesterday I hadn't noticed the door. Probably because I hadn't been looking for an exit. Today it was unmistakably there. Unassuming, as long as you ignored the giant AUTHORIZED PERSONNEL ONLY sign at eye-ish level.

"This door?" I asked Nikki.

"That's the one."

I went through the door.

Nothing exciting or strange happened. This wasn't Willy Wonka's factory, with snozzberry wallpaper. I'd entered a generic corridor that contained a dozen more doors in total, including the exit behind me. No wall art. No signs. No door plaques announcing the contents of the rooms. Wait—there was a restroom doohickey on the last door on the right. Skirts and no-skirts welcome.

What had Nikki told me? Straight ahead and don't deviate.

None of the doors had warning signs, so I took that as a good omen.

Okay, I thought. Next door. I was getting good at this.

Hopefully there wasn't a surprise "You're a loser, Penny!" party happening in my honor. But what if there was? I needed a plan. A short plan that involved me laughing it off and skedaddling without bursting into tears. I checked my bag for tissues. Yup. I was all tissued up. Maybe I should pretend to be on the phone. That way if a crowd of people leaped out at me, I could hold up a "please be quiet" finger, pivot, and slam the door before the party really started to rock and roll.

My phone stayed put.

The handle turned easily in my hand. Cool air rushed past me, desperate to escape.

Freaky.

I'd expected a room or another stretch of institutional beige corridor. Instead, I was staring down a steep set of stone steps, the old battered kind you normally see in places like medieval castles and Greek ruins. Did Nikki and her invisible boss really expect me to go down there? Were they nuts?

"It's quite safe," said the disembodied voice of the boss. This time his words bobbed close to my ear. I spun around and slapped the air.

Nothing. I was alone.

"Well, not *entirely* safe," he continued. "But safe enough, as long as you do *not* deviate from the map. I can't stress enough how important that last part is."

"Where are you?" Better question: "What *are* you? Where am I?"

"There will be time for that later. For now, please proceed. And remember what I said about not deviating from the map."

My feet remained glued to the ground for several moments while I tried kickstarting my common sense. Years of watching horror movies dictated that going into a dark and suspiciously old cellar alone was a spectacularly bad idea.

"I'm not walking into the dark. I've seen this movie. It never ends well for ninety percent or more of the cast."

Lights flickered on. Not electric. These were old fashioned torches fixed to stone walls. The illumination was all fire-based.

"Do you have carbon monoxide detectors? Just asking …"

My common sense threw a curve ball at me. *Think about the money*, it said. *That's a whole lot of cat support. If Chunky needs an emergency trip to the vet, you'll be covered. Maybe you could finally move out again. Get your own place—one you don't have to share with your stupid ex-husband. Who marries a guy named Chaz Trent Burke anyway? Like a horror movie, that was never going to end well.*

"Fine," I muttered to no one in particular. "I'm going in."

The flickering light swallowed me up. The comfortable, professional high heels I'd dragged out of storage for the occasion squeaked in protest.

At the bottom of the steps where the map said to turn right sat a brazier giving off more light and carbon monoxide. In between torches, the puddles of darkness were thin and spooky. The weirdness didn't end there. Other people's experiences told me the place should smell stale, with a hint of mold and dead things.

Wrong. No mold. No bold stench of rotting flesh.

The air bore a definite aroma of briny water. Impossible. The Pacific Ocean was an hour and change away from Salem, heading west. We didn't even have an aquarium nearby. The Oregon Zoo was forty minutes north. And how was all this under a strip mall anyway?

Think about the paycheck, I told myself. The financial freedom. The never having to style hair again. No more waiting tables. Or cleaning rooms at a motel. No more scraping used condoms off the floor in the movie theater restrooms.

In the distance, there were sounds. Sometimes they weren't distant enough. At one point I heard bellowing coming from another direction. Occasionally I got the feeling something was on the other side of the wall, mirroring me. The path twisted and turned. Strong *Labyrinth* vibes. I half expected David Bowie's codpiece to pop out at me at any moment and slap me on the chin.

What felt like hours later, I ran out of map. An industrial metal door appeared. The blazing red EXIT sign was a welcome giveaway. Relieved, I pushed through and into the eye-jabbing sunlight.

My relief lasted a split second.

This wasn't Oregon. Or California, or Washington.

I was on a beach. Definitely not the Oregon Coast. Not unless someone had swapped the sand for pebbles and turned the heat up to broil. Summers on the Oregon Coast were generally a good twenty degrees cooler than inland. Also missing from Oregon's beaches: little half-goat, half-human dudes playing pipes under what appeared to be a gnarled olive tree.

Alrighty then. This was fine. Everything was fine. This was my anxiety throwing an "I'm back, sucker!" parade.

What if it wasn't my brain taunting me? I fanned my face with my hand. Maybe the Dutch Bros spiked my coffee.

"What the heck?"

"Language." That now-familiar voice was coming from inside my head.

"Where are you?"

"In your thoughts."

I checked my phone. No signal. How was there no signal? Almost everywhere had a signal. Yes, except the high forest areas between here and the coast. But this was the coast, not the in-between bit.

"Note to self: Make appointment to see therapist. Also acquire health insurance."

"You are not crazy, I assure you," the boss said in my head.

"Then why don't I feel assured?"

"Low self-esteem."

"My self-esteem is fine! I'm just a recently divorced Greek-American woman who lives in fear of flying slippers and the constant judgment about my lack of husband and children. Also, for some reason, everyone is upset that I'm not a doctor *and* a stay-at-home mother at the same time. And don't get me started on all the times I've skipped church lately ... for several years."

His confidence wavered. "Maybe I misjudged you when I said you're not crazy. I'm not infallible."

"That's what I'm telling you! And now it's raining gold coins. Where. The. Heck. Am. I?"

True story. A patch of the sky had opened up and now it was raining coins a scant few dozen feet from where I was debating my sanity with an invisible person that may or may not be a voice in my head. The coins were thick and round, and they sparkled where the sun struck their gilded surfaces.

"Gold coins, you say?"

"They could be chocolate covered," I said optimistically.

"Get out!"

"What?"

"Back the way you came. Shut the door behind you and run."

"What?"

The golden coins began to coalesce into a humanoid shape. My instincts kicked in—the scaredy cat flight ones, thankfully. Not the run-toward-danger ding-dongs that had pushed me to extinguish Betty Sue's head. I scrambled back through the doorway, slammed the door as something struck against the metal.

The boss, no longer in my head, barked instructions close to my ear.

I didn't stop running until I fell through the door that opened into the office. Nikki was busy inspecting her face in a hand mirror.

"Dang Greek genes," she said. "I'm turning into my mother and my father. I can't live with a mustache."

"Wax is your best friend," I said, panting against the door.

She set aside the mirror. "How did it go?"

"Gold ... sky ... coins."

"Ugh, what a creep. He *never* lets up. All our Greek myth agents have this problem. Ninety-five percent of the drama in Greek mythology is because Zeus can't keep it in his pants."

"Zeus? What? Huh?"

"He likes to make a big impression with a golden shower. Nobody likes a golden shower on the first date, I don't care how broke they are. How was the tour besides that?"

My breath gravitated toward normal. My heart slowed its beat. "What the actual *heck* just happened? What is this place? Why wasn't it here yesterday? I mean, there was nothing here yesterday. Nothing!"

"That was just the boss messing with you."

"I had to be sure she wasn't a crazy person," the boss said. "So I had the labyrinth do a little cloaking thingy."

Nikki eased out from behind the desk. Vanilla and sugar clouded my senses as she looped her arm through mine and steered us both to the sofa. The way she looked at me—hesitant and mildly apologetic—I half expected her to tell me my beloved *Stila Stay All Day Liquid Eyeliner* was being discontinued.

"In a nutshell, the Labyrinth Agency is all that stands between our world and the mythological. We're a port. A transportation hub and the only agency that tracks and polices mythological creatures and beings who visit or live here."

"Ungh," I said.

"The fun part is that we don't just do Greek mythology. Everyone comes through the Labyrinth Agency. Norse, Egyptian, you name it."

"Roman?"

That got a snort out of her. "They're knockoffs—and they look like it."

"And this agency is here in Salem, Oregon, of all places? I mean, *why*?" Not to knock Salem, but the country had other, more famous Salems. And Oregon had Portland, where it seemed like mythological beings would have an easier time blending.

"Just one branch. There are others around the world. Basically anywhere the Labyrinth has an opening into our world, we have an agency."

"I ..." I eyed my coffee cup. "Is this drugs? I always assumed they'd be more fun—at least in the beginning."

"Tell her to go see Grim," the boss said. "He'll knock some sense into her."

"I'm standing right here," I said. "I can hear you."

"Here." Nikki went back to her desk and fired a text message at my phone. "Call Grim."

"He's not one of those little dudes with the goat legs, is he?"

"Satyrs? They're mostly harmless," she said. "Unless you get one that's tone deaf and they insist on playing their latest composition for you. Luke lost his hearing for a week after one of those."

Dazed, I saved this Grim person's contact info. "How was the, uh, boss's voice in my head when I was ... *there*?"

"Magic," the boss said.

"Who *are* you?"

"Er ... you can call me the boss. Everyone else does."

"The boss?"

"The boss," he said with more certainty this time. "Are you going to stand around all day asking stupid questions or are you going to do the job?"

"Okay." I waved Luke's file. "I'm going to go eat my feelings. Then I'm going to take a look at this."

"One more thing," Nikki said. "Avoid the Minotaur. The mission is to find Luke and make sure he touches base with us."

Avoid something that didn't exist. I could do that with both hands tied behind my back. "Easy peasy," I said.

Nikki made a face. She did that a lot. A hazard of being Greek.

Even when our mouths were silent, our faces did a whole lot of yapping.

CHAPTER 3

MOM WAS LOADING up the minivan. Because Yiayia and Grandpa always bickered like a pair of old hens, they were permanently relegated to the backseat. When she was driving, Mom cranked up the easy listening music to drown out their commotion. Grandpa was an unrepentant backseat driver. Before having his license revoked, he'd collected speeding tickets like people collect Pokemon and Funko Pops, so he figured he knew a thing about how to drive. Not Yiayia. She'd been raised in the time of the donkey and knew about Stop and Go.

"You're home early," Mom called out. "Want to come to the store?"

"Go ahead," I told her. "I've got work ... uh ... stuff."

"There's cake on the counter," she said. "If you love me you will eat the whole thing."

In the backseat, Yiayia made hippo noises.

Mom didn't have to tell me twice. I waved goodbye and headed inside to cut a slice of vanilla caramel cake the size of a baby's head. Any food guilt I might have felt vanished as I climbed the two flights of stairs to my place. My goal was to flop down on the couch, cram cake into my mouth, and pretend Zeus didn't just try to give me a golden shower of actual gold.

I dropped the folder on the coffee table and kicked off my squeaky shoes. Something told me I could wear any old thing for this agent job. Maybe something suitable for running like the dickens when the need arose. My fantasies of wearing sleek black clothes and shades evaporated.

This was insane. Or maybe I was the one with the loose screws. Maybe this was a dream. Probably that was it. My brain was roleplaying a weird mythology-is-real fantasy and I was trapped in the dream state until the neighbor's loser son zoomed his lowrider down the street at 3:00 AM.

I wished I was dreaming. But the comforting thing about being steeped in a kooky dreamworld was that some piece of me was always aware that the kaleidoscope of insanity was just my mind working through its issues so I could be a sane and functioning person during the day. After coffee, of course. Unfortunately, in thus particular moment, I was offensively aware that I was wide awake.

Curiosity seized the wheel again. I leaned forward and flipped to the page with the man-bull. The Minotaur on the run. According to the file, he'd busted through the labyrinth without permission and was loose in our world. Last known location: a weed dispensary in Keizer, where he was cramming grass into a bag. Luke lost him after that, then he vanished, too. Included was a brief bio and a list of places the man-bull had visited before he disappeared. He (it?) was classified as Highly Dangerous. No mention of him (it?) rampaging through a china shop.

That was it. That was the file.

I blew out a long, frustrated sigh. None of this was real. It couldn't be. Who wouldn't notice a half-bull, half-man charging around the city? Yes, Salem attracted some oddball characters the way capital cities tend to do, but surely someone would notice a Minotaur. Hoodies didn't come in Volkswagen size, so he couldn't be hiding downtown with the city's homeless population.

Where to start?

I had strict instructions to find Luke and avoid the Minotaur at all costs. Which was fine by me. I did my best to avoid livestock unless it resting in peace on my plate. If I wanted to find Luke, I'd have to follow his trail. Starting at the end, at the last known Minotaur sighting seemed smart —but was it? I decided to begin with the low hanging fruit. Or my version of Occam's Razor: if someone wasn't around, check out their house. For all anyone knew, Luke Remis was relaxing on his own couch, eating snacks and watching football. Had anyone at the Labyrinth Agency checked?

I glanced down at the plate. Someone had eaten my cake.

Me. It was me, damn it.

The file had me so engrossed that Mom's cake hadn't registered. I'd eaten the entire slab without stopping to enjoy a crumb. How was I supposed to eat my feelings if I didn't realize I was eating them?

The injustice of it all propelled me off the couch and into action. Time to get a move on. First step, change clothes. Out of the slick agent clothes and into something more casual. Given that I was about to sniff around Luke's neighborhood, I wanted to project an image of someone who was entitled to be there. Didn't want to look like I was peddling pest control or Jesus. I located a sundress in my closet. Flowery. Sweet. Benign. No one would suspect me of anything more than visiting a friend. Not sweet little ol' me.

I kept the ponytail and ditched the squeaky heels for cute, comfortable sandals.

On the way out, I stopped by my parents' kitchen for another brick of cake. Calories didn't count if you didn't taste them.

I was pretty sure that was one the laws of physics.

Luke Remis lived in a quaint bungalow a couple of blocks away from his grandmother's house. Mrs. Remi had expected him to move into the second floor of her house, the space his parents occupied before they were killed in an unfortunate goat trampling accident while vacationing in Greece. The way I heard it, Luke smashed his grandmother's heart when he took his share of the inheritance and blew it on a modest house and put the rest in savings. Eating at Mrs. Remi's house every weekend and accompanying her to church was his restitution. That and he mowed her lawns every week, whether they needed them or not.

Not even ten minutes and half a slice of cake later, I pulled up to the curb at Luke's house. The driveway was empty but I didn't want to be presumptuous. I finished the cake and contemplated the various outcomes.

What if he wasn't home?

What if he was?

If I knocked on his door and found him scoffing chips on the couch mid-Netflix marathon, would he think I'd come back to flash him again?

I sat there until I realized I'd have to get out soon or risk my reputation. Last thing I needed was for the neighbors to consider my hovering presence suspicious and call the police—or worse: Mrs. Remi. This wasn't her street but these were her people.

Get it together, I told myself. So what if Luke was home? I was a professional, wasn't I? A professional what, I still wasn't sure yet. Myth agent didn't sound like a real job. And was I technically a professional if I hadn't collected a paycheck yet?

Damp cotton clung to my legs as I eased out. I spent a couple of seconds unsticking my dress so the neighbors didn't catch me in a wedgie situation. Once I was presentable, I trotted up the path to Luke's porch. Luke Remis had bought a house too close to his grandmother's for any sane person's comfort. Only a couple of streets separated me from her withering gaze. Like my parents' neighborhood, Luke's was middle class with well-established trees, neat yards, and trimmed grass—except for Luke's, which was veering a couple of inches above decent, by neighborhood standards. I pictured more than one neighbor quietly seething about how that Remis guy hadn't mowed this week.

Deep in the folds of my shoulder bag, my phone rang.

Lena Cooper's words charged my eardrum. "My Virgin Mary, are you sitting down?"

Lena Cooper was still my best friend. We'd been tight since we both wet our pants on the first day of kindergarten because some asshole fifth grader told us we'd be getting zombie flu shots before we were allowed to play in the school playground during recess.

"Standing. Should I sit?"

"Lean. Sit. Something. Anything. There's a rumor going around that you went over to Luke Remis's house. Alone. Everyone is talking about it."

"What? Already? But I just got here!"

You can take the Greeks out of Greece and dump them in Oregon, but they'll find a way to band together and form the world's most judgmental neighborhood watch program anyway.

"So it's true? Virgin Mary …" A few miles away, Lena was crossing herself.

"Well, yeah." I glanced around, wondering which home was responsible for touching the light to the gossip fuse this time. "But it's a work thing, not a sex thing."

"You're doing his hair?"

Typical. The gossip train had priorities. Me losing my job was a step down from me standing alone on Luke Remis's porch.

I dropped my voice down to a whisper. Where there were eyes, there were big ears. "It's a new gig that's way too weird to explain right now, but Luke is missing and I'm looking for him."

"Missing?" The word was threaded with excitement. I could hear Lena calculating the gossip value of a vanished Luke Remis.

"But you can't tell anyone," I said quickly. "His cousin Nikki knows—"

"Which Nikki?"

Because of Greek naming conventions, Greek kids usually wind up with at least a couple of cousins—frequently more—with the same name. Firstborn children of either sex are blessed (or cursed) with their paternal grandparent's given name. Nobody gets a new name until a third boy or girl is born and the parents run out of grandparents to honor. Luke's grandmother had seven kids, all of whom did the Good Greek Thing and spawned at least three children of their own. So now Luke has seven first-cousins named Androniki—Nikki for short— after their grandmother.

"Nikki Kyrios George."

Another Greek quirk. Identifying kids by tacking their parent's name to the end. (*Kyrios* is the Greek word for Mister.)

"Don't they work together? Luke and Nikki, I mean."

"And now I work with them," I explained. "Nikki knows he's missing but no one else does. I have to find Luke before the rest of his family finds out, so you can't say a word about it."

"Not even to Matt?"

Matt is Lena's not-Greek husband. He sticks out like a hammered toe at family get-togethers because he won't touch retsina ("tastes like paint stripper smells") and he passes out if he makes eye contact with a lamb carcass spinning on the spit. Everyone in Lena's family talks to him in loud, careful English, despite the fact that it's his first and only language.

"Okay, fine, you can tell Matt but not the kids."

Lena and Matt have three kids under the age of five and another one on the way. Four grandkids still isn't enough for Lena's family to accept that she married an American.

"So what are you going to do?" she asked breathlessly.

"Right now? My big plan is to knock on his door and see if he's home."

"Do it," Lena said. She made eating sounds. I heard the crinkling of a chip bag. My stomach growled. Now that it was digesting Mom's cake, it wanted chips as a salty chaser.

I poked the doorbell. Luke had installed one of those video contraptions so he could vet visitors before deciding whether or not to get off the couch. My parents had the analog version: Yiayia and Grandpa. I put on what I hoped was a friendly but also professional expression and waved. "It's me, Penny Post."

"What's happening?" Lena said through a mouthful of chips.

"Nothing."

"Maybe he's ignoring you. Could be he doesn't recognize you. There's been a lot of water under that bridge, and by water I mean a parade of *mounis*. After a while I bet they start to all look the same."

"Some have hair and some don't," I said.

"I can't even tell what I have anymore. The last time I saw my feet was two months ago. Matt said everything looks fine down there, but who knows if he's lying? He's just happy to see it."

"Luke's not here," I said. "That or he's ignoring me."

"You should go around back and see if you can get in that way. That's what I would do if I were you."

"Would you do that if you were you?"

Lena snorted. "Heck no."

I weighed my options. If I went around back, the wagging tongues would go up in flames from the flapping friction. But if I bailed now, maybe I would miss something important. Could be Luke was inside, injured and in dire need of medical help. If that was the case, I wanted to savor the moment and snap commemorative photos.

"What if he's hurt? Maybe I should go around and see."

"Or what if he's naked in the shower."

Oh boy. I leaned against the porch railing. I hadn't laid eyes on Luke Remis in years. Not since my wedding day. The real reason I skipped church every Sunday now was because I was doing my level best to avoid him. Twenty-five-year-old Luke Remis had been a physical masterpiece. Hard, built body that looked like he'd earned it swinging fists and bench pressing trucks. Between high school and my wedding day he'd lost the last of the softness in his features. After time doing who-knew-what had had its way with him, he was formidable, dangerous, devastating.

That was five years ago.

Now he was thirty he'd probably swung the other way. That's the bedtime story I told myself to feel better. Probably he had a beer gut and could belch the alphabet in two languages.

Yeah, that version of Luke I could handle. No wonder he'd gone missing hunting the Minotaur. Probably he was stuck in a fence, trapped by his own excess.

"I'm going in. Or around. Around and in, maybe."

"I'll be right here, eating these chips in solidarity. Crap, they're gone. Let me get another bag."

While Lena crunched in my ear, I left the porch and scooted around to the side gate. Luke didn't keep it locked. I went straight through and closed it behind me.

"Incoming," Lena said through the chips. "I just got a text from Mom, who got a text from her cousin, who got a phone call from about five other people, saying you went through Luke's gate."

"Imagine if the Greek community used their powers for good," I said. "They could solve everything overnight. No more wars, hunger, or people who don't return the shopping cart to the corral."

"Then what would they talk about?"

"I'm sure they'd make up enough lies to sustain themselves for years."

Luke's yard contained all the suburban basics. Neatly coiled hose. Gas grill that looked brand new, and a separate charcoal grill that did all the heavy lifting. Garden shed. Unexciting but clean outdoor furniture. A few plants potted in red containers. Definitely his grandmother's touch. Like the front lawn, the back hadn't been mowed in a couple of weeks, at least.

"Someone really needs to mow," I said.

"Maybe you should do it for him. I bet he'd be super grateful."

"I don't want him to be grateful. My business with Luke Remis begins and ends with me finding him and collecting my paycheck."

"Mrs. Remi would probably say nice things about you."

She had a point. Everyone in our community wanted to stay on the blunt side of that sharp tongue. If I did Mrs. Remi's grandson a favor, maybe she wouldn't curse me or tell people I was a loser.

"Fine. Okay. I'll mow the lawn. But just this one time, and only because there's nothing around here to see." I peered through Luke's back windows and sliding door. "There's no sign of him."

I helped myself to the garden shed, where I found an electric mower. When I was done with both lawns, I wheeled the lawnmower back into the shed.

"Do you want the bad news?" Lena asked.

"Wait—what bad news?"

"Luke's grandmother is telling everyone you mowed his lawn because you're madly in love with him and want him to notice you. She's calling you sad and desperate."

"In love with him," I spluttered. "I'm not *in* anything with him, and I don't care if he notices me or not."

"Right? It's not like he didn't notice you plenty in the past."

Ungh. I couldn't win. I grabbed my bag, said goodbye to Lena, and schlepped back to my car, grass clippings plastered to my sweat. I started the engine and cranked the air conditioning to high.

My phone rang. Unknown caller. Normally the kind of call I ignored, but I was in a mood and I was all out of consolation cake or candy. Who better to bear the brunt of my bad attitude than a robocall from some bottom-feeding scammer?

"What?" I snapped.

"Why did you mow my lawn?"

Shock stopped my heart. When it picked up the drumsticks again, it began pounding like I was bingeing amphetamines.

"Who is this?"

As if I didn't know.

"Cupcake, just how many lawns have you mowed today?"

I slouched down in the driver's seat. Was he watching me right now? My gaze darted from window to window, up and down the street. Every last one of them looked lacy and suspicious. Sheers reigned supreme in this neighborhood. "Remis."

"What's the deal? I don't see you for three years and now you're mowing my lawns?"

"Five," I said.

"You've been counting," he said, entirely too smug.

My molars ground together. Luke had that effect on me, among other, even less welcome effects. "I didn't want you to get robbed."

That confused him. "What?"

"Your lawn was a mess and your garbage cans were still at the curb. Do you know what that says? 'I'm not home, so come on in and rob me.' Plus I didn't want your Home

Owners Association to ding you. I'm helpful like that. I'm practically a good samaritan."

"I don't have an HOA. Refused to buy a house with one."

"You're welcome anyway." Something occurred to me. "How did you get my number?"

"Same number you've had for years. You still haven't told me why you're skulking around my house, mowing my lawns."

"I wasn't skulking!"

"Is this your way of apologizing? Because I have to say, it could use some polish. Maybe if you do the weed-eating and edging we could pick up where we left off."

"Pick up where we left off? Are you kidding me right now? We didn't *leave off* anything in the first place! You showed up to my wedding and stuck your tongue down my throat—"

"Yeah, yeah, and then you shoved my face in the cake, kicked me in the balls—"

"Kneed."

"—Excuse me, kneed me in the balls, and then hit me over the head with a Waterford crystal bowl."

"I didn't know it was a crystal bowl! It was still wrapped!"

"You ruined your cake because of a kiss."

"I was getting married!"

"Yeah, to Chaz Douchebro."

"He is a douchebro," I admitted.

"You backed the wrong horse."

"I hear you're a horse with a lot of backers these days."

He went quiet for a minute. I figured he'd hung up.

"Remis?"

"How did you explain the wedding cake?"

"I told everyone it was attacked by geese."

"Geese." I imagined him shaking his head. "And they bought that?"

"Have you ever met geese? They're capable of anything and they love cake."

A motorcycle zipped past me, doing fifty, easy, in a residential twenty-five. It took me a second to realize that I'd heard that same echo in the ear pressed up against my phone.

Luke Remis was around here somewhere. Maybe not at home, but certainly close by. Somewhere he could see me.

"Well, it was the opposite of nice talking to you," I said. "Let's never do this again." Before he could pop his mouth off, I ended the call and tossed my phone onto the passenger seat. I shifted the gear into D and rolled away from Luke's house at a modest and perfectly legal twenty-five miles per hour.

A couple of blocks away, I stopped at the curb and mentally reexamined the houses in Luke's street. This was an established neighborhood filled with single family homes and the rare duplex, frequently owned by elderly women with cats or a small dog with a size-related inferiority complex. Trees were tall and regularly trimmed. Families rarely moved, unless situations changed drastically.

So where was Luke hiding? Yeah, there was a distinct chance he was hiding out in his own house, but I didn't think so. He'd had every opportunity to answer the door when he saw I was on the other side. And he would have, I was sure of it. Even if it was to berate me in person for the cake and balls thing. I crossed his house off my list.

Could he be hiding out in a neighbor's spare bedroom? The neighborhood was riddled with Greeks, several of whom were on the Mrs. Remi phone tree. Any of them could be sheltering Luke to stay on his grandmother's good side.

I crossed that idea off the list, too. If Luke was actively hiding out with someone in the neighborhood, there would be talk. No one in the Greek community could keep a secret, unless it was their real age.

On a whim, I checked a real estate website, curious to see if anything in the street was on the market—or had been.

Nothing

I called Mom to ask if she knew of any houses for sale in the street.

"Not yet, but Helena Mouto's house is going on the market next week. She caught her husband watching Turkish porn and now they're getting a divorce. She moved back to Greece in June and her husband is renting a studio apartment near downtown. Why?"

"I heard a rumor that it's haunted," I lied.

"Probably the ghost of their marriage."

So. The Mouto house. That had to be where Luke was hiding out.

But why watch his own house? Why hide in his own street?

Only one way to find out.

Marching up to the house in broad daylight would give the game away. Someone would see me—again—and they'd be frantically calling Helena Mouto in Greece, and possibly Luke. If he was hiding in that empty house, spying on his own place, there had to be a reason. I reminded myself that he and I were on the same team, that I'd been hired to locate him. A simple wellness check sort of mission. If I gave away his hiding place, I might put him in harm's way. But what harm? Had his pursuit of the Minotaur turned deadly? If news that I was mowing Luke Remis's lawns had reached every open ear in our community, then you could bet your cotton socks that a Minotaur charging around the neighborhood would be an even bigger gossip scoop. But no one had mentioned a giant bull with a man's legs jogging around the street. Which led me to believe Luke Remis was hiding from someone else.

I wasn't about to lead anyone right to Luke—not before I completed my mission—so I scrunched down in my seat and waited.

Around dinnertime, my phone rang.

"Are you coming home for dinner?" Mom wanted to know. "Your grandfather wants spaghetti and meatballs. He's the meatball, if you ask me."

"Doesn't look like it, sorry."

"Don't leave me alone with your grandparents," she pleaded.

"Pretend you've got a headache?"

"Great idea. I think I'll do that. Your father can deal with them alone for once."

In the background I heard Dad say, "Do what, now?"

"Nothing, *vre malaka,*" Mom said. "I'll leave a plate for you," she whispered.

My stomach growled at the thought of dinner. I could go for some spaghetti and meatballs right now, and Mom's were the best. Good comfort food. I really needed some comfort because things were weird.

Around 8:00 P.M., night started dragging itself west. Wouldn't be long now before I could creep over to the empty Mouto house, hopefully without Luke or anyone else realizing what I was up to. It occurred to me that sneaking up on any house was a great way to get shot. Here in Oregon, people were proud of being Ore*gun*ians. But I decided to take my chances. Luke was great at maintaining control.

I tried not to think about that too hard. Good Greek Boys weren't supposed to do the things Luke had done to me in the past. Or excel at them.

As soon as the neighborhood was wreathed in shadows, I left my car behind. I stuck to the deeper pools of darkness. Eased down the street. Sneaked up alongside the empty house. The about-to-be-former owners had done a great job landscaping. Lots of shrubs and bushes. Perfect for hiding. I definitely didn't think about how many bugs were brushing up against my skin, touching me with their tiny bug legs.

I eased through the side gate and moved around back. Somewhere in the street, a dog barked. Lights flicked on in a nearby yard. I pressed my back against the house and pretended I was a stinkbug. A moment later, its owner called the pup inside. The lights went off.

Phew.

I crept up to the sliding door.

Locked. Because of course it was, damn it.

Then something grabbed me around the waist and a hand slapped itself over my mouth.

CHAPTER 4

MY BODY KNEW EXACTLY what to do. Yes, I was twenty-eight, but somewhere deep down inside, I was still a toddler with latent toddler skills. Instead of fighting, my entire body went limp. My center of gravity shifted. The arm around my waist slackened. I licked the hand over my mouth. That hand wriggled away in disgust.

Light shone in my face, dazing me.

"*Gamo ton Christo*, Penny?"

"Do you kiss your grandmother with that mouth?"

"Where do you think I learned it?"

Luke Remis tried to haul me up off the ground but I slapped him away. He flicked off his flashlight, grabbed me by the arm, and dragged me back to the Mouto house via the backdoor. He closed it quietly behind us and led me through a dark, empty house to the upstairs front room—the only room in the house with evidence of life. There was a sleeping bag, a small coffee maker, and a cooler sitting in front of the windows. Could be he'd been using it as a seat. A pair of binoculars on the ground told me I was probably right.

"What are you doing?" His tone said he was disappointed in my life choices, which made two of us. Since taking this job I'd spent hours in my car and mowed his lawns.

"Huh." I made a show of looking around. "I'm here for the open house. I guess I'm early. Or late."

The only light in the room came courtesy of the streetlights, but they were enough for me to see his eyes narrow. "What open house?"

I faked wide-eyed surprise. "Oops. Did I get the wrong house? I thought this was Helena Mouto's place."

"What's your problem? Are you trying to get me fucking killed? Was the whole cake and balls thing not enough for you? For all I know, I can't even father kids now."

"I hear you've been getting plenty of practice."

"Checking up on me?" Was it my imagination or did he sound like that idea wasn't totally awful?"

"In your dreams. This is business, not a trip down sewer lane." I reached for my phone. He smacked it out of my hand.

"Who are you calling?"

"Uh, work?"

"Who's that? Who are you working for? Last I heard you were doing hair."

"That ended with a whole fireball incident that wasn't my fault."

He folded his arms. Glared until I crumpled under the weight of his judgment.

"Fine, okay, we're on the same side, I think."

"Elucidate."

"Nikki gave me your file. She and the weirdo voice dude want me to find you."

He stared at me for the longest time. Then: "You expect

me to believe Nikki and the boss sent you after me?"

"It's just a wellness check, okay? I've checked on you. There. We're good. Now I'll just be moseying out the door—that's if I don't trip over in the dark and break something."

For whatever reason, a grin sprawled across his face. "Pull the other one, cupcake."

"What? You don't believe me?"

"You honestly expect me to believe the Labyrinth Agency hired *you* as an agent?"

"I know, right?" I muttered, "I'm as surprised as you are."

He laughed; a cold, hacking sound. "Oh, I doubt that."

"It's true! I went there because your grandmother told my grandmother they needed a janitor. Then things got weird, a mythological figure tried to shower me with gold coins, and now here I am." I gestured at everything.

"Shit." He pushed his hand through his hair. "You're not lying."

"Of course I'm not lying! That's your thing, not mine."

He paced for a moment. "Does anyone know you're here?"

"At Helena Mouto's house? Nope. But everyone including Lena knows I was at your place earlier. Mowing your lawn was her idea. Don't worry, she won't tell anyone you're missing. Well, except maybe Matt, but no one talks to him. They treat him like he's a potted plant."

"You can't tell anyone you've seen me."

"I can't? Why not?"

"Plausible deniability. If no one knows where I am, they can't be forced to talk."

"About what? What does this have to do with the Minotaur?"

"Forget the Minotaur," he said. "The Minotaur is dead. Which is kind of the problem."

"*I* know you're alive. Am I in danger. Wait—the Minotaur is dead? Does work know?"

"If not, they will soon." He rolled up his sleeping bag. "It's not too late for you, I hope. Go home. Forget you saw me. Call Nikki and quit, but don't—I repeat don't—under any circumstances tell her you saw me. I don't care what excuse you give her as long as you quit. Go marry another douchebag with a stupid name. Get a normal job. Have some kids and try not to kick anyone in the balls."

"Argh! You are the worst, Luke Remis!"

He grabbed me by the shoulders and planted a long, deep kiss on my mouth, the kind that had turned my life upside down in the past. Against my better judgment, I melted into him. The kiss traveled through my body, setting a hundred tiny fires.

He pulled away. The world got a bit colder. "Remember when you said I was the best?"

As if I could ever forget. "No."

"Liar."

He got back to stuffing his supplies in a military duffel. "Got to go, cupcake."

"What about your family? What happens on Sunday when you don't show up for church and lunch? You think your grandmother isn't going to launch a manhunt?"

"That's a problem," he said. "Go see her. Make something up."

"What? Me? No!"

"Scared of a little old lady?"

"Just that one," I said.

"This is the way it has to be until I figure out—" He stopped. Shook his head. "Time to go." He threw his duffel over one shoulder, hoisted the cooler, and steered me out with his spare hand.

"Forget it! I've got a bunch of money riding on this. I need that money. Chunky needs new clothes!"

He burst out laughing. "Who?"

"My cat. He lives with Chaz. I have to pay cat support. The judge said so."

He shook his head. "What a world we live in. Cats don't need clothes, cupcake. Tell your moron ex-husband that. I'm sorry about your money, but better you don't get it if you're going to spend it on cat clothes."

While I'd love to say I didn't give a crap about his opinions, his open mockery hurt. Dressing Chunky up in clothes wasn't my idea. Yes, I went along with it because that was a condition of the custody agreement, but that didn't mean I was the mastermind of that particular piece of ridiculousness. It stung that Luke thought I was silly. We'd known each other forever. It was true, I'd stuffed his head in my wedding cake and kneed him so hard it was a wonder he couldn't still smell his own underpants, but he'd brought that on himself.

"You started it with your kissing and your hands and that tongue!"

"Now I'm finishing it."

He took off down the stairs. Outraged, I stormed after him. He didn't get to have the last word. I had a paycheck to collect, damn it.

"You don't have the right to finish it!"

I elbowed him out of the way, blocking his exit. Probably I looked like a giant starfish spread out across the sliding door.

Luke blew out a sigh. "I'd love to stay and fuck you for old time's sake, but I've got to go. Could be it's already too late."

"I didn't come here to ask for sex!"

"Then what's with the cute dress? It's sexy. Got that girl next-door thing that gets me hard."

"I wanted to look respectable and non-threatening!"

"Mission definitely not accomplished."

He shoved me out of the way and pushed through the back door. I half ran, half walked to keep up. The man had long legs and here I was, stuck with this thirty-inch inseam.

"We're not done here!" I hissed.

That didn't slow him down. He took a right, toward the street where I'd parked. He stopped at a small, sporty SUV. The lights flashed, he threw his stuff inside, and went to climb in.

I pressed my hand against the handle. He couldn't just take off like this. "Tell me what's going on? What are you running from? The Luke Remis I know doesn't run away from anything—not even me after I've rearranged his goobers and shoved him in a cake."

A flicker of that old Luke came back when he slipped his arm around my waist and lifted me up and out of the way like my favorite food group wasn't cake. His face turned from hard Greek marble to something softer and infinitely hotter.

"You're small and maneuverable. I always liked that about you."

"I already told you, I'm not here for sex!"

"Who said anything about sex?" Now that I was no longer obstructing the door, he yanked the handle and angled inside. The car came to life and he rolled down the window an inch. "I meant it's easy to get you the hell out of my way."

"You can't get rid of me this easily!"

He revved the engine. "Cupcake, I already did."

CHAPTER 5

THE LIGHTS WERE OFF and nobody was home at the strip mall. Only the dispensary across the street was doing brisk business. I didn't want drugs; I wanted answers and maybe a basket of fries. Luke Remis was alive and in one piece—for now—but the most cocksure and confident man I'd ever me struck me as scared. Someone was after him. At various times in my life I wished Zeus would shove a thunderbolt up Luke's ass, but now that I knew Zeus was real, I wanted take-backsies. If anyone was going to shove a blunt object up Luke's rear, I wanted it to be me and my foot.

The door opened. Nikki ushered me in.

"If you stand there too long, people will think you're selling the *mouni*." She winced. "That was my grandmother talking."

I got it. Greek DNA was pushy.

"Working late?"

"A lot of unauthorized traffic lately. Someone has to do the paperwork, and the boss doesn't do paperwork."

"Unauthorized traffic?"

"Everyone and everything wants to vacation in our

world. We have electricity and we don't have a bunch of petty gods waiting for us to screw up. We're discerning, though. Some things are too dangerous to unleash on our world."

"Like what?"

"The gods, mostly. They're too childish and bossy. The last thing mankind needs is Hera berating every server and cashier on the planet, and demanding to speak to the manager."

That made sense ... for something that made no sense whatever. I was still struggling to believe.

I flopped down in one of the armchairs and flung an arm over my face.

"Why do you smell like you've been rolling in grass?"

"I mowed Luke's lawn—front and back."

She shook her head. "That's what I heard but I figured it was just talk. Bad idea. Never mow a man's lawn. No *poutsa* is that good. I don't suppose you found Luke."

"I found him."

Nikki crossed herself, forehead to chest, shoulder to shoulder. "He's alive?"

"For now. But it seemed like he was really worried he wouldn't be for long."

The boss cut into the conversation. "Yeah, if you could bring Luke in, that would be great."

I sat upright. "Wait, what? Bring him in? What's that supposed to mean?"

"You heard me. Bring Luke here. Doesn't matter how you do it, but getting him back here is imperative."

"Why? He's alive. I did my part. Come to think of it, shouldn't you be tossing money at me right now? Wait— does this have anything to do with the Minotaur being dead?"

"I'm going with yes," Nikki said,.

"Another five thousand of your American dollars if you manage to get him here," the boss said.

Dollar signs danced in my eyes. Five thousand was a lot of dough, on top of what the boss had already promised. Still, I'd fulfilled the first part of the mission. Shouldn't he be paying up?

"I need to live," I said. "And to live in this world a person needs money."

"Don't you live at home with your parents?"

"That's hurtful, that's what that is. Also yes, I live with my parents. But I have my own place above their place. So I'm sort-of independent."

"If you say so," the boss said. "You there, girl. Give her a thousand of your dollars to bridge the gap until she brings Luke Remis in."

I salivated at the thought of finally having some cash. The salon had barely paid enough for basics. A thousand would get Chaz off my back for another month.

"How am I supposed to persuade Luke to come here?" I asked. "He didn't even want me to tell you he was alive."

"I don't know," the boss said. "Use your feminine wiles, if you have any. Offer him one of your father's goats."

"My father doesn't have goats."

"That's not a thing here," Nikki told him. "Nobody uses goats as currency."

"I miss the goats," the boss said in a wistful voice. "Made it easy to count your wealth."

"Remember the number I gave you?" Nikki said. "Call Grim. He's our best Norse myth agent. He'll hook you up with everything you need to bring Luke in."

"Grim has a goat?" the boss asked.

"Still no goats," Nikki said. "Grim dragged the Kraken

back when it was sitting off the Oregon Coast, pretending to be an offshoot of the Haystack Rock. We didn't lose a single tourist thanks to Grim."

"The Kraken." I was feeling woozy. Which was weird, seeing as how I loved seafood. There was nothing like a heaping plate of fried calamari. "How did it, uh, get here?"

Nikki shrugged. "It climbed the World Tree."

———

When he wasn't slinging cephalopods—was the Kraken a cephalopod?—Fargrim "Grim" Gunnerson's regular hangout was a downtown bar that believed less was more in the decorating department. The place was built like a long-house. Glowing fire pit in the center. Small wooden bar off to the side. Clientele came in two flavors: Thor cosplayers and bikers.

Grim slid behind the bar and poured us a couple of beers. I didn't have the heart to tell him that my palate had decided early on that all fermented beverages tasted like they'd done time in a corpse's bladder. I nursed the drink while I wondered what the heck I was doing here, sitting across from what had to be a Norse god.

Fargrim Gunnarson wore his blond mane long and loose. Women paid a fortune to get his soft, beachy waves, and here he was acting like they were no big deal. His arms were thick and corded branches, and his torso dared people to "fuck around and find" out at their convenience. His eyes were a deep, discerning and ageless blue, although if I had to guess, we probably ticked the same age box on forms. He towered over me by at least a foot.

He raised his glass. "So you're the boss's new Greek myth agent."

"Wasn't exactly my idea. I was gunning for the janitorial position when I turned the tables on him and forced him to take me on."

"Why?"

"Because I'm broke and I don't like it. I especially don't like the constant phone calls from my ex-husband telling me what a loser I am because I haven't sent him this month's check."

"He's taking money from you and *you're* the loser?"

"We have a cat. He's the primary custodial parent and I get visitation."

Grim's laugh boomed through the bar. "You pay child support for a cat?"

"Hey, good food and vet care are expensive."

"If you say so. So this is financial for you, no problem. We've all got to make our own way in this world. What do you need from me?"

"Tips, I guess. The boss hired me to find someone. I found them. Now the boss has upped the ante and I'm supposed to bring that person in. His best idea was to lure in my target with a goat."

"The boss has goat issues."

"Can I ask you something?"

"That's why you're here, right?"

"Am I losing my mind?"

"You look sane enough to me, but what do I know?"

"No—I mean the mythology thing. Is it really real?"

He took a long pull on his beer. A couple of human mountains stalked past. They raised their hands in greeting. Grim raised his glass.

"Real as real gets."

"But they're just stories."

"Stories have to come from somewhere, and the truth is

as good as anywhere. The old stories endure because of that spark of truth."

"Before yesterday I would have said they came from our imaginations."

"Imagination, belief, DNA memory, it's all the same well we draw on. The point is that myths are real. How much did the boss and Nikki tell you?"

"Just enough to get myself into trouble and not nearly enough to get myself out of it."

"Yeah, they do that. Okay, I'll do my civic duty because you're cute and I hate to see a cute woman get hurt. It's like this. Mythology is real. All of it. Some of the details aren't right in books, but the shape of them is accurate enough. Given that you've been hired on as one of the Greek myth agents, I'm gonna assume you've seen the labyrinth."

"And the goat dudes and Zeus's golden coin shower."

Grim laughed. "Yeah, Zeus does that. A punch to the dick puts him in his place. Alright, so the other mythologies are real, too. Norse, Egyptian, Roman, although they plagiarized off the Greeks and just changed the character names. All of them have entrances that lead to that one strip mall. They have them in other places, too, but our branch of the Labyrinth Agency only deals with the Salem area."

"Ha-ha," I said weakly.

"What myth agents do is locate and apprehend anything that comes through without permission. Then we send them back."

"That's what Nikki said. What about the reverse? Does anyone try to go back the other way? Humans sneaking into the various myth worlds?"

"Not supposed to. The other side has its own authorities. But sometimes it happens anyway. They do that and they're on their own." The look on my face made him shake his head. "It's no cakewalk in there."

"So you just leave them there?"

Grim shrugged. "Not always. Sometimes we send in a lone agent or a small team. If the authorities on the other side allow it. There are treaties, and one of the biggest rules is that nobody sends assassins or recover agents across worlds without permission. Violate the treaties and things will turn to shit fast. So what did the boss send you to bring in? Dryad? Runaway satyr? You're new so I'm guessing he's going easy on you."

"Another agent. Luke Remis."

He laughed so loud the whole joint went quiet. Heads turned in our direction. Grim didn't care. He drained his beer and slapped the glass on the table.

"What?"

"What the hell is the boss thinking, sending you after Remis?"

I felt an uncomfortable squeeze of mild outrage. Obviously the boss and Nikki had confidence in me, even if this Grim character didn't. I had dozens of skills on my resume beyond styling hair, waiting tables, and pumping gas, and I could dodge a flying shoe and dance a pretty good *sirtaki*. That had to count for something.

"Obviously he thinks I can do it. What I need is help bringing Remis back."

"Forget about Luke Remis. Tell Nikki to give you something you can handle. He's a dead man walking right now if what I heard is true."

That caught my attention. I sat bolt upright. "What do you mean?"

He shook his head. "They really did send you in unprepared, didn't they? I gotta ask myself why."

"Luke and I have history."

"Old flame?"

"So much messier and briefer and longer and more complicated than that. Talk to me about why he's a dead man. What's going on? He didn't look dead when I saw him earlier. I already found him once. I can find him again and bring him back in."

"Damn, you found him?"

"What, like it's hard?"

"So why didn't you haul him in then?"

"The boss moved the goal post after I located Remis. Not that it would have done any good. He seemed to be pretty keen to vanish."

"Yeah, I bet. Look, the word is that Remis bagged himself the Minotaur, the one he was supposed to locate and return to the other side. Instead, he killed the creature. King Minos of Crete is protective of his bull. It's his kid. Now he wants Remis's head on a pike. That's why the boss wants someone to bring him in."

"The Minotaur is this king's kid?"

"Don't think about it too hard. They're not like us there."

"Damn right they're not if those kinds of shenanigans are genetically viable." I drummed my fingers on the table. "Why would Luke kill the Minotaur?"

"Don't know. Probably had a good reason. Know your mythology? The Minotaur's favorite snack is people. Wouldn't surprise me if Remis did what he did because he there wasn't a better option. It was the bull or a person."

"Why was the Minotaur here in the first place if he's a people-eater? Shouldn't he on a no-fly list or something?"

"Don't know about the Minotaur specifically. A lot of myth folks live here full-time, part-time. Some work here and commute. Like I said, there are all kinds of treaties in place. The boss isn't about to risk it all for one agent, even if it's his second-best guy, I know that much. Someone has to hold Remis accountable."

"What's the best?"

"You're looking at him."

"So why not send you after him instead of me?"

He reached over and tapped me on the forehead. "Because this is a Greek Mythology problem and I'm strictly Norse Mythology, remember? But it's interesting that he's sending a neophyte. Either he thinks you're good or he doesn't want Luke brought in that badly."

"Do you think you can teach me how to catch Luke?"

He gave me a long, level stare. "Are you sure you want to?"

"Why wouldn't I?"

"What happens after you bring Remis in? Have you thought about that? Given that you've got history, you might not like what happens to him next—or you might love it."

Acid churned in my empty stomach. My last meal was hours ago and a hundred percent cake. The money. I was doing this for the money because I was out of other ideas. Right? If the job required bringing Luke Remis, then that's what I had to do, didn't I? "Can I get a basket of fries?" I asked weakly.

"Forget the fries," Grim said. "You're gonna need to fuel yourself right if you want to find your man." He left the table for a moment and returned with a protein bar. Low in sugar. "This work isn't for the soft. You want to catch anything, you're gonna need to toughen up, inside and out. You think you can handle it?"

Did I have a choice? As far as I could tell, being an adult mostly involved paying bills and sucking things up to survive the bad times.

"I have to," I said.

"Good attitude. You'll never catch Remis but maybe you'll last the night. Now, you want to catch yourself one of our agents, you're going to have to be prepared. That means you've got to be able to defend yourself.

"Defend myself?" I gulped. This job was shaping up to be a lot. "You mean there's a chance I might die?"

"There are worse things out there than death."

It wasn't all bad news. As Grim mentioned, preparation was important. According to him, he was the guy to help me line my defensive ducks in a quivering, jibbering row.

"You mean weapons?"

Grim peered down his nose at me. His significant acreage of muscle flexed as he folded his arms. "You ever used weapons before?"

"Do sarcasm and insults count?"

His lips twitched at the corners. "Know what you call an untrained person with a weapon? A victim. You want a weapon, you need to train."

"How can I train if I don't have a weapon to train with?"

"Got to keep you alive first. C'mon." His long blond locks flipped as he tilted his head at the back of the bar. He pushed back his chair. For a big guy he was graceful.

"Is this like a *Men in Black* thing? We go to a seedy pawn shop run by a hydra in disguise, who is secretly hoarding mythological weapons and defensive equipment?"

"You watch too much TV."

"But are we?"

"None of a hydra's heads would be caught dead in a pawn shop, unless it was on the water."

Grim drove. He owned a big black pickup truck with all the fancy trimmings, including a bone-rattling audio system. He turned the Nordic death metal down low so he could answer half my questions and ignore the rest. About fifteen minutes after we left the bar, he pulled into the parking lot outside a store that sold hot tubs.

"Really?"

"Hydras dig water," was all he'd say.

We didn't go into the hot tub outlet. Instead, he opened the door to the business next door: a weapons store. Syne of the Times, the painted sign said.

"I don't really do guns," I said.

"Couldn't get a gun here if you wanted one."

A bell tinkled as Grim held the door open for me. This had to be a joke. Not a funny one either. The store was empty, save for a counter and a beaming cashier with a waterfall of golden hair and t-shirt with the store name emblazoned on the front. She smiled as us as though she couldn't do anything else with her face.

"Grim," she said. "Did you take a wrong turn?"

"New Greek myth agent," he said, pushing me forward. "Give her the starter kit so she can survive the night."

If the starter kit included nothing and zilch, we'd come to the right place.

The cashier hurried around the counter. She kissed me on both cheeks, Greek-style. "I'm Philophrosyne, daughter of Hephaestus. You can call me Syne. Welcome to my weapons store."

"Hephaestus? The" —my brain blipped and blooped— "the god?"

"Yes." She hugged me. "You feel like a small, so we'll start there, okay?"

"Okay?"

A white pedestal appeared out of nowhere. Waist-high. Doric style. Atop the pedestal were three items. Pepper spray. A stun gun. One letter opener. Could be a dagger.

Syne presented me with the items one at a time. When she got to the letter opener she said, "Sword."

"Aren't swords bigger?"

"It's not the size of the sword that matters."

"It's how you use it?"

"Ah!" Her smiled flared another twenty watts. "You know swords."

CHAPTER 6

THE HOUSE WAS QUIET. Everyone was tucked in their beds except Mom, who was passed out on the couch with a book on her face and an empty plate on her chest. I carefully extricated the plate and book and draped a blanket over her.

She sat bolt upright. "Plastic surgery!"

With that sleep-fueled exclamation out of the way, she flopped backwards and began rattling like an old truck.

I crept to the kitchen, desperate for dinner. Didn't matter how cold. Mom had left a covered bowl, along with a slab of cake—also covered. I carried both upstairs to my own kitchen and hunkered down at the coffee table.

I was about to fork the first twirl of spaghetti into my mouth when the toilet flushed. The fork fell back into the bowl. I scuttled sideways, reaching for my bag.

Yiayia hobbled into the living room. "Huh. I got lost on the way to the bathroom and ended up here. You are late. What time is this that you come home?"

"I was working."

"Working, working, always working. I will speak to

Androniki about sending my granddaughter to the sweat shop! How many pairs of pants did you make, eh?"

"Today was a zero pants day. I'm not working in a sweatshop." Although come to think of it, I'd done more than my fair share of sweating today, most of it while mowing Luke Remis's lawns. "I'm less of a consultant and more of a secret agent. At least I think it's a secret. Come to think of it, nobody mentioned anything about keeping secrets."

"A secret agent!" She shook her hands at the ceiling. "*Ahpa-pa*! That is the job I wanted when I was young. Instead I got married. What a mistake that was. When you get married, eh? Today a woman can be a wife and a secret agent."

"Tried that. Didn't work out."

"Because that *malakas* was not a Good Greek Boy. Marry a Good Greek Boy and you will not have problems. A Greek husband will do anything you tell him to do, yes?"

"I don't want a husband."

"Every woman wants a husband."

"Lesbians beg to differ."

"Lesbians! Pah! Where I come from we call them wives, same as any other woman."

Probably that wasn't true. Didn't matter either way. I was a hundred percent sure of my sexuality and I definitely didn't want another husband. The first one had scarred me for life with his weirdo mommy attachment.

"I'm not interested in a husband right now. What I want to do is succeed at work, make money, and eat this spaghetti."

She patted me on the cheek. "You will have my money when I die."

The only money Yiayia had was her pension. "I'd rather

have you around. The good news is that I got a thousand bucks today. But I had to buy some things."

"Did you get anything good?"

"Pepper spray, a stun gun, and a sword." The sword was less of a sword and more of a dagger, but Grim had told me I had to start somewhere. He wanted me to practice opening mail with it before I took it out in the field.

"A stun gun! *Po-po-po*! I have never seen such a thing. Can I touch it?"

What could it hurt? I dug around in my bag and handed Yiayia my stun gun.

She held up the black stick. "That does not look like a gun."

"I think they were just looking for something that rhymed with 'stun' and 'gun' was an easy target."

"How does it work?"

She waved it around.

"Wait. Don't."

ZAP.

I blacked out. When I woke up, Yiayia was cackling.

"Can you get me one of these?"

"What? No! Why?"

"I need it for that man."

"Forget it. Dad won't be happy if you start zapping Grandpa. Besides, he probably has a dickey heart." That part was probably true. Grandpa's favorite food groups were sugar and fats—and not the good kind either. He was a go-lard-or-go-home guy, unless bacon fat was on the menu. Mom tried, but there were limits to her powers. You can't stop a grown man with a debit card and a Walmart+ account.

"Okay." The way she shrugged I suspected the conversation was over but the idea of acquiring a stun gun was very much alive.

"Yiayia ..."

She raised both hands. "What? What? I am going to bed now. Maybe I can sleep. At my age all I do is lie awake and count."

"Sheep?"

"Sometimes regrets, sometimes my enemies. The other night I counted the number of *poutsas* I have seen. Do you know how many of them were that one man on the TV, the Harvey Keitel?"

I stared at her.

"Okay, okay, I go now."

Sleep started to knock on the back of my eyes. I wasn't going to last much longer. Resting up was imperative. Tomorrow the manhunt would begin in earnest.

Friday arrived fast and with the threat of rain. An empty threat. Salem's summers were frequently warm, increasingly scorching, and drier than a lost sock in the Mojave Desert. By the time I'd finished pouring coffee, the clouds had fizzled up and it was nothing but blue skies all the way to the horizon. My phone was lit up with text messages from my ex-husband. One was from his mother, admonishing me for not returning his messages. Given that the advance from work had already hit, I sent him a couple of hundred bucks and hoped that would shut him up for now.

He texted right back.

Chaz: *Where did you get the money? Rob a bank?*

Me: *From your mommy.*

Yes, it was immature. No, I didn't regret it.

Chaz: *Loser.*

Me: *Go try on your mommy's clothes again, Norman Bates.*

Still fuming, I rifled through my wardrobe and took stock of my potential outfits. What did I have that was appropriate yet still professional for engaging in a manhunt? The sundress was a no-go. Too girly and no pockets. The pencil skirt was also out. Too hot for jeans. I scrounged up shorts, a white tank top, and hiking boots. My Lara Croft outfit. If she could do adventures in this outfit, then I could hunt down Luke Remis, potential Minotaur slayer. In the shower I'd mentally sketched the world's roughest plan.

"Waffles?" Mom called out as I was leaving.

"Can't. I have to work."

"They're chocolate chip."

"Really?"

"No, they're blueberry because your grandparents need the antioxidants."

"I guess I could go for some waffles," I said. "Blueberry is fine."

I tried helping in the kitchen but Mom shooed me away. "This is my punishment," she said.

"For what?"

"I don't know, but I bet it was something bad."

The center of the table was loaded with several kinds of syrup. Grandpa was hogging the maple.

"Go easy on the syrup," Mom told him. "All that sugar, it's not good for you."

"Drink the syrup," Yiayia muttered. Mom rolled her eyes.

Grandpa scoffed. He wasn't about to give up his precious syrup anytime soon. "It's natural. Straight from a tree. That makes it a fruit. Heck, maybe even a vegetable."

"A vegetable," Mom muttered.

Yiayia wasn't eating her waffle. She never did until no one was looking. She refused to be seen consuming American breakfast foods. They were beneath her. Back in her village, during her youth, breakfast was coffee and a cigarette, and occasionally toasted bread slathered with olive oil.

I smothered my waffle with butter and selected my go-to table syrup.

"Penny has a stun gun and she let me use it," Yiayia announced.

All eyes swiveled toward me.

"I don't have a stun gun," I lied because it was the first thing that popped into my head. "Okay, maybe I do. But it's only a small one."

"Penny said she would get me one, too."

"I never said that," I said.

"And she has pepper spray."

"I need some of that for cooking," Mom said. "Seems like it would be good for seasoning."

"Stun guns," Grandpa said with a mouth crammed full with waffle. "Pepper spray." Flecks of syrup and waffle launched across the table. "Those are girl weapons."

"They're more for defense," I said.

"Defense!" Mom and Yiayia crossed themselves. "What are you defending yourself from?" Mom asked.

"Uh, probably small animals. Definitely not bad guys."

My mother didn't look convinced. She crossed herself again and went *ptou-ptou*. The spit was fake but the magic was real in her mind.

"Time to go," I said before she could chain me to my chair. "The waffles were great, Mom."

Before she could whisk my plate away, I carried it to the

kitchen, rinsed it off, and placed it in the dishwasher. She opened the dishwasher, moved the plate, and closed it again. "I heard on *Good Morning America* that today is *Take Your Grandparents to Work Day*," she said.

"You wish."

She sighed. "It was worth a try."

I fled before anyone else could beg me for weapons. Thankfully Yiayia had fixated on the stun gun and pepper spray. The sword went forgotten, probably because anything can be a sword if you have access to a kitchen. The blade was something Grim had called adamantine, but if you asked me it looked like a big diamond. I didn't want a sword but Grim and Syne had insisted. They said I'd need it, sooner or later, because creatures from Greek mythology had their own special aversion to adamantine. I didn't want to stab anything or anyone. Maybe I could work on my intimidation skills. Look threatening while waving the sword.

With my new toys, I set out for the first place on my list. Once again, the plan was to start with the lowest hanging fruit and work my way up the tree. I hid the diamond sword under the seat when I parked at Mrs. Remi's place. Something told me a sword wouldn't faze her. Probably she ate weapons for breakfast. That or I'd wind up with the blade stuck in a hole where no sharp things should go.

I steeled myself. Fixed my wedgie. Straightened my ponytail and hoped this encounter wouldn't end in the death of my self-esteem.

Mrs. Remi cracked the door. Her nose appeared first, followed by her hawkish eyes. She scraped her gaze over me and came to a decision. "*Vre*, what are you doing? What happened to the rest of your trousers?"

Be still my freaking-out heart. "I was wondering if Luke was here."

She stared at me like I was a grubby window. "For what?"

I winced on the inside. "Hiking?"

"My grandson is not here. Try his house. But put on some more clothes first."

The door closed.

Well. That was that.

I skulked back to my car and tried to figure out who else might know where Luke Remis was hiding out. Given that he was Greek like me, his family tree was a sprawling behemoth with hundreds of branches. He could be hiding out on any one of them. But I didn't think so. Like my own Greek relatives, none of them could keep a secret. If Luke was sleeping in one of their spare rooms, it would be all over the community. Same as the neighbors.

I tried to think over what Grim had told me last night. Luke was on the run from King Minos—utterly bonkers—after killing his pet Minotaur. Plot twist: the king's pet was also his child. In this country, we had laws and therapy for that sort of thing.

How was I supposed to find him again?

KISS. Keep It Simple, Stupid.

I sketched a flowchart on paper. In the first box I wrote *Find out Why*.

Step One: Figure out *why* Luke had killed the Minotaur. If Grim was right, Luke wouldn't have felled the creature without a good reason. I needed to figure out that reason. Why would he risk the wrath of King Minos, who was apparently a pretty wrathful guy?

"Maybe he didn't do it," Lena said when I called her and explained the situation, minus the mythology bits.

"You don't think he did it?"

"Think about it. What did Luke do when you smushed his face in your wedding cake and kicked him in the goodie bag?"

"He left."

"Yeah, he left without retaliating, right? What I'm saying is that Luke Remis isn't a violent guy. He wouldn't put the hurt on anyone unless there was a great reason. Self defense maybe. Or he was protecting something or someone else. Or maybe he didn't do it. Maybe it just looks like he did, so everyone is assuming he's the perp."

"Lena ..."

"I know, I know. I've been watching too much *Law and Order* and *CSI*. I can't help myself. It's so easy to binge watch TV these days. Baby kicks in time to the gavel sound now."

She was right, though. Luke Remis was a guy who ended fist-fights. He didn't start them. If he was involved, chances were he was wading in to separate the swinging fists. Yes, if rumors were true, these days he went through women like I did cake, but that didn't make him violent. Just easy.

I was back to where I started: tracking the Minotaur's path. If I followed in Luke's footsteps, maybe I could find out if he had actually killed the half-man, half-bull and take it from there.

———

I had questions. Because I didn't want to bug Grim again—he struck me as someone who slept during the daylight hours, when he wasn't plundering—I decided to hit up Nikki and the boss.

"You're back," Nikki said. "Did you find him?"

"That's a negative," I said, letting my bag slide to the floor. "I have questions."

"Hit me."

"Okay, here we go. What happens to creatures, like, say, the Minotaur when they die?"

"Easy. If they kick the bucket in their world, they dissolve and wait to be reborn from the primordial goop."

"And if they die here, in our world?"

She made a face. "Some turn to goop. Others leave a body, so we send in a cleanup crew. They're meticulous."

"We have a cleanup crew?"

"Given that we're privately funded, we have a lot of cool things."

I filed that away. "So is it here? The Minotaur, I mean. Or is it goop, waiting to be reborn?"

"I don't know if I'm supposed to say."

There was a big sigh from the boss. "I suppose it's time you got to see the guts of this place. Come on back. Through the same door and down the steps. This time take the first left."

"You heard the boss," Nikki said brightly. She kissed me on both cheeks before returning to her snack: a chunk of bread and a lump of feta.

The boss's instructions involved entering the labyrinth again, which I really didn't fancy. There's no way to make an ancient stone maze *not* creepy. But this time there was no sign of old stones; today I descended into a library, where the stacks ran forever in every direction, including upwards. Everywhere I looked, a forest of shelves and books blocked my view.

"My Virgin Mary, what the heck is going on here?"

"The labyrinth has a mind of its own at times," the boss explained.

I got my adamantine letter opener sword ready, just in case. In case of what, I wasn't sure. A falling pile of books? I added an angry expression and hoped that would be enough of a defense.

"Oh, put that down. You're perfectly safe down here. Well, not *perfectly* safe. There's always a chance of death or random acts of mutilation. But the odds are quite good that you'll be fine, I must say. Did Syne give you that sword? It looks like her doing. Fond of swords, that one. I'm more of a fan of adamantine bullets."

"Now I'm even more determined to not put the sword away."

"Can you even call that a sword? It's quite small. Practically a dagger."

"The Salem Police tend to frown on swords. I'm happier with something I can keep in my handbag."

He quit blabbing.

I took a right where I'd turned left last time, walked a short way past the art history section, and wondered where I was supposed to go next.

"Through the door," the boss said, reading my mind. One minute there wasn't a door, then there was. That should have been enough to send me scampering back upstairs, but I was committed to the insanity now. The door was a heavy bookshelf—Danielle Steel's entire catalog—that wheezed when I shoved it open.

I gawped. Glanced behind me. Peered into the room again and performed some more gawping. What had Nikki said? They were privately funded? Well, it certainly showed. Down in what should have been a sewer, someone had set up a state-of-the-art lab. Lots of cool science doodads. Weapons you couldn't buy from a shady figure lurking in the shadows of an overpass. Disinfectant hovering in the air.

In the center of the room sat a cylindrical fish tank—except this tank was devoid of marine life.

It was a habitat for a head. A male human head, the approximate size of the average male human head. The noggin had a neat, short beard and a nest of curls.

I bit my tongue and definitely didn't make any jokes about getting head. Inappropriate jokes and laughter were frequently my way of dealing with sudden stress.

"Um ... hello?"

The head swiveled around. "Took your time," it said in what was definitely the boss's voice.

My eyelids fluttered frantically as my brain struggled to make sense of the nonsensical.

"Got something in your eye?" he asked dryly.

For several long seconds, my brain tried to reconcile the weirdness. Once it managed to file everything in a way that made sense, I gestured at everything. "All of this."

"Yes, well. I've had centuries—millennia, actually—to accumulate belongings. But I really love modern times. You can buy anything on the internet if you know where to look."

"Excuse me," I said, "but who the heck are you?"

"The boss."

"And you're a brain in a vat?"

"How very simplistic."

"So you're not a brain in a vat?"

"Well, yes. But that's not all I am."

He was snooty for a no-body.

"Where are your" —I tried to be tactful in case his missing body was a sore subject— "other parts?"

"Long gone. But lucky for me, I've got everything I need right here."

"In your fish tank?"

"It's not a fish tank!"

"Yeah, okay. If you say so."

Now that I was relatively sure that nothing was going to leap out and attack me, I moved around the room, inspecting gadgets while keeping my hands to myself.

"What you are looking for is in the fridge," he said.

Refrigerator ... refrigerator ...

Ah. There it was. In the corner. Not exactly the ideal positon for a good kitchen triangle. But then this wasn't a kitchen. Wow, the Minotaur must be tiny. This was a standard refrigerator with the freezer on top. The kind you see in apartments. Maybe they'd put the Minotaur in a blender first. Or he was a miniature. Sometimes that happened in nature. Miniature horses came to mind. I pictured a teeny, tiny man-bull, small enough to fit in a teacup.

"Not that one," he said. "That one."

"Which one?"

"That one."

"Can you point to it?"

Ten long seconds crawled by.

"No."

For a moment I felt bad. Mocking the body-less was completely uncalled for. But I had a sneaky suspicion the boss wasn't disabled as such, and that if he wanted to he could produce a body fairly quickly.

"Okay, so can you describe the direction?"

"Follow my eyes."

His eyes flicked to the end of the room, which I realized was a wall full of lockers, exactly like a morgue. What were they doing down here?

"Have you been a bad, bad head?"

"You'll find the Minotaur in the bottom right," he said, his tone chilled and sprinkled with salt.

Okay, I'd play along. I made my way across the room and tugged on one of the jumbo lockers on the lowest row.

I steeled myself for the potential horrors contained within. How bad would it be?

A drawer slid out easily.

Human feet. Human legs. Not so bad. I dared to exhale and kept pulling. Yikes. Huge penis. Horrifying, actually.

"Yes, I know it's big," the boss said with an exasperated sigh. "And despite what that overblown egotist Minos would tell you, the Minotaur gets it from its mother's side."

I kept on pulling.

Yup. There it was. From the waist on up, the man was a bull with a football field of chest and a set of horns only a poacher could love.

My brain hit its weird-o-rama limit. I pushed the drawer in and went back to the boss's tank.

"How did it die?"

"Multiple gunshot wounds."

"And you think Luke Remis is responsible."

"He was the myth agent in charge of apprehending the creature."

"So someone else could have shot the Minotaur."

"Possibly, but probably not. Occam's Razor, girlie."

"It's Penny Post. Do you have a name?"

"Of course I have a name!" he spluttered. "Okay, I had a name once, but it's irrelevant to this conversation!"

"What will happen to Luke when I bring him in?"

"If you bring him in."

"Oh, I will." My confidence was in the toilet, but my tongue was making it look like I was staying afloat and rowing a boat. The truth was I was in so far over my head that I couldn't see the light above. Although there were vague shadows that I suspected were floating turds.

"We have treaties to uphold!"

"Still not answering my question."

"Minos is vindictive and cruel, as kings often are. It's the bowing and scraping, it goes to their heads. But he's not very imaginative. Minos has always relied upon the brilliance and genius of others, turning on them when things soured."

"You mean like when Daedalus trapped the Minotaur in the labyrinth on Minos's orders and then he revealed the secrets of the labyrinth to Minos's daughter, and she turned around and helped Theseus kill the Minotaur?"

"You make it sound like a silly story! But yes. Daedalus was trapped in the labyrinth for a long time after that incident."

"This labyrinth?"

"Yes."

"Is he still here?"

"Sometimes I hear him scream."

Yikes. "How is the labyrinth here and not in Greece?"

"Of course it's in Greece! It's all over the place. It's just got a bit of a mind of its own and does all kinds of things for fun. It was built to be ever-changing and evolving, you know."

"It's made of stone—and apparently books."

"So? What's that got to do with the price of olives? The point is that I don't know what Minos will do with Remis when we hand him over, but it won't be good. Boring, yes. Good, no. But I don't have a choice. Like I said, there are treaties between our worlds."

"If you ask me, that's stupid."

"Did I ask?"

"So that's it. You're going to just hand Luke over to be tortured and killed?"

"Oh come on, it's not the first time an agent's been tortured!"

I stormed out and left the head to whatever business heads had. Haircuts. Thinking. That sort of thing.

"Did you get what you needed?" Nikki asked.

I leaned on her desk with both hands. "Who else besides your cousin would want to kill a Minotaur? Besides possibly the beef industry."

"From what I understand, Minotaur meat is tough. It's not even good enough for a long, slow pot roast, so burgers are absolutely out of the question." She tapped on her computer. "Everyone hates King Minos, even his own family, so the list is long. That's not including the trophy hunters and the thrill seekers. What's going on?"

"Trying to figure this out. Why would Luke kill the Minotaur?"

"He wouldn't. Not unless he was doing it to save an innocent life."

"Are you sure he killed it? Because I'm not a hundred percent on this, and I'm not bringing him in unless he really slayed the thing."

Nikki crossed herself. "My Virgin Mary, it's a miracle. I didn't think Luke was guilty, either. Murder isn't really his style. Okay, if I were you, I'd work the case like you were looking for the Minotaur."

Nikki and I were on the same page.

"Where did the Labyrinth Agency's cleanup crew find the Minotaur's body?"

"Downtown at Waterfront Park, by the giant globe."

I thanked her for her help, made promises I hoped I could keep, then set off for Waterfront Park.

CHAPTER 7

PEOPLE FREQUENTLY ASSUME Portland is Oregon's capital city. It's an easy mistake to make. Portland is the only Oregon city that ever makes it onto the national news or TV shows. Case in point: *Portlandia*. Nobody would ever think to create a TV show based on people living in Salem. We're too not-Portland. An excess of pickup trucks. A whole lot of livestock. Farmland. We've got more than our fair share of coffee shops, but hipsters are thin on the ground.

Downtown isn't much more than a handful of city blocks shoved up against the Willamette River. Sandwiched in between, on a narrow strip of land, is Riverside Park, featuring a children's museum, an old-timey carousel, and— further down—a giant sculpture of our planet. On a warm day, you can see people flicking garbage into the river or dumping the critter they just used as a speed bump.

Given that it was a summer morning, the park was filled with children, most of them leaping and shrieking at the splash pad while their parents hid inside their phones and tried to remember the BC—Before Children—days. I went the other way: toward the humungous Earth, where River-side Park blurred into Waterfront Park.

Walkers marched past me, swinging their arms to kill a few more calories. We smiled our good mornings and went back to ignoring each other.

When I reached the planet, I slowed down and did my best to inspect the area without looking like I was cruising for drugs or someone to spank me for cash. There was no sign that a Minotaur had been shot here. The paths appeared to be clean—as clean as paths in a public park can be. A cup of sticky soda was drying by a bush. Not exactly a murder weapon. Further down, I discovered a faint blue stain. Paint, probably. Or an ice cream that died by suicide in the hands of a preschooler.

No signs. No addresses. Definitely no casual note, giving me the name and location of the Minotaur's real killer.

I walked back to the blue stain. Something rattled around in my memory banks. Probably a loose screw. I performed a quick search on my phone. According to competing sources, the ichor—blood—of gods, monsters, and other assorted creatures in Greek mythology was either blue or gold. Regarding the color, there was no consensus because it was all stories. Except, you know, not.

Was this Minotaur blood?

I took stock of the area and found nothing else useful.

Were there any electronic eyes on the park? The other side of the street was home to a number of businesses and apartments.

Time to find out.

Despite my divorce and the fact that I'm not a physician, my stitching is close to one hundred percent Good Greek Girl. I don't do crimes. I have a healthy distrust of the government. I itch when it comes to paying taxes but I do it anyway because tax evasion is the bailiwick of Greeks who live in the homeland. Because of all this, and because I score low on the anarchy scale, I pressed the button and waited patiently for the traffic lights to turn red and the little walking figure to flick to a watery green. After I crossed over, I spent the next few minutes, strolling up and down the street, trying to figure out if anyone had security cameras aimed at the park.

"Hey!"

I focused on the canopies and overhangs and avoided eye contact with the person going "Hey." Salem's city sidewalks are cluttered with small camps, where the homeless dwell until they're occasionally swept off the pavements and into a different pile.

"Hey you."

The hey-ing was moving closer. Fear grabbed me by the throat. I didn't want to get mugged or caught up in a conversation with the voices in someone's head. My own inner voices were already pushy enough.

I walked faster.

"Hey lady."

"I don't have any money," I said.

"Don't want your money. Got a whole inheritance of my own, don't I? My dad's a king."

Burger King, maybe. The USA was fresh out of other royalty. But she had me, damn it. There was a hint of humor in her voice that spoke to me. Also there was an oddball hissing sound close by that I hoped wasn't someone urinating against a wall.

I pivoted.

Huh. Not what I expected. The woman had the requisite youthful indigent uniform of hoodie—hood up—torn jeans, and battered Converse Chucks in what was originally a cheerful shade of yellow. That part I totally expected. But the designer sunglasses? Unexpected. Probably a gift from her dad, the king. That or someone lost them at the park across the street.

"What's up?"

She shrugged. "Saw you prowling around the park, and now you're sniffing around over here. I should ask you what's up."

"I wasn't prowling!"

"Creeping, then."

"I wasn't creeping, either." I hoisted my bag further up onto my shoulder and tried to look like a professional. A professional what, I wasn't sure. "I'm working."

"Oh yeah? Well, this corner is taken."

"I'm not a woman whose services can be purchased with a menu! Also, sex work is valid work and I totally respect your choice, although I have to question your wardrobe. Not very skimpy, is it? Mind you, I'm way behind on what's trendy in sex work, so maybe" —I gestured at her outfit— "that's all the rage."

"Sheesh. Is that what you think? That I'm a streetwalker?"

"You're the one who said this was your corner. Wait—is it drugs? I don't want to sell or buy any of those either."

"Shut her up," someone else called out. Another member of her pack. They were clustered around a dead critter—mouse? rat?—further down the sidewalk. The woman in yellow Chucks sighed. She reached up and took off her sunglasses. Her eyes were a luminous sea green.

I froze.

Time passed.

Passersby gawked at me.

My phone rang.

A bird crapped on my head and I couldn't shoo it away.

Finally, I managed to shake loose.

"Did I have some kind of weird seizure?"

Yellow Chucks shrugged. Her glasses were back on her face. "Dunno what you're talking about. Just FYI, you have bird shit in your hair."

"What happened?"

"Nothing."

Yeah, right. She was lying through her teeth, but I let it go. Arguing with people downtown was never a smart idea.

"Wait," I said. "This is your street corner?"

"You got a problem with that?"

"Not at all. Actually, now that I think about it, I'm glad someone, uh, owns this corner. You see anything weird at the park lately?"

The woman and her compadres—all women, I noticed —laughed up a lung apiece.

"Weird is all we see over there," Yellow Chucks told me. "Every freak in town winds up in that park sooner or later. People are attracted to open spaces with trees and water to do their weird shit. Crazies doing nasty deeds where anyone can get a good look."

"That's what gets them off," one of the other women called out. Probably she was right.

"I'm talking about something specific," I said. "Weirder than your usual weird. Maybe someone in a costume?"

Yellow Chucks thought about it. "Like a cosplayer?"

I snapped my fingers. "Exactly. This guy was dressed up like a Minotaur. Dude on the bottom half, bull on the top."

"Huge junk?"

"Probably that was part of the cosplay, but yeah."

The other women, done ogling the dead rodent, saun-tered over. A half dozen in total. They were all dressed the same, hoods up, glasses on, none of them caring that the temperature was already hovering close to ninety. Sweat was having a pool party in my bra. How they weren't passing out was a mystery.

"What do you care?" the one in the red hoodie asked.

"He's a friend of a friend."

"Uh huh. Sure he is. What friend?"

I pulled out my phone and wandered over to Nikki's Facebook page. We were friends, and she was friends with Luke, so I had no problems pulling up a picture of him grinning into the camera at a Remis family shindig. A baptism by the looks of it. One of the other Nikkis had recently added a new Greek-American to the population.

I showed her the picture. "Have you seen him?"

"Don't know. We see a lot of people. Could be we've seen this one. What did he do?"

"He's my real dad."

Yellow Chucks snorted. "Yeah, right. He's not anybody's father yet, although I bet a lot of women wish he'd knock them up."

"So you know him?"

"I know how to keep my mouth shut and my eyes open."

Definitely a yes. "What about the Minotaur cosplayer?"

"Why?"

"It's dead."

"We were busy that night."

They were dropping breadcrumbs all over the place. Not enough to form a loaf, but enough to bread a cutlet.

"Maybe you saw my friend here" —I waggled my phone at them— "with the cosplayer?"

Red Hoodie grabbed her yellow-shoed pal by the arm. "We didn't see nothing."

"A-ha! The presence of a double negative implies that

you saw something. You didn't see nothing, therefore you saw something."

"This bitch ..." Red Hoodie whipped off her sunglasses. She had the same ethereal green eyes as her friends with the yellow Converse.

I froze.

Damn it. I still had bird crap in my hair from my first seizure or whatever this was. It had to be neurological. Mental note to self: Talk to Nikki about the Labyrinth Agency's medical plan.

While I was frozen—Oh my God, was this locked-in syndrome?—Red Hoodie turned on the others. "We've got to get rid of her, otherwise she's gonna fuck us over."

"She seems okay," Yellow Chucks said. "A bit stupid, but that's humans for you."

Whoa. Who were these women? And where was the dead rodent? As soon as this whatever was over, I had to skedaddle.

"She's thicker than pig shit if she's coming here, asking about King Minos's kid. She's in way over her head."

I broke loose again.

"Okay, well, if I said talking to you was fun I'd be lying. Got to go make an appointment with a neurologist," I said.

"Neurologist." Yellow Chucks snorted. "You're better off seeing a shrink. You're all kinds of paranoid. I bet you spend way too much time on YouTube, hunting down conspiracies."

Boy, did she have me pegged wrong. When I fell down a YouTube hole it was because one cute cat video led to another.

I waved in a non-threatening way and took off.

That's right, scram!" Red Hoodie yelled at my departing back. "We got a corner to maintain."

The corner looked fine—very corner-ish—but what did I know about corners except that they were the point where two streets converged?

I power walked back to my car at a fast clip, doing my best not to look back. There was something weird about those women. They'd referred to me as human. That struck me as something a non-human would say. Unless it was a new, ironic type of slang. Anything was possible. Probably the Urban Dictionary would know. I hated new slang; it reminded me that time had its running shoes on.

Safe in my car, I checked my hair in the rearview mirror. Yup, that bird got me good. Not that I was a bird expert, but it seemed to me like it needed to drink less and eat more fiber. I cleaned up as best I could with a tissue and plotted my next move.

Where to next?

I'd started at The End. Time to take the next step backward into the Minotaur's final hours.

Truth be told, I'd considered knocking on doors up and down the street across from the park, but the corner women had me spooked. Something told me if anyone had seen anything, they'd be blabbing all over the internet—

Synapses fired. Conclusions crouched to give my thoughts enough space to leap over them. Yellow Chucks had mentioned YouTube. What if that wasn't a casual mention? What if she was ponying up an oblique clue? What if the answers were on YouTube where anyone could find them?

If I was going to watch a bunch of Youtube, I needed to go home and get comfy. Some one-on-one time with my couch and snacks. But first I wanted to at least swing by the next place on my list.

Before the Minotaur met its blue and sticky end at

Waterfront Park, it had been sighted at a Greek bakery, the kind that specializes in cakes and sweets and leaves the bread and savories to the bakers that work with yeast. What a Minotaur wanted with a bakery, I had no idea. Maybe it liked cake. Not surprising. Who didn't like cake?

I doubled back and crossed over to West Salem, temporarily dying of old age on the bridge. For whatever reason, absolutely no one with the gift of foresight was involved when planning the city, and now we were all stuck struggling to go west across one lousy bridge. It wasn't even a good bridge. Just a two lane thing when we needed at least four.

The Hellas Bakery was perfectly located next to a dispensary in yet another strip mall. An enterprising cannabis shopper could buy their weed and feed the munchies in one trip. A real timesaver. The bakery itself had Greek flag in the window next to a wedding cake and a blue and white awning shielding its segment of the sidewalk from the elements. One of the few exterior ashtrays in existence in the city was outside the bakery. Even transplanted Greeks of a certain age loved their cigarettes.

I parked across the street outside a BOGO Burger and watched the bakery. I scrunched down and tried not to look like a creep. The dispensary was doing brisk business. Probably people loading up for a Monty Python marathon later tonight. None of the traffic appeared to be interested in the bakery next door. Maybe the clientele didn't fancy any of that foreign food. They were missing out. Nothing temporarily cured a craving for sugar like a slab of baklava, or a crisp pastry horn filled with crème pâtissière and sealed with a whirl of freshly whipped cream. Maybe brownies were more their style.

In the rearview mirror, I checked out the BOGO Burger

at my back. They had a few locations around town, and for a while they tried to pretend they were a Five Guys or a Nancy Jo's or an In-N-Out. In the end they gave up and decided to play to their strengths: cheap burgers for customers with no interest in flavor or nutrition. The building had electronic eyes on the entrance and drive-thru. The entrance faced the bakery.

It was a stretch, but my brain was capable of all kinds of ridiculous flexibility.

I left my car and went into BOGO Burger. The aroma of grease seduced my sense. Pictures of golden fries, bobbing in bubbling oil filled my head. I imagined patties of beef-like substance sizzling on the griddles. My stomach wanted a sack of burgers and fries. Good thing my brain was watching out for me.

I bellied up to the counter and asked if I could please speak with the manager.

"Okay, Karen," the acne-dotted kid behind the cash register said.

Geez. All I did was ask a question in a nice tone, using the magic words, and I get attitude from a toddler.

"Spare me the lame internet jokes. Just get the manager. Please," I added, in case anyone who knew my family was within earshot. Last thing I needed was anyone running back to my Greek relatives, breathless with excitement because they caught me not using my "please" and "thank yous."

The boy-baby rolled his eyes and threw some words over his shoulder. "We've got a situation."

"What? No! There's no situation."

A soft, doughy figure appeared from out back. He projected a pleasant and non-threatening aura that I pegged immediately as fake. His eyes were dull marbles that were unaffected by his thin-lipped rictus smile. He wore creased khakis and a red polo shirt that hugged his rolls.

He pointed to his name tag which labeled him as Kevin, Manager.

"There's no situation," I repeated. "I was hoping you could help me."

"We're always hiring here at BOGO Burger," Kevin, Manager said.

"I'm not looking for work, thank you." I swung around and pointed to the front door. "Those cameras outside, do they work?"

"That's classified information." His voice was cheery but his smile was starting to slip.

"Classified by whom?"

"Our corporate office. We can't go around giving out that sort of information willy-nilly. Has there been an incident?"

"My husband is cheating on me," I lied. "Or at least I suspect he is. I think the other woman—or man—works across the street at the bakery." I hit him with my best puppy-dog eyes and threw in a bucketload of sad, betrayed wife.

Kevin, Manager sighed and leaned across the counter. He glanced left and right like he was anticipating the arrival of the corporate cops, who'd revoke his polo shirt and name tag. "Look, you didn't hear this from me, but they're for show. Corporate is too cheap to spring for the real deal, no matter how many burgers scumbags steal."

"People steal your burgers?"

Hard to imagine anyone was that desperate. Maybe it was a slow death by nutritional suicide thing.

"Oh, yes. Usually it's people from *that place* across the street." He tilted his head toward the dispensary. "They buy their drugs and then they steal from me."

"Have you called the police?"

"What's the point? They won't do anything. It's just burgers. If it was donuts they'd be falling over themselves to make arrests."

I was pretty sure that was a stereotype and the police didn't discriminate between burgers and donuts when it came to their snacks. But Kevin, Manager looked so serious that I let it go without correcting him.

"I don't suppose you've seen him—my husband—over at the bakery?" Time to stroke the ego a bit. Kevin, Manager had that crestfallen, soulless look about him. Common amongst people who'd served at least a couple of tours in customer service—and Kevin, Manager looked like he'd been struggling with the public his whole adult life. "I'm confident you don't miss anything around here. You strike me as a man who pays attention to the details."

His spine straightened. "Yes, well, I try. It's part of being a good manager. You can't lead a team if you're not observant." He turned around. "Dwayne, stop eating the fries or I'll dock your pay!" He adjusted his collar. "They don't get a lot of storefront business over there, seems like. Not a lot of people around here are into those fancy foreign cakes. Too expensive, for one. But they do a lot of catering. Got a van around back that does deliveries. They must be doing okay. They've been here since BOGO Burger moved in, and that was some fifteen years ago."

"Have you been here that long?"

He beamed. "Started as a cashier. And look at me now: I'm the manager." He chucked his chin at me. "You got a picture of your husband? Maybe I've seen him."

Earlier I'd saved Luke Remis's picture in case I had to show it off again. I tried not to notice that he looked good with his shirt button open just a notch.

"Okay, yeah, I saw him the other day." Kevin, Manager did a lot of nodding. Dandruff flakes rained on the counter. "Late afternoon. I was wiping down tables because a couple of our team members couldn't be bothered showing up to work. He went inside, then came back out with a white paper bag."

"Sounds like he bought a pastry."

"Yeah, he ate it right there on the sidewalk while he was playing with his phone. When he was done he drove away. He came back later on foot and went around the back. That's where they keep the van."

"Did you see him with anyone?"

"Nope. If he's cheating, maybe it's an online thing. He was more interested in his phone than an actual person."

"You're so helpful, thank you. I don't suppose you've seen anything ... strange over there."

"I see all kinds. That depository brings in every sort of weirdo to the neighborhood. A lot of regular folks, too. Not the kind you'd peg as stoners. Marijuana has really gone mainstream."

"This would be irregular even for the depository. Say, a cosplayer."

"They get a lot of those, too. Can you believe it?"

"Anything like a half-man, half-bull?"

"You mean a Minotaur where the top half is a bull, or where the top is human?"

"Wait—you've seen the second kind?"

"No, but it could happen. Definitely seen the first kind, the one with the bull on top. That was one heck of a cosplay. He was huge. Probably one of those basketball players inside."

"Did you see my" —I almost gagged slightly on the word — "husband with him?"

"Nope. But he was with a couple of women, maybe."

"Can you tell me anything about them?"

"No can do. I was too busy contemplating what Minotaur guy was going to order and how he was going to eat it in that costume."

"Probably he was going to eat it later."

"Could be right. But I never did see him come out. We got busy about that time. Never saw him again. Or your husband."

"And the women?"

"Wouldn't know them if they were standing in front of me." He pointed at me. "One of them wasn't you, was it?" He laughed at his own joke. "Just kidding."

Since I owed him something for his help, I bought a bag of burgers, two orders of fries, a large chocolate shake, thanked him for his time, and went back to my car.

I dumped everything on the passenger seat and sifted through my thoughts before jotting down a few notes on my phone. The Minotaur had been here. Ditto Luke Remis. He'd eaten cake—without the Minotaur. Also, two people had been sighted with the Minotaur. Both maybe female, with no particular features, clothes, or mannerisms. That ruled out approximately nobody.

Time to take my burgers and go home. Hopefully the YouTube thing would pan out. So far I had nothing but lying junk food. I knew the taste would never match the delicious, mouth-watering smell, and yet here I was, reaching into the bag, digging out fries.

Before I hit the road, I crossed over and tried to look cool and calm as I approached the bakery. The sign in the door was flipped to OPEN. I pushed the door open, breathing deeply as the aroma of sugar and baked goods enveloped me. It smelled like Yiayia's kitchen when she and bunch of friends from the old country got together to bake sweets and shred reputations.

Behind the counter was a mustache pinned to a bowling ball. The woman was shrouded in a navy blue housedress printed with geometric patterns. Her hair was permed tight and high. Not to be judgmental, but her scowl wasn't great customer service. Maybe she could hit up Kevin, Manager for lessons on how to play well with others.

She squinted at me.

"What?" she said in thickly accented English.

I tried to look like my intentions were all cake-based.

"*Ti kanes,*" I asked her in Greek. Direct translation: What are you doing? Greeks are more interested in what you're doing than how you feel about it. Only one of those things is gossip-worthy, and it's not your emotions.

She grunted, unimpressed with my linguistic skills.

"What do you want? Baklava? Only *xenes* come for baklava. That is the only Greek dessert they know."

"*Kataifi,*" I said, referring to baklava's more obscure (outside of Greece) cousin. I held up two fingers. She stared at me. I held up four fingers. May as well be honest about my intentions. Oh, fine. "Make it six."

Another grunt.

While she was slinging nests of pastry into a box, I glanced around the shop, curious about what could have drawn a Minotaur to this place. On the surface the bakery seemed normal enough. Cold cabinets for items that required refrigeration. Room temperature cabinets for sweets that could easily survive in air conditioning. A freezer for ice cream. Mural of Greece on one wall. Posters on another. The place was clean. The air was still. The only sound was a radio playing Greek music, barely above a whisper.

I took a risk. A foolish, barely calculated risk. While the mustachioed woman was boxing up my sweets, I retrieved my phone and slid to Luke Remis's photo.

"I don't suppose you've seen this man?"

She didn't look up. "I know nobody. I see nothing."

I wiggled the phone. "Maybe take a peek?"

"I no know him."

"His name is Luke Remis. Does that sound familiar at all? The Greek community is pretty tight knit about here, maybe you know his *yiayia*? Androniki Remi? Or mine? Penelopi Pappa?"

She cupped a hand to her ear. "What you say? Speak Greek."

"What about a man dressed as a bull."

"What man? What bull? He look-a like-a man, he look-a like-a bull? My eyesight no good."

Frustration was building up. I waited while she charged my card. I glanced outside. The shadows inside my car shifted. They weren't right for this time of day and the direction I was parked.

"You know," I said absently, most of my attention on the strange shadow, "a Minotaur. *Minotavros*."

There was a commotion behind the counter as the woman whipped out a shotgun and leveled it at my head

CHAPTER 8

VIRGIN MARY, she was crazy!

I hit the ground and scuttled toward the door.

Ungh. My *kataifi*. I'd already paid for them.

"Stay still so I can shoot you," the woman told me.

"I don't think you can miss with that shotgun. I'm kind of a captive audience."

She moved behind the counter, in my direction. There was something odd about the way she walked. It became apparent when she emerged around the side. Instead of legs, she was using a pair of snake tails to get around.

My brain tussled with my body. The smarter of the two —my body—flailed at the door. It knew snakes that size were terrible news, whether they were huggers or biters, and that guns were bad if you were on the wrong end.

In my head, things were getting philosophical. The part of my brain responsible for my insatiable curiosity wanted to know what kind of creature had snakes for legs. Was her appetite human or snake? Did she cook actual food or flop down on the couch to binge watch Netflix with a bucket of mice for snacks? How much money did she save not having to buy razors for her legs? Did she moisturize?

I threw my weight against the door but it was an innie not an outtie.

Snake Legs fired.

Drywall exploded above my head. On all fours, I scooted backwards and lunged at the door, hoping I could reach the handle before Snake Legs fired again. She burst out of her dress. It was snakes all the way down. Only her head and arms were human. What I'd mistaken for a fondness for sampling her own wares was just more snake bunched together and covered with a dress. Talk about false advertising.

The shotgun fired a second time. The ceiling began to snow.

"You no ask about *minotavros!*"

"Sorry!"

"You no ask! I tell nothing!"

"Can you stop shooting? I'm a paying customer!"

She fired again. This time the shotgun swung low and blasted through the refrigerated cabinet, splattering me with cold whipped cream and custard.

I felt rather than heard the door swing open. Warm air gushed in. Someone grabbed me by the ponytail and hauled me out just as Snake Legs was waving her shotgun around, gearing up to miss her target—me—again. Pain tore through my scalp, radiating downwards. Tears bubbled down my cheeks. My heart was freaking out, hammering blindly in all directions.

"Run!" my rescuer said. He let go of my hair. I bolted without looking back. "Not that way!" he yelled, exasperated. "Get in your car!"

I pivoted and hurled myself at the driver's side door, but the seat was already taken by none other than Luke Remis.

BANG. The cake shop's front window exploded outwards, showering the pavement with glass and bits of wedding cake.

I yanked open the rear driver's side door and threw my body across the backseat.

Luke hit the gas. We shot backwards out of the parking lot. Horns honked. An SUV slammed on its brakes a split second before impact. We jolted to a stop.

Snake Legs appeared in the broken window. She scratched her tight curls before returning to her place behind the counter.

Luke hit the gas. Less force this time. He waved to the SUV driver—using all his fingers and thumb—and we were on the move again.

"What the fuck were you doing?" he demanded.

"Buying *kataifi*. Which I didn't get, by the way."

"Like hell you were. Something you said or did pissed off the dracaenae."

"You mean the mustachioed snake lady?"

"Aphrodisia. That's her name. She owns the Hellas Bakery."

My teeth clacked together. Shivers rolled through my body in waves. Now that the adrenalin was wearing off, the weirdness and the danger to which I had exposed myself set in.

Luke's gaze met mine in the rearview mirror.

"You're an idiot," he said.

"Kiss my ass."

"Lady, you're too much of an idiot for me to kiss anything of yours ever again."

"Good! I wouldn't want those man-whore lips of yours touching me anyway."

All I could see in the rearview mirror were his rising eyebrows. They had an issue with my description. "Man-whore?"

"If the crate of condoms fit."

"Sounds like you care about my love life."

"Pull over," I barked.

"There's nowhere to pull over!"

"Pull over anyway."

He jerked the steering wheel and cruised to a stop. His finger jabbed the hazard lights.

I got out and yanked open the driver's side door. "Get out."

"What are you talking about?"

"Get. Out. Which word don't you understand? Need it in a different language? Okay. *Vyes exo.* Want me to be less polite?"

"Show me what you've got."

"*Gamisou.*"

"You offering?"

I slammed the door and climbed back in.

Luke Remis stabbed the hazard lights and melded seamlessly back into the traffic flow. "My ride is back at the bakery. I left it there to save your ass."

"I didn't ask you to save anything!" Since he wasn't about to give up the steering wheel, I scrambled over the console and plopped down in the passenger side. "Where are we going?"

"To find me another ride, then you need to go home and call Nikki and tell her you quit. You're a fucking menace and a disaster all rolled into one. The boss is out of his mind for hiring you in the first place."

Ha. As if that was going to happen. Ooh, look. Cream and custard. I scooped a blob of custard off my leg. Delicious.

"Snake Legs—what did you call her?—freaked out when I mentioned the Minotaur."

His jaw hardened. When he glanced over at me, his eyes were flat and dark with rage. I'd never been scared of Luke Remis in my life, but right now he looked like he wanted to shake me until I snapped.

"What the hell were you thinking?"

"I was just trying to do my job!"

"So you thought harassing the mother of a murder victim was the way to do it?"

"What?" I deflated. "I didn't know! She's the Minotaur's mother? Wait—if she's the mother, where did the bull part come from?"

"Not the Minotaur."

"Then who? Or what?"

"Aphrodisia's daughter."

"So Aphrodisia's daughter was murdered, and the Minotaur fits into this how?"

Luke looked uncomfortable. We had crossed back into downtown Salem, heading south. "He ate her."

Shock stunned me into silence. Temporarily. "The Minotaur *ate* her?" I snorted and thumped my head against the headrest a couple of times, hoping the movement would shake some sense into the situation. "He ate a half-snake girl?"

"Her adult, fully human daughter."

"How's that work? Wait, don't tell me. Wait, tell me. Wait—"

"Aphrodisia's husband is human. Their daughter was human from top to bottom."

"Why did the Minotaur eat her?"

Nothing.

"Did you kill the Minotaur?"

Luke's jaw clenched tighter. He didn't answer. He kept up the silence all the way to the public library, where he pulled into the parking garage.

"The library? Really?"

"No."

"No?"

"No, I didn't kill the Minotaur, and I need a vehicle."

"What about the other one?"

"Wasn't mine. Can't have them tracking me."

"Who? Minos's men?"

"That's *King* Minos. Biggest way to piss him off is by dropping the 'King.'"

"Let me guess: second biggest way is by killing one of his weird kids?"

"I'm amazed."

"That I know so much?"

He found a parking space and cut the engine. "That you know nothing."

"Hey—"

Luke checked all the mirrors. The man was paranoid—possibly for a good reason. "Here's what's going to happen. I'm gonna find a new car—"

"Stealing from library patrons? That's just rude. They're *readers*."

"—And you're going to prowl the stacks for mythology books. Section 292.13. If it's too much, start with children's guides to Greek Mythology and work your way up. Stock up on your Percy Jackson and Lester Papadopoulous."

Library card. Where was my library card? I dug down in my handbag for my purse. My hand brushed up against the stun gun. I couldn't believe I'd forgotten about it until now. One good zap and I could truss up Luke like a Thanksgiving turkey and wheel him back to the Labyrinth Agency. I tried not to think about how I'd probably be imprisoning him indefinitely in a mythological oubliette or wherever Greek kings kept their prisoners. And I definitely didn't think about the probability that he'd wind up tortured—or worse. Mostly I was annoyed that he kept brushing me off like I was lint.

"Huh?" I said.

"Rick Riordan. He mostly gets it right, especially the bits about the monsters. I gotta go." He reached over to open the door.

I made my move.

ZAP.

Luke slumped in the seat.

The *driver's* seat.

Damn it. Letting my anger (and, yes, greed) get the best of me was stupid. I should have wrangled him out of the car first. Ungh. Then someone might have spotted me zapping Luke.

This job was turning out to be a major pain in my butt. Yes, it was thrilling. No, I didn't have to listen to women jabbering about people I'd never met and places I'd never been all day long. And yes, the money, when it eventually came, was amazing. But was it worth having Luke Remis passed out in my car with no way to get him out?

What now?

Think, Penny. Think.

Find a way to move him over, then restrain him in case he woke up on the way back to the office. That was the ticket.

I got out and went around to the driver's side. Luke

slumped sideways. I managed to stop his descent with my knee. Once I'd stabilized him, I pushed his top half into the passenger seat. I looked up in time to see a woman and her passel of kids heading back to their car, loaded up with books. The woman was staring—hard.

"My husband," I lied. "He's a diabetic. A bit of juice and he'll be as right as rain."

She ushered her children toward their car, glancing back nervously.

I shoved one of his feet up, bending his knee in the process, then scooted it over to the footwell. I tried my best not to notice that he smelled warm and musky, pure Luke without the cologne or aftershave. My ridiculous hormones could have found him in a dark room full of strangers. I resented their stupidity.

The second leg went over easily, his left foot joining the right in the footwell. Now I had to get his butt over the console's hump.

I pushed my hip up against him. Shoved.

Nope. Wasn't happening. Luke was stuck like that for the foreseeable future. No problem. I could drive with his denim-clad ass covering the console. Next I needed to secure him.

I gave him another *zap* for good luck, then hoofed it to the trunk to find a rope or zip ties or anything I could use to truss up a grown man like a Thanksgiving fowl. Logically I knew I didn't make a habit of keeping items in my trunk that might be misconstrued by law enforcement if they were searching my vehicle. That didn't stop me from hoping I'd stashed something useful there, just in case. Even a bungee cord might work.

Nothing. Only the donut, lug wrench, and basic jack in

case I got a flat. Even then, I had AAA to do the tire-changing deed if necessary.

I slammed the trunk.

I was useless. Definitely not cut out for a life of apprehending runaway mythological creatures or the myth agents who policed them.

My car started up.

What the—?

Luke grinned at me from the driver's seat. He waved, a full five-fingered thing that was a low key insult in Greek culture. In one move he was rubbing figurative crap in my face *and* accusing me of masturbating to a brain-mushing degree. That wasn't true. My brain was fine.

I did the *moutsa* back at him.

Luke Remis laughed harder through the closed window of *my freaking car.*

I performed another appalling gesture, inviting him to suck a body part I didn't have.

My window buzzed down. He made a wide enough gap to toss my handbag out.

"Go read a book," Luke Remis said.

He hit the gas and peeled out of the parking garage, leaving me stranded at the library, covered in cream and custard.

CHAPTER 9

EVERY WOMAN NEEDS one ride-or-die friend who drives a minivan and always keeps a steady supply of juice boxes and Goldfish snacks. For me, that friend was Lena.

"Get in," my best friend called out through the rolled down window. "I managed to escape without the kids. Well, not counting the stowaway. Let's go find some drugs and get super high."

"Can't." I held up my stack of mythology books. "I have homework and you're knocked up."

Lena made a horrified face. "Ugh, I wish I'd known being an adult sucked as much as being a teenager—but with more bills. What kind of asshole gave you homework?"

"Luke Remis."

She gawked at me for the longest time, until I was sure she'd frozen in place. I struggled into the minivan and waved my hand in front of her face.

"Please tell me that's euphemism for his dick."

"No, it's literal homework. This is it. No dick whatsoever. Unless you're counting the nudie pictures of gods, dudes, and other creatures. Then yes, I'm about to be drowning in penis."

She cranked up the A/C and exited the parking garage. "Please explain to me how, exactly, Luke Remis came to give you homework that's not his middle leg."

"It's a really long story with me getting shot at and Luke rescuing me. Then it all went bad when I zapped him with my new stun gun and he stole my car."

She hit the brakes. "You've got a stun gun? I want one. I feel like my family would take me seriously if I could stun them. Right now, I talk until I'm blue in the face. Nobody pays attention to mama until she starts screaming."

"Yiayia wants one, too."

We both made a "yikes" face. Lena crossed herself.

"Are you going to do it?"

"The homework?"

"Ha! No. You're definitely gonna do that or you wouldn't have checked out all those books." She elbowed me. "Are you gonna bone Luke Remis again?"

"He stole my car."

"And your virginity."

"I'm pretty sure I gave him that on purpose."

———

Lena dropped me at home then peeled away while yelling, "I'm going to Target! By myself! For an hour! If the police call you looking for me, tell them I need me-time."

Boy, being a mom seemed like it was hard work. It made getting shot at feel like a walk in the park.

With my arms loaded up with books, I tried to sneak around the side of the house and upstairs to my apartment, but the neighborhood watch was on high alert.

"Here is my girl!" Yiayia called out. Her face was soft and wrinkled liked the syrup-drenched pastry on *galaktoboureko* —custard pie. She pressed gummy kisses on my cheeks and went back to glaring at Grandpa, who was picking his teeth with a toothpick and licking the bits off. He gestured at my sagging arms.

"Are those books?"

"Bravo," Yiayia said. "He knows what are books. Next we work on animals and numbers. Soon he will be a big boy. But he will always need diapers."

Grandpa settled back and smoothed the *Kiss My Grits* t-shirt over his belly. "Forget about the books. You know what you need?"

"A husband," Yiayia said.

"A husband," he said.

Their gazes snapped to each other. Glares were exchanged. Then there was movement at the end of the street and they were suddenly on high alert. Only thing missing was the yapping. I used the opportunity to make a getaway before they realized it was just the mailman.

Upstairs, my place was quiet and dark. I shoved open the living room curtains to let light in, then I closed them again because it highlighted the dust bunnies. I needed to clean.

Later.

Right now I had work to do, starting not with the assigned homework, but following up on Yellow Chucks' maybe-tip.

Probably I should have reported my car stolen, too. Taught Luke a lesson by throwing the cops at him. He stole my car. He abandoned me at the library. Now how was I supposed to get around? It wasn't much but the Honda was my car, free and clear. What if he crashed it? What if he dumped it to find another vehicle and left it for someone else to steal, like a chain letter on wheels?

My body screamed for sugar. Too bad I'd left my *kataifi* at the Ellas Bakery and I'd cleaned the custard and cream off my body and clothes in the library restroom. I contemplated calling my bank, but a pang of empathy kept me off my phone. Aphrodisia, Snake Legs, had lost a daughter to the Minotaur. Could be I'd whip out a shotgun and shoot, too, if I were in her shoes. Not that they made shoes for snake tails. What had Luke called her? A dracaenae. I grabbed a mythology book off the pile and pecked through the index until I found the relevant entry. I flipped to the page. There was Aphrodisia, all right. Or at least one of her kinfolk. Woman from the waist up. Snake from the bottom down. Aphrodisia had more snake in the torso, though, and human arms. A different book told me there were a few variations on the woman and snake combo. I guess it depended on how the genes expressed themselves.

I shoved the books back on the coffee table and reached for my laptop. I clicked to YouTube and searched for Waterfront Park in Salem, restricting the filters to videos from this past week only.

One video popped up.

My hands were cold and shaking slightly as I clicked PLAY. This whole thing felt like I was fighting to shove an octopus into a bag after I'd already screwed up by letting it escape in the first place.

Waterfront Park appeared. Slightly out of focus, and obviously captured using a potato, but very definitely Salem's park. There was no mistaking the big Earth. A few seconds in, the camera moved a fraction and the Minotaur appeared. Shock sucked the breath out of me. This wasn't my first encounter with the half-man, half-bull so I shouldn't have been breathless and covered in cold sweat. Seeing the man-bull dead was like looking at a prop. The corpse could have easily been crafted out of latex and whatever else expert movie magic folks used to create their amazing effects.

This was different.

Alive, the Minotaur was something else. Massive, obviously, and yet agile. Possibly the offspring of Gene Kelly and Blossom, the Holstein that had stood at over six-feet tall. Maybe King Minos was a dancer, because his kid sure could move. He boogied around the Earth for several minutes, putting on a show. The camera shifted slightly right, revealing his audience of two. Both women. The same pair that Kevin, Manager had mentioned?

Then suddenly, the dancing stopped. The women walked away. Once they vanished out of frame, the Minotaur staggered backwards. Slowly, it swayed and then toppled over backwards, landing with what had to be an almighty *crash*.

The camera shook.

A figure clad in a nude bodysuit walked up to the Minotaur and kicked it a few times for what appeared to be funsies.

The Minotaur didn't move.

It was history. Or mythology.

The killer took off.

Finito.

I hit REPLAY, pausing when I reached the women who'd been present. I took a screenshot and sent it to my phone, repeating the moves of the killer, when they appeared. In the dark, the Minotaur's foe could have been almost anyone. All I could discern was that they dug nude bodysuits and were possibly male. Anything more would be speculation on my part. A person can hide a lot of details in shadows.

With an *oof*, I flopped against the couch back and let the pillows hug me.

Questions swirled around in my head. Who killed the Minotaur? Was it Luke? Right now I was going with "no" because there was a time when I had obsessed over him just a teensy bit and was intimately familiar with his body shape. The figure in the nude bodysuit didn't have Luke Remis's strong, stocky build or his height. Luke was probably telling the truth when he insisted he didn't do it.

More questions.

Who captured the footage? Judging from the angle, it was easy to surmise that the amateur filmmaker was standing across the street, probably on the corner. Yellow Chucks or someone else? Where did the women from the video go?

Once again, I had more questions than answers.

"Lunch!" Mom called out from downstairs.

Oh boy, I was starving.

I jogged downstairs to find Mom slinging slabs of moussaka onto plates.

"Foreign food. Again." Grandpa glared at his plate, no doubt trying to use his mind to transform the layers of meat and cheese and vegetables into his favorite chicken fried steak. That didn't stop him from lowering his mouth to the plate and shoveling food with the zeal of a Labrador Retriever.

Dad was already digging in. Moussaka was one of his favorites. Yiayia was picking at the layers, inspecting each one before moving on to the next.

"You okay?" I asked her.

"She calls this moussaka?"

"It's Akis' recipe," Mom said.

"Akis? What is Akis? I don't know any Akis from my *kolos*. Why you not make my recipe?"

"He's a celebrity chef," Mom said. "Look him up."

Yiayia Googled him. "He is very pretty, like a girl. I will ask him if he is married."

"What for? He wouldn't have a mile of ruined road like you," Grandpa said.

"For Penelope! She needs a husband. This one looks rich."

"Chaz was rich," Grandpa said.

"Chaz's mother was rich," Yiayia said. "Chaz was poor until my granddaughter married him. When they separated, he threw his riches away—"

"Aww, thanks," I said.

"—like old garbage!"

"I'm not *that* old," I said.

"You are a princess," Yiayia said. "Chaz is *skata*."

Grandpa stopped forking food into his mouth. "God-damn, is she talking about shit again?"

"Language," Mom said.

"Shit, shit, shit," Grandpa said.

"That better not be a verb," Dad muttered.

I took a bite of the moussaka and all my problems went away for a few moments. Mom had outdone herself—and probably Akis Petretzikis.

"Where's your car?" Grandpa said.

My fork froze midair. Truth or lie? Both paths were lined with peril. I chose lie. "I loaned it to a friend."

"What friend?" he wanted to know. "Not that Lena. I saw her screeching away in her minivan."

"Another friend."

"You don't got any other friends," he said.

"What does he know about friends? His friends are dead," Yiayia said. "Died to get away from him." She thought about it a moment. "Same as mine, now that I think about it"

Mom was crossed herself, silently begging for sweet death.

"That happens when you get old, I guess." I loaded up my fork again. It had things to do and places to go, like my mouth. This bite was as delicious as the first and the tenth. "People start dropping like flies."

"Eddie Morrison was the first of our crew to croak," Grandpa said. "On the job, too. We were rolling the asphalt and he keeled over while he was holding the STOP and SLOW sign. Got run over a dozen times before someone realized he weren't a speed bump."

"*Mouni* cancer took my friend when she was just fifty-five," Yiayia said.

Grandpa squinted at her. "Moo-what?"

"*Mouni*," Yiayia said.

"What's that?"

Dad had a death grip on his fork. His face was pale. Beads of sweat were popping up all over his forehead. He knew a few Greek words—the sex ones, mostly. "Don't say it."

Yiayia forged onward, undeterred by her sweating son-in-law. "What you are: a *pussy*."

Grandpa purpled. Dad choked. Mom rushed in and Heimliched Dad. Moussaka shot up and out of his throat, hitting Grandpa's face with a *splat*.

Yiayia cackled.

CHAPTER 10

WITHOUT WHEELS, I was grounded. Which stank because I had a to-do list that needed doing before it spiraled out of control. Luke Remis's case file on the Minotaur suggested that he'd tracked the creature to several other businesses in the area prior to his visit to the Hellas Bakery and subsequently Waterfront Park. I needed to check them out and see if anyone recognized either of the two women who had been with the Minotaur before he went to the big pasture in the underworld.

Bottom line: I was going nowhere without my car.

I called Nikki. "Your cousin stole my car."

"What happened?"

I relayed the whole torrid tale, including my faux pas with Aphrodisia. In retrospect, mentioning her daughter's killer was a bad idea. But in my defense, I hadn't known. Seemed to me like that sort of thing should have been in Luke's case file.

From across town, I felt Nikki wince. "Can you borrow a car?"

"I guess I could ask Mom for her minivan."

"Okay. Great." There was a noise in the background. A hideous mashing of killer geese and metal. "Bit of a situation here. Want to earn some quick cash?"

Did bears poop in the woods and wipe with soft, pillowy paper?

"She's not ready," the boss said in the background.

"More ready than you, Mr. No Arms. I've been shot at and robbed today. I think I can cope with whatever you throw at me, as long as it's not clowns."

That got a snort out of the boss, whatever his name was. "You can't even bring in Luke Remis, and he's one of ours."

"Yeah, because he's been maybe falsely accused of slaughtering a Minotaur. Is it murder, given that he's only half man? I'm really confused here. How sentient was the Minotaur anyway? Could he read?"

"Those are good questions," Nikki admitted.

"Bring in Remis and we will see about another case," the boss said.

"She's the only one available right now," Nikki said. "Normally you'd give this to Luke. This one should be easy."

"I like easy," I said. "I'm great at easy."

The boss sighed like I was tapping on his tank. "Fine. Give it to her."

"I'm sending the file to your phone," Nikki told me. "Ganymede took off again. He does a runner on the regular. Ganymede is—"

"Zeus's cupbearer," I said. "He pours nectar for the gods, right?"

"If by cupbearer you mean phallus holster, and if by nectar you mean ball sweat, then yes," the boss said.

I waited for Nikki to correct him. She didn't.

"How do these runaways get through? If the Labyrinth

Agency controls traffic through the labyrinth, then why aren't they stopped before they escape?"

"There are a few places where the barrier between worlds is threadbare," Nikki explained. "We patch them when we know about them. But sometimes things and people can get through without our knowledge."

"Alrighty then," I said. "One Ganymede, cup holder to the gods coming right up."

"Watch out," Nikki warned me. "Ganymede is a delicious snack, but when he's liquored up he's a much bigger fan of coming than he is going."

Between lunchtime and 2:00 PM the sun had scrounged up a bigger, hotter stick and was beating Oregon with the dry end. Full from lunch, and sporting a wicked food baby, I swapped out my shorts for different shorts, these ones with an elastic waistband. Apprehending a mythological drunk would be easier if I didn't have to suck in my stomach. Now that I could take full, deep breaths again, I dug into the file Nikki had sent to my phone.

Wowza. Ganymede was one cute guy. Full lips. Fair hair. Piercing blue eyes. Cheekbones made for slicing ham. According to the file he loved cruising the local gay bars for drinks and dancing. Apparently he loved pop music, which wasn't a thing in mythological Greece. This was a regular jaunt for the cupbearer. He didn't have Zeus's permission to cross over between worlds—another issue with treaties—so whenever Ganymede escaped, Labyrinth had to send an agent to extract him from whatever mess he'd gotten himself into this time. The file listed some of his favorite haunts, but it wasn't out of the realm of possibility that he'd picked a new place to shake his nectar-maker. I figured I'd start with the list Nikki had given me and take it from there. Clubs and bars opened and closed all the time.

Because it was mid-afternoon, I wasn't confident I'd get a hit, but I'd dug my heels in and wanted to prove to the boss that I had what it took to be a myth agent. What I needed now were wheels. I jogged downstairs in my stretchy shorts to find Mom. She was bent over her phone, thumbs dancing over a mobile game.

"Fun game?"

"It dulls the pain of my existential dread," she said.

"I think you need therapy," I said. "This isn't normal. Maybe they can prescribe antidepressants."

She smiled up at me. "Look! I am fine now. Ha-ha!"

Yeah, right. "I have to get back to work. Can I borrow the minivan?"

My phone rang. I stepped outside and sat on the bottom step leading up to my place to deal with my ex-husband.

"Where did you get the money?" Chaz demanded.

"My new job. And you're welcome, by the way."

"What new job?" He laughed. "Did the salon fire you?"

"I guess you could say I fired them. How is Chunky?"

"Prince Charleston is at the kitty salon, getting his nails done. Mommy took him."

My skin crawled. At the same time, my heart hurt. I missed my cat. "Can I see him this weekend?"

"That's a negatory. We're going to a show in Portland tomorrow. We're hoping for Best in Show."

"But it's *my* weekend."

"And I'm his custodial parent. I decide when you see him."

I ended the call with a whimper. With the heartache of

missing Chunky riding on my shoulders, I slouched back inside to get back to Mom about the minivan.

Mom handed over her keys. "Drive safe. I packed it with a few supplies."

"Supplies? What supplies?"

"You'll see."

When they were handing out moms, I scored a good one. She loved me. She loaned me her minivan. No, her minivan wasn't cool or new, but it was reliable and fast when it needed to be. She also thoughtfully included snacks.

I took the keys and went to the driveway. The sliding door was open. Yiayia and Grandpa waved at me from the backseat.

"Supplies!" Mom said behind me.

"Mom! No! I have to work."

"Please. I beg of you. They never go anywhere except church, and I'm pretty sure when your grandfather says he's going to church he means a taxidermy shop down in Albany. Look at them. Don't you feel sorry for them?"

Yiayia and Grandpa were slapping at each other, complaining about who was taking up more space and breathing more air. Any minute now it was going to devolve into an argument about who was touching who.

Mom looked hopeful ... and tired.

"Fine," I said. "I'll take the kids. Go nap or something."

"I'm going to cuddle with Ben and Jerry's Cherry Garcia."

Resigned to my fate, I climbed into the minivan and swiveled around to face my grandparents.

"Saddle up, folks and listen. First thing's first, there are rules," I said. "My rules."

"This is America. I don't have to follow rules," Grandpa

said. "There's a document that says I have the right to not follow rules. You know what it's called?"

"The Constitution?"

"Nope. This." He handed me a punchcard for a local coffee shop.

"Okay, well I'm not a coffee shop, nor do I play one on TV, but if that ever changes I'll let you know. First rule, buckle up. Second rule, stay in the car."

"What if I need to pee?" Grandpa said. "Got a prostate the size of a bowling ball. Feels like sitting on a nest of fire ants."

"Go in your underpants like you always do," Yiayia said.

"If that's true, I'll take you to your doctor later," I told Grandpa.

"I hate that guy," he said. "Says he graduated at the top of his class, but I don't see it."

Oh brother. "Anyone needs to pee, let me know. Third rule, be nice or I'll make you walk home."

"You sound like your mother," Yiayia muttered.

I was sure that wasn't a compliment, so I ignored it.

"Ready?"

Yiayia crossed herself. "*Theos, Christos*, and the *Panayia* will protect us."

"Amen," Grandpa said.

I rolled my eyes. God, Jesus, and the Virgin Mary were Greece's favorite motor insurance plan. My parents and I had Geico because we wanted to save money instead of our souls.

I backed out of the driveway and pointed the minivan north. My starting point was downtown—again. Ganymede liked the hustle and bustle. Especially the hustle.

First on the list was Uncut, a glitzy club for men who liked men and also money. At night the place sparkled.

During the day the exterior looked sad and cheap, like Vegas at the crack of dawn.

My passengers peered out.

"What is this place?" Yiayia wanted to know.

I parked at the curb. "It's a club."

"What kind of club? Bingo?"

Grandpa lit up. "Is it a titty club?" He peered out. "I don't see any women or champagne glasses on the sign. Usually there's women and champagne glasses."

"It's a club for people who'd gladly sell their grandparents to roving bands of nomadic persons," I told them.

Yiayia elbowed Grandpa. "She means *tsiganes*."

I left them in the car with the air conditioning blasting because I got the feeling Mom didn't mean it when she said she wanted my grandparents gone. Also, I didn't fancy some well-meaning samaritan smashing Mom's windows to save the elderly folks from the sweltering heat.

Uncut's door was unlocked. I took that as a sign that they'd be okay with me entering, even though it wasn't technically business hours. Someone had to be here, and maybe that someone had seen Ganymede shaking his groove thang.

The door closed slowly behind me, helped by a self-closing arm. As it clicked shut, the noise from Salem's busy streets died. I was in a tunnel that probably lit up at night, flickering strobe lights that came with seizure warnings. During the daylight hours it felt like a dark, cloying box. There was sound coming from up ahead. Glasses clinking.

Sure enough, glasses were bumping against other glasses as the bespectacled guy behind the bar ferried drinking vessels from a dishwasher to the racks overhead. He was cute and he smelled good even across the bar.

"We're closed," he said not unkindly. Then he did a

double-take. "Wait—Penny Post? It's me, George Bitzios. How's it going? How's your family? I haven't seen you at church in ages."

I stared. I knew the name but not the face—not at first. Then he smiled and it hit me. George and I were in Greek school together, and our families attended the same church. He was right, our paths hadn't crossed in years.

"George! Sorry, it's been a weird day."

"Doesn't help that I had a huge glow up, right?"

That was putting it mildly. "So you're—"

"Gay now? Depends who's asking. I'd never hear the end of it if my grandparents knew."

We shared a smile. For a country that practically invented sex between two dudes, the old guard moved slowly towards acceptance, if they did at all.

"Actually I was going to ask if you're working here," I said stupidly. "Which obviously you do."

"Five nights a week. The good nights. The tips are amazing."

"I guess I don't have to ask if they're uncut."

He busted out laughing. "So what brings you here?"

"I'm looking for a man. Not like that," I said quickly, figuring it was best to clarify. "He's a missing person." I'd worked on my cover story on the way over. "He's taking medication and he really needs to stay on them."

George took a long look at Ganymede's picture on my phone.

"Yeah, I know him. Haven't seen him in a while, though. He's pretty. Always gets a lot of attention when he comes in here."

"Because he's pretty?"

"He's like catnip to all our customers. There's something about him ..." He shook his head, gave a half laugh, fanned his face. "What's funny is your boy there loves to dance but doesn't have a coordinated bone in his body. That man gets out on the dance floor in his skimpy shorts, and a glass in each hand, and lets whatever happens happen. No shame. Boyfriend just loves to party."

"Do you know where else he likes to party and show off his sweet dance moves?"

He closed the dishwasher, picked up a bar mop and threw it over one shoulder. "Unless I'm seeing them on the side, I don't pay attention to where patrons go when they're not here. But your boy strikes me as a low key thrill seeker. I'd check out some of the other local bars. Or anywhere that the drinks are cheap and the music is free."

"You're a star, George."

He grinned. "Only on nights we do drag. I'm the world's tallest Lady Gaga. Come see the show sometime. Last Saturday of every month."

I promised I'd swing by—probably I wouldn't—and braved the dark tunnel before bursting back out into the moody sunlight.

The minivan was missing, along with my grandparents.

Damn it.

Bringing them to work was a terrible idea. Why hadn't I listened to my brain? It had been practically screaming and waving signs in my head. On some level, it knew this would happen.

Frantic, I called Mom. "Someone stole the minivan. Yiayia and Grandpa were inside."

"That's okay, we have good insurance on the minivan."

"Did you hear the part where my grandparents are missing, too?"

"Huh. I finished the ice cream."

I looked up and down the street. Which was stupid

because the street was strictly one-way unless a wrong-way driver was on the loose. No sign of Mom's minivan or my grandparents in either direction.

Terrifying scenarios flashed through my mind. They'd been carjacked and kidnapped by God only knows who—or what.

The latter was definitely possible, given my recent work-related discoveries. For all I knew, Yiayia and Grandpa had been abducted by Cronus. At this very moment he might be slurping senior citizen soup and moping up bits of Grandpa with bread. Or was that just his own kids? Wait—was Cronus still staying at the Tartarus Inn? Curse my inability to read all those library books in one sitting.

A horn honked in the distance.

As I watched in horror, Mom's minivan inched around the corner. The vehicle jerked as whoever was behind the wheel bunnyhopped across two lanes of traffic.

"Crap!"

Mom groaned in my ear. Apparently I'd managed to disappoint her. "Oh no, did you find them?"

"I think so?" I heard a crinkling sound. "What are you doing?"

"Putting the party favors away. You know, it's not too late to hide."

The minivan rolled closer at the speed of whatever was slower than molasses. Frozen molasses, maybe. Yiayia's eyebrows were barely visible over the steering wheel. Grandpa was missing. As I gawped, Mom's vehicle lurched to a stop twenty feet away.

"Got to go," I told Mom.

"This called started out so well, too."

I jogged over to the minivan, waving politely to other drivers who were swerving and waving Greece's other favorite flag: the raised middle finger. (Who knew there were so many Greeks in Salem?) I yanked open the door.

Grandpa was slumped down in the footwell, working the pedals with his hands, while Yiayia was in control (although that was debatable) of the steering wheel.

"What are you doing?"

"Trying to park this van," Yiayia said. "Did it work?"

"Course it worked!" Grandpa said. "We ain't moving no more."

"That sound you hear isn't the welcoming committee," I told them. "Get in the back!"

Nobody moved.

"Now!"

"I cannot move until this one moves," Yiayia said.

"Grandpa?"

"I'm not saying I'm stuck." Grandpa grunted. "I'm just saying my back don't want me getting up off this floor too soon."

For crying out loud.

I put my arms around Grandpa's waist and pulled. He groaned, then something popped and he made a sound like a pen full of squealing pigs.

"Sorry!" I said.

"Do it again," Yiayia said. "I like that sound."

"Shut your pie-hole, woman," Grandpa said. "I think something broke. Probably my spine."

I inspected his foot, naked in flip flops. "Wiggle your toes."

His toes wiggled.

"Most likely not a spinal injury. Now you've got no excuse to not get in the back." I went around to the driver's side. "Your turn."

"This was not like driving a donkey," Yiayia said as I helped her out. "The car-o is too fast."

"You were crawling."

"That was him."

With the two of them safely (also debatable) in the back-seat, I moved us out of traffic and snugged up to the curb. I swiveled in my seat.

"What were you two thinking?"

"You left us here alone!" Grandpa said. "What else were we going to do?"

"You did not even a leave a bowl of water!" Yiayia said.

"You're people! You're not dogs!"

"That one is a dog," Yiayia said, chucking her chin at Grandpa.

"The AC was on," I told them. "If you wanted water you could have waited five minutes."

My grandmother changed the subject. "Who did you see? What did you do?"

"Nobody we know," I said.

"You are lying," Yiayia said. "I hear it in your voice."

"Okay, fine, it was George Bitzios."

"Which one? The fat one or the one with glasses?"

"Glasses."

"What was he doing at that club?"

"Working?"

"I did not know he worked at a club. What kind of club is it?"

"It's for queers," Grandpa said. "I looked it up on my phone."

Yiayia stared at him like he had two heads. "Is what?"

"It's a gay bar, Yiayia," I explained. "For men who enjoy the company of other men."

"Eh?"

"It's not natural," Grandpa said. "That's what. Putting your mouth on another man's ding-dong and taking it up the poop shoot."

"That?" Yiayia said, wafting her hand through the air. "Greeks invented that."

"Figures," Grandpa said.

"What consenting adults do is their own business," I told Grandpa. "Love is love."

He belched. Yiayia elbowed him in the gut.

"And you say George Bitzios, the one with the glasses is a *pousti*?" Yiayia asked. "Funny. I would have said the fat one, his brother. He has too many cats and that little dog. He drives an electric car."

"It ain't right, driving a toaster," Grandpa said.

I stared at them both and shook my head. Thankfully this apple had rolled away from the tree.

The next bar on my list was further down the street. It was locked up tight and nobody was inside. We were way too early for nightlife.

If I were a smoking hot guy who loved to dance, on the run from my controlling literal god of a sometimes-lover and employer, where would I go for a good time on a Friday afternoon?

Singalongs in the Park.

My phone lobbed the location of today's Singalongs in the Park at me. No GPS required; right now, people were grooving to the sounds of their own voices at the Keizer Rotary Amphitheater.

"Anyone want to go dancing?" I asked my passengers.

Yiayia snapped her fingers in the air above her head. For an old woman she sure could shimmy. Yes, there was a possibility she'd put out an eye with a flying boob, but she'd have fun doing it.

"I will do the *tsifteteli*!"

"I don't dance," Grandpa announced. "Dancing is for women."

"Dancing is for everybody," I told him.

"Tell that to my hip."

Because I couldn't stand listening to the adult kids squabbling in the back, I pulled a Mom and cranked up the music until their voices faded behind a backdrop of pop music. Every so often I glanced in the rearview mirror. Their mouths continued making shapes, but in my space I didn't have to hear them scream.

The Keizer Rotary Amphitheater is part of the larger Rapids Park Complex. They have the usual park stuff. Playground. Dog park. Trails. And the amphitheater, which harkens back to the Ancient Greek days in its cunning simplicity. The stage is a simple stone slab, and seating is basically rows of grass and stone rising in gentle tiers.

Today the area was swarming with sticky children, rocking out to a woman playing guitar. She was singing a song about a llama with an addiction to cake. That llama was all of us.

I parked in the designated parking area in the shade.

"You gonna leave us here again?" Grandpa asked.

"Can you behave?"

He thought about it a moment. "Probably not, but I'll try. Can't say the same for her, though."

Yiayia was already out of the minivan, fingers snapping in the air around her head, wiggling her hips, grimacing every time something pulled the wrong way. With each swivel, her knee-high stockings sagged lower.

Oh boy. Best to scope this out quickly before Yiayia sprained something.

I spotted the scantily clad Ganymede almost immediately. He was at the front surrounded by preschoolers. He had a sippy cup in each hand and every so often a tiny hand would reach up and he'd pass the kid their cup. For whatever reason, none of the parents were freaking out about the loin-clothed man dancing with their kids.

From the back, his gender could have gone any which way. He was smooth and tan and not overly muscular but not soft. Strong shoulders, but not broad. His curls were cut in a soft bob.

Okay, time to roll. According to his file, Ganymede was a peaceful guy who went willingly with whoever had been designated to reel him in that day. I trudged down the steps with my grandparents behind me.

"These stairs will be the death of me," Grandpa said.

"I will pray," Yiayia said. "Virgin Mary, please, take him."

I ignored them. I had an apprehension to make.

I waded through the dancing toddlers and preschoolers and tapped on Ganymede's shoulder.

He turned, and gave me a slow, full beam smile.

I blinked. Ganymede's photograph depicted a cute guy. After my divorce from Chaz, I'd developed an immunity to cute, unless the cute thing had fur. Ganymede wasn't cute. Zeus's cupbearer was beautiful in the most devastating way imaginable. He was male and female and full lipped and blue eyed and soft and strong, and suddenly, for the first time in my life, I was horribly confused. This must have been how people felt meeting Prince in person.

"You must be my ride back," he said with a silky voice.

"I'm afraid so."

"It was fun while it lasted."

My nipples hardened.

His gaze dropped to my chest. "Sorry about that. It happens a lot."

Behind me, Grandpa cleared this throat. "Excuse me, m'am."

I turned and raised my eyebrows at him. My grandfather had his hat off and he was blushing like a virgin bride from some bygone era.

"That happens a lot, too," Ganymede explained.

Yiayia grabbed onto his arm, eyelashes fluttering. "My husband is dead and my bed is empty."

A woman appeared on his other side, balancing a baby on her hip. "My husband *could* be dead if you want."

"We should go," I said.

"Stay." A serving suggestion from a guy carrying his kid in a backpack. "Please."

Ganymede bent down and offered the sippy cups back to their knee-high owners. "I have to go now."

The kids started to cry.

"Can we at least wait until the end of the concert?" he asked me.

"Let him stay!" the parents begged.

"No can do," I said. My primary focus was on the Minotaur case. Ganymede was supposed to be a quick and easy filler to get some experience and cash. A successful extraction would boost my cachet with Vat Man.

"I understand," Ganymede said sweetly. "We should go."

My hormones suggested less than politely that I should hold Ganymede's hand to make sure he got back to the minivan safely. Unfortunately, both sides were presently hogged by my grandparents. Grandpa had his arm around the cupbearer's shoulder. Yiayia was snuggled up to his side, clinging to his arm. Ganymede didn't seem to mind.

I stomped back to the parking lot, mentally grouching about the unfairness of it all. My grandparents had already experienced their fun and their youth. Now it was my turn, damn it. I wanted a tussle with Ganymede.

I jerked to a stop. Something was wrong. Mom's minivan had vanished, and in its place was my car.

My phone pinged. Text from Unknown. No number.

Unknown: *You're welcome.*

I typed back, *Who is this?*

Unknown: *That's the thanks I get for returning your car?*

Luke Remis. That lowdown, dirty car and minivan thief.

Me: *Remis? You stole my mom's minivan!*

Luke: *It's got snacks and drinks.*

Me: *Go steal from your own family!*

Luke: *No can do. I'm less scared of your family than mine.*

Me: *You should be terrified of me.*

Luke: *Nah. You're a cupcake.*

Me: *Tell that to your balls and face.*

He sent back a wincing emoji. I lobbed back a raised middle finger. Annoyed by his existence, I stuffed my phone back in my bag.

"Everybody saddle up," I told my grandparents and the cupbearer. "Please," I added sweetly, holding eye contact with Ganymede.

My grandmother blinked at my car. "What happened to your mother's van?"

"Dang, it got stole," Grandpa said. "The world ain't what it used to be, that's for sure."

"Nothing happened to it," I grumbled. Hopefully that would suffice as far as explanations went. Without complaint, they all piled into the backseat, with Ganymede squeezed in the middle like jelly in a donut. My car was built for me and a few groceries and maybe a dog riding shotgun, not two grandparents and a mythological hottie. "You can sit in the front seat," I told Ganymede.

"Turn around and drive," Yiayia said. "Mind your own business."

Not fair.

I kept stealing glances at Ganymede in the mirror. I got it, why Zeus fired Hera's daughter Hebe and disguised himself as an eagle to kidnap Ganymedes. I wanted him to pour my coffee all day long. Did I really have to take him back?

Sadly, yes. If I wanted to keep this job, I had no choice but to return the cupbearer. But maybe I could be Nikki's first call next time Ganymede busted out of mythological Greece.

"Why do you do it?" I asked him. "Is it really the music?"

"Leave?"

I nodded.

"Zeus is relentless. He needs his cup filled all day and night long or he throws a tantrum. He's exhausting. Sometimes I need to break out and dance or I'll cut a god."

"Aren't they immortal?"

"Yes, so their booboos hurt longer."

I filed that bit of information away.

We arrived at the Northeast Salem strip mall. I parked out front and played passenger Tetris as I tried to get Ganymede out while leaving my grandparents inside.

"Where he goes, we go," Grandpa announced.

"You can't go where he goes," I told him.

"Where's he going then?"

"Home," I told my grandfather,

"We will visit later," Yiayia said, giving a flirty little wave. "I will bring my famous *galaktoboureko*."

For the record, her custard pie wasn't famous. Nobody knew about it outside our family.

Ganymede stood awkwardly outside the door. "Do I really have to go back?"

"You really do, as much as I hate it."

"Couldn't we ... have dinner? Dance? Have some fun together?"

Yes, oh yes, oh—

"Not this time."

His smooth, perfect forehead puckered up. "Where is Luke? Usually he picks me up."

"Luke Remis is ... uh ... kind of on the run right now. Bit of trouble with King Minos."

"Did he kill the" —he glanced around furtively— "Minotaur?"

"So they say, but I don't think so." Wait a minute, here was a real being from the myth world. Probably he knew things—things I could know, too, if I asked the right questions. "What made you ask that?"

"It's Zeus. He's out of sorts at the moment. Even more grumpy than usual. He's been pounding me like I'm a nail. It's a miracle I can sit."

Poor baby. I had lotion back at my place. And a bathtub where he could get naked and soak away the pain.

Focus, you ding-dong. "What does Zeus have to do with the Minotaur?"

"King Minos is his son."

"That means the Minotaur is—was—his grandchild? That's messed up."

Ganymede tilted his pretty head. Blond hair tumbled into his sky blue eyes. "How?"

Wow, values in his world sure were different. Around here we had laws about violating animals. In Greek mythology it was a feature, not a bug.

"Never mind," I said quickly. "Can you think of anyone who might want to kill the Minotaur?"

He shrugged. "Everyone? The Minotaur had no friends, only enemies. He was kind of an asshole. No manners at parties. Rude. Always showing off. Every last being in our world hates him."

I remembered the man-bull's dancing by the Earth sculpture at Waterfront Park. "He was a pretty snazzy dancer."

A cloud passed over Ganymede's face. "Was he? I never noticed."

"One more question before we go in." Nikki was waving at us through the window. No, wait, she was waving at Ganymede ... and wearing a whole lot more makeup than usual. Now she was unbuttoning her blouse slightly. That cheap hussy. Ganymede was *mine*. "When and where did you sneak through the labyrinth this time?"

He wafted a hand through the air. Long, slender fingers. Yet strong. Perfect for piano or guitar or doing that thing I liked. "I don't know where, only that I did. And time ... time is different here. Seconds and minutes shuffle forward in a line. Ours time is like a wheel that never stops turning. What goes around, comes back around. What dies is reborn. What is lost returns to us. We fight the same wars. Love the same lovers. Carry the same cups." He blasted me with his smile. I melted on the spot. "And when I can, I dance."

Nikki threw open the door, bosom heaving. "There's my favorite cupbearer," she said breathlessly.

We stepped inside. The boss's voice was waiting for me.

"Well, I suppose you're not entirely incompetent, but this was an easy one. Escort the runaway home, girl."

"No need for that," Ganymede said. "I know the way."

The boss made snorting sounds. "Please. We've tried that. Last time you hid in the labyrinth for a month before we found you, and I know that labyrinth better than anyone."

"Almost anyone," Ganymede said. "Oh well, it was worth a try, old man."

"It's okay," I said. "I'll come with you. I don't mind."

Ganymede bestowed a smile on me. My heart fluttered. We headed for the labyrinth. This time the maze was masquerading as a cubicle farm. We walked for what felt like hours, before the same metal door and EXIT sign appeared. I paid more attention to the otherness of the myth world this time. The sweetness of the sun. The gentle breeze. The dancing satyrs playing their cane pipes.

No golden shower today, so that was nice. Instead of Zeus, our greeting party was a woman in a long white dress, her hair coiled in a pile of braids that made me think she had at least one maid on hand just to do hair. Not the kind of 'do one normally saw outside of weddings. She was what they called "handsome" in the old days. She didn't look happy about anything—ever.

"Hello, pervert," she said. "I was hoping you would never come back."

Ganymede winked at her. "I always come back."

"Too bad." She chucked her chin at me. "What is this?"

"A mortal female," Ganymede told her.

She made a dismissive sniffing sound.

Well, excuse the heck out of me. Lady Fancy Braids didn't get to discard me like I was toilet paper in a Greek bathroom. (Seriously, in the homeland, TP isn't flushable. Everyone leaves their skid-marked paper in tiny trashcans parked next to the toilets.)

I waved. "Penny Post. Hi."

"Do I look like I care? Leave my husband's ball-fondler here and go home before I decide to ruin your life for fun."

Lights flickered on in my head. "You must be Hera."

She raised both eyebrows at me. "What is it you mortals say? Well, duh!"

"She seems nice," I said to Ganymede.

Hera snapped her fingers. Suddenly, I didn't feel so good. My stomach rolled. My bones were on fire. Everything was getting bigger. Wait. No. I was getting smaller.

"What the heck?"

"Language!" Hera said.

I looked down. My feet weren't feet. My hiking boots had vanished and I was sporting hooves, front and back. Everything was hooves.

"What did you do to me, you crazy—"

Ganymede slapped his hand over my mouth. "She didn't mean whatever she was about to say."

Hera waved her hand. "Whatever." She vanished in a cloud of pink smoke.

Panic surged through me. My eyes weren't working properly. Now I had a peripheral vision and regular vision combo. Too much stimulus. Argh!

"What am I? Am I stuck like this forever? Where are my clothes?"

Ganymede crouched down beside me. "You're a goat." He patted my back.

"A goat!"

"A vey cute goat. One with long, floppy ears. But you should leave before someone eats you. They love goat meat around here."

"Can you, uh, get the door?"

Ganymede reached over and jostled the handle. The door swung open. "Do you need me to close it?"

"Thanks, but I've got it."

I trotted through the door. It took me a moment, but I managed to coordinate my hooves to give it a swift kick.

———

Nikki stared at me.

"Yeah, I know. I'm a goat now."

"Hera?"

"Hera. What's her problem?"

"She's married to the manager and he won't listen to her customer service complaints."

I winced. Or I tried wincing. Goat faces didn't do expressions the same way. "Am I stuck like this now?"

"No," the boss said. "It will wear off soon."

"How soon? I need to drive my grandparents home."

"Not that soon," he said.

"Nikki, any chance you can drop them off?"

"I have to watch the door and desk, but let me call someone. Grab a—"

"Hay bale?" the boss said.

"I'll just stand in the corner and eat a newspaper, if that's okay."

"Go ahead," Nikki said. "It's yesterday's anyway. It'll save me from dropping it in the recycling bin."

CHAPTER 11

HELP ARRIVED.

Help, unfortunately, was Grim.

He glanced at me, then at Nikki. "That the new agent?"

I wanted to say something, explain why I was a goat and why I needed someone to take my grandparents home, but my mouth was full of newspaper. It's not polite to talk with a mouth full of the funny pages, even when you're a ruminant.

"That's Penny," Nikki confirmed.

"Hera?"

"Hera."

Grim had Nikki sweet-talk my grandparents into taking a ride in his pickup truck, the black behemoth with a mirror shine. Probably Freud would have things to say about that, but what did I know? I was a goat.

An adorable white and brown goat with floppy ears.

But I digress.

"Somebody catch that *katsika*," Yiayia said. "I will have my daughter make *stifado*."

Yikes! Who had four hooves and didn't want to wind up as stew? This goat.

I scooted around back of the truck, out of sight and hopefully out of mind.

"Nobody eats the goat," Grim said.

"That is too bad," Yiayia said. "Goat is good for eating. It puts hair on your chest! That is what happened to my aunt. Too much goat."

"Foreigners," Grandpa muttered.

Grim raised his eyebrows at me. Please, like he didn't have his own crazy relatives. Mine were my grandparents. Ten bucks said he had at least one whacko uncle who was no longer invited to family functions unless he was wearing a gag and straitjacket.

With my grandparents shut safely in the cab, Grim moved to the next phase. He came around back and dropped the tailgate.

"Your chariot awaits."

"You expect me to ride in back?"

"I just got my truck detailed."

"What if I promise not to eat the upholstery?"

He thunked his knuckle on the tailgate. "Let's go."

Fine. Okay. Whatever. I'd get in the back of his truck. But later, once Hera's voodoo wore off, I would have things to say, and Grim would have to listen.

I put my front hooves on the metal flap. The back refused to cooperate. "A little help."

"I'm wearing black."

"Nice mud flaps you've got there. Be a shame if somegoat happened to them."

"I can buy new mud flaps."

"I'll eat those, too."

He came to a decision—the right decision. In a flash, he scooped up my hindquarters and deposited me in the bed of his fancy truck.

"Are you going to tie me up?"

"Not in your current condition."

Blushing is impossible in goat form. Instead of pitching a witty comeback at him to cover up my sudden confusion, I curled up on the truck bed floor and kept an eye out for flying objects and anything else that might endanger a small goat riding the back of a speeding truck. Grim dropped my handbag in next to me.

The nice thing was that after surviving an afternoon with my grandparents and Zeus's favorite servant, I had plenty of peace and quiet. Going home in this goat body was out of the question. I needed someplace to sleep it off.

By the time Grim cut the engine outside my parents' house I'd come to a decision. He walked my grandparents up to the door and loped back to his truck.

"You getting out?"

"Ha! Looking like this? My mother is on the verge of a psychotic episode. I don't want a surprise goat daughter pushing her over the edge."

"Want me to drop you off at the park? You can eat grass until the spell wears off."

"No, I don't want to go to the park, clever clogs. Can we cruise past Luke Remis's house? And by cruise I mean you park out front and leave me there."

"Why? You looking for trouble?"

"I want to flip off his whole house with my hoof, then I'm going to eat his plants, even if it takes me all night."

Grim laughed. "Petty."

"I'm at peak petty right now. Also, I'm strangely hungry for whatever he's got growing in his flowerbeds. There was a geranium that looked tasty, in retrospect."

"Got an address?"

I told him where Luke lived and he did a U-turn. He parked at the end of the street and came around back to drop the tailgate.

"Figured you'd want to keep this away from the neighborhood watch and their doorbell cameras."

I jumped down and waited while he slung my handbag around my neck. The corners of his lips kept leaping around.

"Puh-lease. Like you've never been transformed into squirrel or a wolf or a whatever by your Norse gods."

"Nobody ever turned me into anything."

"What's your secret?"

The edges of his lips turned upward. "I know when to keep my mouth shut."

I trotted along Luke's street, feeling like Donkey from *Shrek*. I ixnayed on the melancholic singing incase someone captured a singing goat on their security cameras.

Because I'd lost access to my thumbs—temporarily—I was forced to eat my way through Luke's side gate. Unsure about the safety of consuming treated wood, I spat instead of swallowing. Maybe he could glue the damp pieces back together when he returned home.

Damn it. If I'd known I was going to pop my mouth off at a bitchy goddess I wouldn't have mowed Luke's grass. Oh well, he had a few plants that looked tasty. Breaking into the house was an issue in goat form, so when I was done gnawing on the plants and grill cover, I curled up on Luke's patio furniture to sleep it off. Hopefully I'd be me again soon.

The evening thickened into night. Bugs made bug noises. Periodically, dogs flipped out. Probably warning their people about a dodgy yet adorable goat spotted in the vicinity.

A car pulled up out front.

Neighbor?

Visitor?

Ha. Probably one of Luke's booty calls, ready to carve another notch on his bedpost. Curiosity seized me by the nubby little horns. I trotted to the gate and peeked out.

Huh. Unless I was mistaken, Luke's bonk buddy was a stick in a black sack. Malevolence and an infinite capacity for judgment rolled off the creature in waves.

Luke's grandmother.

Crap, crap, crap! What was Mrs. Remi doing here? She never went anywhere unless one of her myriad kids or grandkids was ferrying her around. Was she capable of driving? Were pedestrians in peril with her tootling around Salem's streets?

Wait—why was she coming straight toward me?

She bent down and patted her knee. "*Katsika*? Come here, little *katsika*. I know you are there because Maria told Toula who told Voula, who called me and said their cameras saw a *hondros* little goat going to my grandson's backyard."

Rude. I wasn't fat. Well, maybe I was presently curvy in the midsection. But I was a goat, and therefore goat-shaped. This pot belly was a sign of robust goat health.

Which meant I'd be the perfect roast.

I backed up, intending to make a run for it through the other side gate. Did I have survival skills or what?

Definitely *what*.

I had seriously underestimated Luke's grandmother.

Like Yiayia, this was a woman forged in the old country, where tales were told about women's elbows that were registered as deadly weapons. Despite her advanced age, Mrs. Remi was speedy. Someone was *not* suffering from nearly as many maladies as they claimed. She lunged at me. She threw elbows. She did that thing old Greek women do when someone tries to board a bus ahead of them. Then she wrestled me to the ground. A rope slipped around my neck and she jerked me to my feet.

"Tomorrow I will make a feast after Church. Roast goat."

Enough was enough. No way did I want to end up spinning over hot coals with a giant metal rod shoved up my butt and out my mouth. Some holes were sacred.

"You can go pound your Sunday dinner!" I yelped.

Mrs. Remi's eyes were normally buried in a nest of wrinkles. As my words sank in, the wrinkles rippled outwards until her eyeballs were the size of saucers.

Her voice wobbled out on shaky legs. She staggered backwards. "God, is that you?"

"Uh, yes. This is totally God. Step away from me—I mean the goat. This is my goat. Touch my goat and you'll be cursed—even more cursed than you are now!"

She crossed herself. "But ..."

"No goat for you!"

"What about my prayers? Did you hear them?"

Never let it be said that I avoided an opportunity when it presented itself. "I heard them. You've been a bad, bad girl. Be nice to people. Stop gossiping. Mind your own business or I'll give you a one-way ticket to Turkey."

Her eyeballs rolled up in her head and she keeled over backwards.

My satisfaction lasted a split second before reality

bopped me on the head. Panic shivved me above the kidney and dumped me in a tub full of ice. Great. Not only had I pretended to be God (if there was a hell, I'd just bought myself a seat at the pit-side bar), but I'd committed elder abuse. And here I was with stupid do-nothing cloven hooves instead of hands.

I trotted over to my bag. I gripped the zipper between my teeth and pulled. That worked better than I expected. I nosed the bag open and felt around for my phone. I yanked it out onto the patio with a small *plink* and touched the screen with my nose. The screen lit up.

Success.

I swiped up. More success. Now where was that pesky phone app? My goat eyes were experiencing issues with colors.

Ah. There it was.

Boop.

Nothing.

Boop.

Nothing.

With every poke, my goat snout jabbed several apps at the same time. Dumb goat nose. I couldn't even call nine-one-one to get help for the old woman I'd traumatized. Could be I'd even killed her. I couldn't tell.

I sat on my hindquarters and bleated. Woe. Woe was poor, stupid goat-me.

Then a pair of big hands grabbed me from behind. One hand wrapped around my furry snout.

"For fuck's sake," Luke Remis swore. "Keep it down, goat."

He released my muzzle and tethered me to one of the posts holding up his porch cover. He crouched down beside his grandmother to check her for lifesigns.

"It was an accident," I said. "She was going to cook me and—"

Luke whipped around. "Penny?"

"I was trying to call nine-one-one but I couldn't get my phone to work properly with this dumb goat nose. Your grandmother thought I was God."

That got a rise out of his eyebrows. "She thought *you* were God?"

"In my defense, she assumed. I just ran with it so she wouldn't eat me tomorrow. Wait—what are you doing here?"

"I've been watching my place. I saw Yiayia show up, and then she didn't leave. I was worried she was ironing my underwear again."

"Marika told Toula who told Voula that there was a goat here."

"So I see." He was trying not to laugh.

"Pay attention to your grandmother."

"She's fine. She just fainted. Act normal—like a normal goat," he clarified. "I'm taking her home. Wait here."

I decided to make myself scarce by hiding around the back of the garden shed. I heard the sounds of Luke gently bringing his grandmother around and escorting her from the yard. A few moments later, her car started up. He returned after that on foot.

"Penny?" he said in a loud whisper.

I trotted across the lawn. "Still here?"

"I've got to go," he said.

"What? No! I'm like this because of you. Well, I'm like this because of me, but don't leave. I don't know how long I'm going to be stuck like this. What if I die of exposure?"

He was suppressed laughter as he unlocked the back

door and shooed me inside, but some leaked out the sides anyway.

"Could you get my handbag?"

He scooped it up and placed it on the kitchen counter.

"You hungry?"

"Thanks, but I already ate some of your plants."

"I can get new plants."

My goat stomach rumbled. "How soon?"

He laughed. "You're a mess, Post. Midnight."

"Where can you get plants at midnight?"

"Forget the plants. Hera's spells wear off at midnight in our world."

"How did you know it was Hera?"

He shifted his body weight and focused on something behind me. I couldn't tell what without turning my whole body around.

"What?" Realization dawned. "Oh my God, you got Hera'd, too, didn't you?"

"Did I say that?"

"You didn't have to. I've known you my whole life. I know when you're uncomfortable. What was it? What did she turn you into? Was it a goat?"

"Doesn't matter."

"Oh, it does."

"Forget it, okay?"

"Tell me or you're getting head-butted. I can do that now. Wait—you were watching the house? Where are you hiding?"

"Close by." He backed toward the front door. "Look, I have to go. I can't be here. The key is on the counter. Lock up when you leave."

I charged. He ducked through the door at the last second.

SLAM.

I collided horns first with the door. The wooden door. I pulled back. *Ungh.* Damn it. I was stuck.

"Hello?" I called out. "A little bit of help here?"

Too late. Luke had left the building.

There was nothing to do except wait out the clock.

CHAPTER 12

AT THE STROKE of midnight my horns vanished along with my fur, leaving me naked on Luke's entryway floor. Hera's spell had stolen my clothes. Not cool. Those boots were pricey. I'd splurged on good hiking boots when I was still married to Chaz. Later, we'd fought about the boots. He was livid. According to Chaz, I should have spent the money spoiling his mother on Mother's Day. No mention of my mother. Or the fact that I was juggling three jobs while he worked precisely zero jobs whatsoever.

Alone in the house, I prowled through Luke's home and located the bedroom. From the outside his home was quaint. Inside, it was clean and functional. He'd spared every expense decorating and only owned a few basic items of good furniture. Big comfortable pieces for men who enjoyed kicking back and passing out at the end of a work-day. Back when we'd been a thing, Luke lived in a tiny apartment with a roommate and cheap, flimsy furniture. One night we broke his bed, so he tossed the frame and left the mattress on the floor. Now he owned a solid bed that looked like it could take a whole lot of hammering.

There was no female presence—besides yours truly—except the icon stand in the small foyer. The collection of religious imagery and figurines had to be his grandmother's doing. Twenty-five-year-old Luke had claimed to believe in God, but he didn't feel the need to show-off about it. His faith was personal-sized. His Sunday jaunts to church with his grandmother were to please her, not to see and be seen.

Luke's closet was a shallow walk-in, and he'd placed the dresser inside. I opened the drawers one at a time, mostly out of the desire to clothe myself before I wandered into the dark streets of Salem, and partly out of curiosity. Everything smelled like him. I tried not to sniff stuff because that was weird. What if he had one of those nanny cams in his room? I wouldn't put it past him to keep an eye out for mythological beings that wanted to kill him, under the circumstances.

I located a black t-shirt and gym shorts with a drawstring, and thanked my genetics for the moderately flat chest, seeing as how Hera had also stolen my undies and bra. At the bottom of the closet I found gym slides that were too big but would have to suffice.

Lamenting the loss of my boots, I locked the door behind me and set off for home on foot.

———

The night was darker than most, and every time a car approached or something moved in the shadows, I jumped. My slapping footsteps echoed on the sidewalk. I kept my hand in my bag, ready to snatch up a weapon. I wasn't sure which to hold. Swinging even a teeny tiny sword in Salem's streets might get me noticed by the kind of people whose hobby was panicking on neighbor apps. Which left me torn between the pepper spray and stun gun.

I made it home without giving my weapons a chance to shine. Which was nice.

Because it was after midnight, I expected the whole house to be dark, except for the security lighting. No such luck. Grandpa was still up, watching the street from his usual porch rocking chair.

"You're up late," I said, kissing him on the cheek.

"Can't poop, so I guzzled a bottle of prune juice. Now I'm scared to go to sleep."

"You could sleep on the toilet."

He pointed at me. "You're full of good ideas. Must get it from my side." His finger dipped lower. "Wait a minute, those aren't your clothes."

"There was an incident."

"Shame! Shame!" He gave me an exaggerated wink. "Did you get you some?"

"No—no shame. I was working."

"Then where are your clothes?"

There was movement from the second floor. I heard the glass door slide open and Yiayia shuffled out onto the balcony in her nightgown and slippers.

"*Vre*, who is that? Who are you talking to? I am trying to watch my shows."

I stepped back so she could see me. "It's just me, Yiayia."

"There you are, my love. What are you talking to Mr. *Malaka* about?"

Grandpa stepped off the porch. Using his hand as a visor, he peered up at Yiayia. "This one had a wardrobe change. Looks like a man's clothes. Ask me, our grand-daughter is getting some action."

The only action was me narrowly avoiding ending up on Mrs Remi's spit.

"There was no action, I swear. There was an incident. With a goat."

Grandpa's eyebrows took a hike. "We saw a goat when that fancy boy Viking drove us home, didn't we?" he called out to Yiayia.

My gut plummeted. My car was still parked at the strip mall, and Mom's minivan was ...

In the driveway, actually. And someone—Luke no doubt —had taken the time to have it washed. God, what a suck-up. Okay, yes, it was actually pretty nice of him. Something told me he'd returned it with a full tank of gas, too.

"I wish I had that goat," Yiayia said. "It could be marinating right now."

I woke up in bed with a woman. Her hair was neater than mine, so she couldn't have been hogging my other pillow for long. She wore a long, diaphanous negligee and she looked like an old-timey movie star.

I wasn't even surprised, not after a Greek goddess turned me into a goat. This freak show was shaping up to be my new normal.

She wiggled her fingers at me. "Hi."

"Can this wait until after coffee?"

"No."

I sat up and swung my legs out of bed. "Too bad. My night was weird and my morning isn't any better. If I don't get coffee, I'm going to cut someone."

The woman followed me. "You're curious about why I'm here."

"There would be something wrong with me if I wasn't."

"You're going to ask why we woke up in bed together."

"Why did we wake up in bed together?"

"See?"

"No."

"But I do."

"It's way too early for this," I said.

I staggered into the kitchen and seized my mug and carafe. For once I'd remember to set up my coffeemaker the night before—well, this morning—and was rewarded with steaming hot coffee. Thanks, past Penny.

"Coffee?" I asked the woman in the nightie.

"Ugh, no. Never touch the stuff."

I raised my cup. "More for me."

"Great, I can work with this." She grabbed my mug, dumped the coffee, then peered inside. With a snot of derision she thrust it back at me. "This isn't coffee."

I snatched the mug out of her hand.

"Not anymore it's not! What the heck is your problem?"

She made a "come on" motion with her hand. "Where's the muddy stuff? Greeks always have the muddy stuff. It's thick, it's goopy, it sticks to the cup. Great for fortune telling if you have even a speck of woo-woo powers."

"My American genes reject everything about Greek coffee, except the *frappe*. You want mud? Go see my grandmother."

"No can do. I'm here for you." She wandered around, poking through cabinets and drawers. "Guess we'll have to do this the old fashioned way. You like poetry?"

"More than I like muddy coffee."

"Great! Okay. Listen carefully. Grab a pen and paper if you've got them."

Was she saying something? I'd zoned out. That's what happens when someone talks poetry at me first thing in the A.M. "What was that?"

She shimmied up onto my counter and whipped out a bong from thin air. It was made out of a large sea shell.

"What? No! You can't do that here!"

She shrugged. "This is Oregon. The law says I can. I checked."

"No, I mean you can't do that in my house!"

Her head tilted. She looked genuinely confused. "Why not?"

"Because I said so!"

"Oh, is that all? Just FYI, I don't really take orders from anyone except Apollo, seeing as how he's my boss."

"Are you Starbuck?"

Her face scrunched up. "Who?"

Someone had never watched any version of *Battlestar Galactica* and it showed. "Never mind."

"Call me Sibyl. That's not my real name, mind you. It's more of a job title. A name I have to use for the duration of my tenure as the Oracle of Delphi. Okay, hang on. I have to do this or I can't do that thing I'm supposed to do." She sucked a lungful of smoke out of the bong. Whatever was in there, it didn't smell like cannabis. Probably it was some weird oracle weed. I recalled that the oracles of Delphi were apparently drugged, while priests interpreted their high-as-balls babbling. Would I have to interpret her poetry? Nobody mentioned I'd have to do schoolwork first thing in the morning—and ten years after I'd graduated.

Sibyl—allegedly—kept sucking for several minutes, until finally she set aside her shell bong. Her eyes rolled back in her head. She waved her arms and smoke poured out all the holes in her face—thick, purple smoke.

My fire alarm flipped out.

SCREECH. "Fire. Fire. Fire." *SCREECH*. "Fire. Fire. Fire."

Stupid fire alarm. Mind you, it was nice to know it worked.

I grabbed the stepladder, poked the reset button, and climbed down.

"Everything okay?" Mom called from downstairs.

I stuck my head out the window. "All good. Just testing the alarm."

Sibyl was still blowing smoke out her holes.

"Should I get the fire hydrant?" I asked her.

Her eyelids fluttered. I grabbed my phone.

"There once was a King named Minos/Who acted like a giant penis/He sent his best men/Then sent them again/Oh shit, he lost his loincloth." She held up her hand. "Wait. There's more. Minos is a dick/the birds are not what they seem/at least they're not geese."

The smoke stopped. Sibyl sat up and wiped her hands together. "There, how did I do?"

I looked down at my phone. Poetry wasn't my thing, but I recognized a limerick when I heard one, even if the first two lines didn't quite rhyme. The other poem was a haiku. Five syllables, seven syllables, five syllables.

"Am I grading on the curve? Do I have to hold up numbers?"

Sibyl gave me a hopeful smile. "So it was a five figs out of five right?"

"Yeah, okay. Five figs. The door is over there. Don't forget to take your bong. I hope you find your loincloth."

"What loincloth?"

"The one you just mentioned."

"Oh, that. I never listen to my own poetry." She waved. "See you next time."

She headed out the door in her long nightgown and pretty hair. When I peered out, she'd vanished.

Weird. Nobody had ever made me do poetry in the morning. I saved her babblings, just in case a mental health professional contacted me about her state of mind, then I called Nikki in case there was a new side mission.

"Oh, that's just Sibyl," she said. "She shows up at all our Greek agents' houses on the regular. She gets high and blows smoke before delivering some nonsense, usually in a haiku. Did she haiku you?"

"I definitely got haiku'd and limericked. And she threw out my coffee."

"Oh no she didn't. String the *skeela* up." Nikki understood that coffee was life.

"It's fine, I've got more."

"What did she tell you?"

I repeated the haiku.

"Minos *is* a dick," Nikki said, "so she's not wrong. The rest sounds like a laundry mix-up and too much time spent watching 1990's television. Sibyls always love old shows. They never abandoned the VCR like the rest of us. Her prophecies are mostly nonsense. When she gets it right it's usually by accident."

"Yeah, okay, if you say so. See you soon. I need to go beg for a ride."

"I had to do that last month. I thought things would be different when we became adults," she said wistfully.

Thirty minutes later, Mom dropped me off at work with a dozen donuts from the Wicked Sweet Bakery. I couldn't tell her twelve was overkill because my boss was a head in a vat, so here I was: a woman standing alone with a dozen assorted donuts. Poor Nikki and I would be forced to eat them all ourselves. Oh, the humanity!

Alas, Nikki wasn't alone. Half a dozen scantily clad soldiers of some mythological flavor were crammed into the office, and Nikki was giving them a good talking to. Her voice was high and angry, and she was on the verge of—as Yiayia put it—making them eat wood.

That wasn't a kinky sex thing involving a paddle. Eating wood meant somebody was about to get a painful, non-sexy spanking. All the safe words in the world weren't going to help this gang of buff and oiled beefcakes.

Nikki was the only thing standing between them and the door. From the sounds of things they wanted out and she wasn't about to let that happen.

My donuts and I barged in. "Good morning! Although really, is it good when it's this early? Oh well! I brought donuts." I flipped open the goodie box and showed off the fried and decorated circles of dough. "The pink one with the gold bits is mine, so hands off that one." One of the beefcakes reached for it. I yanked the box away. "What did I just say?"

"Sorry," he muttered.

"They're not too bright," Nikki said, "but they're relentless."

"And barely dressed," I observed.

"I have seriously mixed emotions when they show up," she whispered to me.

"What's the problem?"

The wannabe donut thief banged the blunt end of his spear on the floor. "Our mission is to engage in a training exercise."

"Good luck with that," I said.

"We do not require luck. We are Trojans."

"Could I interest you in a horse?"

He lit up. "Horses would help, yes."

"Definitely not bright," I mouthed at Nikki.

She pulled me aside. "If they're here for a training exercise, I'll shave my head and let my mustache grow wild. They smell like Minos's flunkies, and my gut says they're looking for Luke, whatever their paperwork says."

"And that's a violation of the treaties, right?"

"Right. Security should have stopped them, but they presented themselves as having legitimate cause to enter our world."

"We have security?"

Nikki shuddered. "You don't want to mess with Labyrinth's security."

"What happens if they find Luke and bring him in before I do?"

"You don't get paid."

"Stall them," I whispered. I glanced at the watch I wasn't wearing. "Wow, would you look at that time? I have to go do a thing that needs thinging." I grabbed my pink-and-gilded donut and raced back to my car, which was thankfully still parked outside.

As much as I wanted to see Luke Remis flayed alive, he was still a human being, albeit one of occasionally questionable character. But I didn't, for one minute, believe he killed the Minotaur.

If I solved the Minotaur's murder, King Minos could get his cruel and unusual revenge on the real perp and I'd still get my paycheck. And then, yes, Luke Remis would owe me a sizable favor, which I'd hold over his head until it was time to collect. Good chance I'd hold onto it until I was on my deathbed, purely to watch him twitch for the next forty-plus years.

What definitely could not—and would not—happen was those shiny, hunky Trojans collecting my paycheck. There was no way in heck a sextet of glistening hotties was going to steal food out of my cat's mouth.

I spent the morning scoping out the other locations in Luke's Minotaur file. Every last address on the list was a bakery, Greek or otherwise, owned by a family that had relocated from the myth world to the Salem area. This time I approached the businesses with more tact and discovered each family had lost at least one member to the Minotaur. I offered my condolences, bought too many sweets, and assured them the Minotaur was dead. While that was going on, I reminded myself that any one of them had ample cause to kick the Minotaur's male buttocks back to Tartarus. Not that the bull dude didn't deserve it. Eating people without their permission in any respect was bad manners.

Unfortunately, I struck dead end after dead end on the screen captures of the Minotaur's pals at Waterfront Park—and its killer. Nobody knew anything. Nobody recognized anybody. Maybe they were lying, but I didn't think so.

I called Nikki. "Any chance I can get a list of myth folks who live here and who also own bakeries? I'm looking for anyone not already on Luke's list."

"Sure thing. Incoming."

Within seconds I had the names and addresses in hand. According to the list there were just three more businesses. Something told me they would have been next on the Minotaur's menu unless something or someone hadn't take him down.

I drove over to the first place on the list, a bakery up in

Woodburn. I gazed longingly at the outlet mall and turned in the other direction. Another day, when I had money to burn.

Located in an upscale shopping center, The Bread Basket was wedged in between a clothing boutique and a shop called Fancy Feasts that sold gourmet meals for pets. Chaz and his "mommy" were regular patrons. Neither of them cared that Chunky preferred the regular Fancy Feast, straight off the supermarket's shelves. My bitty boy was a big fan of any flavor with gravy.

The Bread Basket's owner was one Ariadne Smith, who had requested asylum in this world back at the turn of the 1900s. That had to be a typo. Or maybe not.

I parked out front and cast a longing gaze at the cakes and goodies on the passenger seat. I couldn't eat them all right now, but later, I would do my best. Effort was everything.

The bakery was doing brisk business. People entered empty-handed and left with their arms full of crisp and crunchy loaves, wrapped in brown paper. The window was full of bread, in a full spectrum of shapes and shades of brown. Some had been scored with a razor pre-bake, resulting in a bloom of geometrical patterns.

I slipped in and waited off to the side while trying to look like I was here for the carbs. Which I kind of was. There's no smell in the world as wholesome and comforting as baking bread, except maybe sheets dried in the sun. I stole glances at the woman and girl behind the counter. Mother and daughter, for sure. The two had definitely been pressed using the same cookie cutter. The woman was tall and willowy and ageless with flawless, glowing skin. Kudos to her surgeon if she had one. If this was moisturizer's work, I needed the name and hoped I could find it at Target. The girl was her mother in a smaller size. A photocopy printed at eighty-five percent of the original.

When it was my turn and the rest of the shop was empty of customers—for now—I shuffled up to the counter. I pointed to a crusty round loaf of sourdough with flower designs cut into the golden bread.

"A loaf of sourdough, and could I please speak to Ariadne Smith?"

"I'm Ariadne Smith," the woman told me.

"Penny Post from the Labyrinth Agency. You don't look over a hundred years old."

That amused her. She played along. "I haven't been a hundred in thousands of years." She exchanged her bread for my money.

"This is going to sound really strange—"

"Stranger than thinking I'm over a hundred years old?"

"So much stranger—"

She paled and reached for the girl. "He's found us."

"Who? What? No. This is more of a wellness check. I'm making sure you're okay."

Her anxiety deescalated in slow, jerky stages. "We're fine, and we intend to stay that way. Why another check up so soon?"

"There was a bit of an issue that has since been fixed. Nothing to worry about."

"What issue? Fixed how."

"Someone did a tiny bit of murder to the Minotaur."

"Zeus's cotton chiton," she breathed. "He'll be out for blood."

"The Minotaur? No, he's totally dead. The deadest kind there is."

"Not my half-brother. I'm talking about our father."

This time I was the one in shock. "Half-brother? You're

that Ariadne? Ball of string? Theseus? The labyrinth? Didn't that all end badly?"

"Don't believe everything you read in mythology books. I ran away to start a new life after Theseus abandoned me on Naxos, because I didn't fancy winding up as Dionysus' consort. And now here I am—with Stella."

"Hi, Stella."

Stella waved. "Hi."

"Are you over a hundred years old, too?"

"I'm fourteen."

A customer came in. I stepped back and waited while Ariadne attended to them. The moment they left, I gravitated to the counter again.

"When you said 'he's found us' did you mean Theseus?"

"No, I wish. Being a single mom and running a business, even when you've got the best kid in all the world is a lot. I meant my father, Minos. He was furious when I helped Theseus solve the labyrinth and kill the Minotaur."

"The Minotaur that was killed here?"

Her smile was tight. "You must be new."

"Less than forty-eight hours old."

"It's confusing, I'm sure. My father has been hunting for me since I fled."

I thought about the Minotaur and its rein of recent terror, eating its way through local bakeries owned by mythological figures and beings. Couldn't be a coincidence that the Minotaur's half-sister owned a bakery.

"Do you think your father would go as far as sending the Minotaur to find you?"

"Yes." She looked me in the eye. "He would go all the way." She tensed. Her back stiffened like a metal rod had been shoved up her spine with a mallet.

I followed her terrified gaze to the window. The half

dozen Trojans were marching across the parking lot with their spears and shields. They were coming this way, armor glinting in the morning sun.

How did they know to come here?

How did they get here *so fast*?

"They're eating my donuts—still!"

"Your donuts? You knew they were here in your world?"

"They faked out security and claimed they were here for a training exercise, but Nikki thinks they're searching for another one of our agents, Luke Remis. King Minos, your dad, believes he murdered the Minotaur."

"Luke can handle himself."

My eyebrows jumped, and they did it without my permission. What was that supposed to mean? There was subtext going on here, and it was too subtexty for my liking. Not that I had the hots for Luke—I didn't. But I needed all pertinent information to do my job effectively.

At least that's what I told myself. And I was darn good at it, too.

Ariadne grabbed her daughter and bolted for the back door. "Take care of them!"

"How?"

"Oh great, that's right, they stuck me with a newbie."

No explanation was forthcoming. She and Stella vanished through the backdoor, leaving me to smile brightly at the six bronzed, oily men when they barged through the front entrance. In their defense, they were polite about it. One soldier opened the door and let the others through.

I scooted behind the counter and tried to look helpful.

"Bread, anyone?"

They stared at me. The last man in—Trojan Six—spoke for the rest of them. "Didn't we see you earlier? You gave us donuts."

"Who, me? Nope. I would never give anyone my donuts. Must be a doppelgänger. Everyone has one, allegedly."

"A what?"

"A doppelgänger. A person that looks like another person, usually. Legend says a doppelgänger is an evil apparition."

"Which one of you is the evil spirit?" Trojan Six wanted to know.

"It's not me."

"That's exactly what an evil spirit would say."

I held up a loaf. "Bread?"

"Where is Ariadne?"

"I think she went to the store to buy some twine. She said something about today being a-maze-ing."

I waited for them to laugh. They didn't. No sense of humor, those soldiers.

Instead, they attacked.

CHAPTER 13

I WASN'T READY.

But then, who is?

Okay, maybe some people are prepared and poised when a group of men in very little armor attack. But not me. This time last week I was doing hair and going "Uh-huh. Really? Jeez, Louise! What a dirtbag," at least a dozen times a day. Today I was rummaging around in my bag, trying to withdraw my sword without spilling my own blood.

I held up a finger. "Hang on. I need to get my thingy out."

They didn't wait. Trojan One and Trojan Two vaulted over the counter and pointed their spears at me.

A-ha. The sword was stuck in the lining. I managed to work it out and pointed it back Trojan One.

The soldiers laughed.

Yes, my sword was short, but it was mighty; although I hadn't tested that theory yet. I could use it to open envelopes, chop vegetables, and stab at anything scary that got too close to my face. Spiders, for instance.

"It's not the size of the sword that matters, it's how you use it!"

They laughed harder. Back at home they probably had big swords to go with their long spears.

I retaliated by snatching up a huge boule loaf and sticking it on Trojan One's spear.

There was movement behind me. I stuck a loaf on Trojan Two's spear, in case he thought I was playing favorites.

"Speaking of spears, have you guys ever heard of Britney Spears? She's been going through some things for a long time now, but her music's pretty catchy. Do you know it?"

Trojan Six's eye twitched. "What is wrong with you?"

"What's wrong with me? Are you kidding? I don't want to die! Not yet, anyway. I haven't even made a will. It's been more than a year since I had sex. I can't die without having sex again!"

"Okay." Soldier Three—directly across the counter from me—set down his spear. He reached for what I assumed was some kind of armor-ish belt. "First sex, then you die."

"I don't want to have sex with you!"

That didn't compute. His face said so. "Pick one of the others, then."

"No! I mean you're all very studly, and so, so hot. But no!"

"Then fight!"

Through the window, I saw Ariadne and Stella peel out of the parking lot in a late model Mercedes. At least if I stayed here and fought, even if I died valiantly if not embarrassingly, they'd have a shot at finding a safe haven.

I waggled my sword. "Fight, I guess. What do I do? Is it like the movies where I just jab, or should I twirl around and hope I hit something?"

Trojan Three waved the tip of his sword. "Er, you can try a combination of both and see what works."

"Okay. Let me get organized." I hefted my pitifully tiny, practically-a-letter-opener in one hand and grabbed a pair of long-handled tongs with the other. A person could do a lot of damage with some tongs. If I timed it right I could pluck out a few eyeballs or cripple some nipples.

Nobody had given me any training. Everything I knew about fighting came from television and watching Greek women trample and maim other shoppers during the post-Christmas seventy-five percent off Christmas ornaments' sales. No one got between a Greek widow and a cheap glass pickle. The most useful tool in a Greek woman's arsenal besides her slippers, wooden spoon, or her shrill, eardrum tearing screech of fury, was a modified windmill. Unlike the regular windmill, which was all about the spinning arms, the modified windmill added elbows and weapons.

My arms began spin. On each swoop, I threw my elbows out and backwards.

"What is she doing?" Trojan Four asked Five.

"It's called a windmill," I said, trying to be informative. "This will probably work better if you come at me one at a time. So can we do that?"

"Our plan was for all of us to stab you at the same time," Six said.

"Yeah, that's not going to work for me." The door opened. "We're taking a play-fight break at the moment," I told the new arrival. "Be with you as soon as we're done, uh, practicing for that movie we're making."

"Don't mind me," Luke Remis said. "I'll be right over here, checking out the bread. Let me know if you need any help."

That got the Trojans' attention. The two on either side of me vaulted over the counter.

"Don't mind me," I told Luke in a singsong voice. "I'll be right over here, hiding behind the counter. Let me know if you need any help."

Spoiler alert: Luke Remis did *not* need any help kicking Trojan butt. Out of nowhere—literally, not figuratively—two swords a whole lot longer and scarier than mine winked into existence, as if he'd shot them out of his wrists. Very Spiderman, but without the sticky, thready goop. In a flash, he leaped forward and sliced the head clean off the closest Trojan. The man exploded in a burst of glitter, that rained down on the floor and vanished.

I felt woozy. The shop began to spin. Luke had killed a man right in front of me. But had he really? Living things bleed when you poke holes in them. Even the Minotaur had oozed blood the shade of a blue raspberry milkshake. And now this soldier's life had ended in a colorful display of craft supplies?

At least the glitter had vanished. Otherwise Ariadne's customers would be picking shiny bits out of their teeth for weeks.

With one man down, the other five decided they didn't want to wind up as sparkly dust. They surrounded Luke, forming a pointy stick circle around him. Luke turned slowly with his swords out.

My breath caught.

He was one man. They were five.

(Boy, I really knew my math. My kindergarten teacher would be proud.)

Bottom line: Luke Remis needed an intervention. What he had was me.

At my disposal I had one fairly useless sword/dagger

combo, pepper spray, a stun gun, and more than enough bread to throw all five soldiers into a carb coma for at least a few hours. The obstacle was convincing them to set down their spears to eat.

I made a decision. Odds were high it was a bad one.

"Hey, Luke? Close your eyes."

Before he could pop his mouth off, I aimed the pepper spray and hit the button. Spray shot out of the canister. Syne had hooked me up with a brand that promised 18 feet of range. Good enough to nail five Trojans in inadequate armor. They clawed at their faces, shrieking.

The bad news was that Luke hadn't closed his eyes. Probably I should have prefaced my command with "Simon says" or "please." Too late now. He was stumbling around, crying and stabbing. One at a time, the Trojans turned to glitter and vanished. When the last one *poofed*, Luke fell against the wall, clutching his face.

I tried to muster up some encouraging and consolatory words. What came out was "I told you to close your eyes!"

"And I told you to stay out the damn way!"

"No, you didn't!"

He opened his mouth to argue. Spray dripped in and triggered a series of dry, hacking coughs.

For crying out loud, he was a mess. I located a loaf of soft, pillowy bread, the kind with a high milk content. I tossed it in his direction. The loaf hit him in the gut.

"You were supposed to catch it."

"Do I look like Captain America?"

"Only in the butt."

That softened him up. "You've been checking out my butt, huh?"

"Sure. It's that thing on your shoulders, right?"

"Yeah, you've been checking me out. Don't deny it."

"The only thing bigger than your ego is your capacity for delusions." Because I wasn't a jerk, and I was directly responsible for Luke being a weeping mess, I scrunched up a couple of sheets of the paper Ariadne used for wrapping bread and offered it to him like a big tissue.

He didn't take it, on account of how he couldn't see.

Fine. Okay. This one time I would baby him.

"Move your hands."

He complied, which was helpful. I dabbed his red eyes and wet face with the paper. It wasn't soft or absorbent but it made me feel useful.

"Thanks for coming to save me," I said.

"I wasn't here to save you, cupcake. Ariadne and Stella are my responsibility. I came to escort them to safety once I realized Minos's soldiers were on the way."

I flung the paper in his face and let him mop up his own man-tears.

"This isn't about the Minotaur at all, is it? King Minos doesn't give a crap about a dead mutant, even if it does have half of his DNA. I bet he sent it here to get Ariadne in the first place, didn't he?"

"Correct."

High on my own cleverness, I kept going. "King Minos wants his daughter back so he can punish her for betraying him over the whole labyrinth and Theseus thing. I bet he knows you're her special friend, too. That's why he wants you dragged back to crazy land."

"Special friend, eh? You jealous?"

"No."

He dabbed his face. "I'm Ariadne's caseworker, the person who makes sure her father doesn't find her or hurt Stella."

"I said I wasn't jealous. I don't care about you. I'm just here to collect a paycheck."

"So you can pay cat support?"

"Don't mock my life."

"Who me? I'm not mocking your life."

"You're mocking my life."

He threw me a lopsided grin. Or could be he was having a stroke from the pepper spray. Difficult to be sure. "Maybe a little bit."

"Do the boss and Nikki know about this?"

"Nikki hands out assignments and runs the office, so yeah, she knows. The boss, too. He and King Minos have been at loggerheads forever."

"Why?"

"Minos hired him to build the labyrinth. He was supposed to keep the solution a secret but he blabbed to Ariadne, who used that knowledge to help Theseus slay the Minotaur. Minos retaliated by imprisoning him in the labyrinth with his kid, Icarus. The boss escaped but his kid was killed during the escape attempt. The boss isn't ever about to forgive Minos for that."

My brain went kaflooey. "Yeah, I know that story. Minos vs. Daedalus. Wait—are you telling me that Vat Man, our boss, is Daedalus? That's crazy."

"The head of Daedalus, which he'd tell you is the important part."

"Didn't he kill Minos?"

"Indirectly. Dead things always come back around in Greek myths. The underworld spits them back out, sooner or later."

"Why? How?"

Luke helped himself to a bottle of milk in the beverage refrigerator. He swished once and swallowed. "Mythological worlds aren't like ours. They're finite. Things die, something needs to take their place, otherwise the gods get pissed about the imbalance. Hades and the others have an ongoing rivalry. He has to kick out the dead regularly to avoid all-out war."

"So the Minotaur ..."

"Has been dead before and will be again, no doubt. Everyone hates him."

"He's a pretty good dancer."

The lines on his face hardened. This wasn't the Luke Remis I used to play with when we were kids. This was a man, and it occurred to me that playing with him now would be like sticking my hand in fire.

"When did you see him dance?"

"Where, not when. YouTube. His last dance and murder are there for anyone to find, if they know what to search for."

"Show me."

I cued the video, but because the videographer had used a root vegetable to shoot the footage, the picture was a smear of vaseline.

"I need this on a decent screen," Luke said. "Send it to me?"

"Number?"

"You don't have it?"

"I lost it. On purpose."

"I'm hurt."

"No you're not."

"Hey, men have feelings, too."

"Yeah, you *feel* hungry and you feel tired."

"You forgot horny." He ponied up his number and I sent him the link and the screenshots I'd nabbed. "Damn it. My computer is at the house. I can't go back there. Minos's guys know where I live. He'll send more once he realizes this batch are gone."

"Why did they turn to glitter? Why didn't the Minotaur? He's just a regular body in the boss's lair. Well, as regular as a mythological half-man, half-bull can get." It was shocking how all this weirdness was already becoming normal.

"Mostly it's affected by the ratio of human to creature. The soldiers went up in a puff of glitter because they're just constructs. They look human, but they're walking, walking cardboard boxes, kept alive with magic. The Minotaur is half human. In a day or two he'll liquify. Eventually, he'll return."

I poked myself in the temples. It didn't help me process faster, but it made me feel productive.

"My laptop, can you get it for me?"

Luke Remis was giving me that look. *The* look. Smooth and sultry and made of promises. And he was using it against me. Ugh.

"Save the whole panty-removing vibe for someone dumber than me." I rattled his house key. I'd put it on my keychain. "I'll get your laptop."

"Thanks, it's—"

"I know where it is. I snooped around your whole place last night. Wore your clothes home, too, seeing as how Hera stole my clothes and my good boots—boots I can't afford to replace yet, thanks to you."

"Yeah, she does that."

"Are you ever going to tell me what she turned you into?"

He sauntered toward the door. "Got to go."

"Wait—where do I take your computer?"

"I'll find you, so keep it handy."

"Where are you going?"

"To check on Ariadne and Stella, hopefully without Minos's next batch of soldiers on my tail."

"Should I get a bigger sword?"

"Cupcake, you don't need a bigger sword. What you need is a different job—or a bazooka."

That wasn't going to happen. Luke couldn't tell me what to do. He wasn't my real dad.

In full blazing daylight, my loaf of sourdough, sweets, and I drove over to Luke's place. I waved at the doorbell camera, unlocked the door, and made my way to the home office, where his laptop was languishing on a large, solid desk. Real wood. Not an arts and crafts project from IKEA.

I grabbed the laptop and its power cord and headed back to my car.

My phone rang as I pulled into Mom and Dad's driveway.

"Everyone is saying you robbed Luke Remis's house," Lena said. "What did you take? Anything good? Are we going to pawn it and take ourselves out to lunch?"

"What? No! I didn't steal anything. Luke asked me to get his laptop. He gave me his keys!"

"That doesn't sound like a robbery," she admitted. "What's his place like?"

"Clean."

"Probably Mrs. Remi cleans it for him. Got to go. My offspring are bouncing a raw chicken on the trampoline and I'm going to watch while I eat a burrito."

I gathered up Luke's computer and my baked goods. I took the bread and pastries to the kitchen and set them on the counter. Mom eyed the bread with suspicion. She sniffed.

"Is that sourdough?"

"Freshly baked this morning."

"Your grandparents hate sourdough. I'll serve it with lunch."

Lunch was shaping up to be what looked like *fakes*—fa-kez—a lentil soup. One of my favorite comfort foods. Mom served it Greek-style, ladled over a small block of feta cheese in each bowl, with a squirt of vinegar to finish.

I hugged Mom and went upstairs to my third-floor apartment. I unlocked the door and stepped inside.

Something was *off*. The air felt different, as if someone had been moving through this space uninvited just moments ago. Light was streaming in through curtains that I was sure I'd left closed this morning. Motes danced through the air instead of gently drifting.

I froze. Listened. There was splashing.

Someone was using my shower.

I sat Luke's laptop on the coffee table. One at a time, I slipped out of my shoes and set them aside. After a short mental debate about whether to equip the stun gun or pepper spray, I went with the spray. Giving myself an electric shock wasn't my idea of fun.

Then, because I was super brave, I crept downstairs and rallied my family—minus Dad, who was in a meeting. Between us we had two wooden spoons, one vial of pepper spray, and one of Grandpa's shotguns. We inched up to the bathroom door.

"On the count of three," I mouthed. One at a time, I ticked off fingers. On three, I turned the handle.

Locked.

Rats! The audacity of this intruder. How dare they lock my bathroom door?

I held up my index finger. This lock and I weren't strangers. I knew how to pop it open from the outside.

BAM!

I hit the ground as wood splintered. Thoughts jostled for dominance in my head.

Was it a bomb?

Oh my God, *was* it a bomb?

Who would put a bomb in my place?

Where did all the sound go?

Holy crap, was I deaf now?

Could someone my age learn sign language?

Frantic, I looked around for my family to make sure they were okay. Mom was on the ground with me. Yiayia was texting someone on her phone, oblivious. Grandpa was grinning at my shattered bathroom door, his shotgun up and smoking in the air. He said something I couldn't hear with all the dead air in my ears.

Not a bomb. A trigger-happy Grandpa was to blame.

You shot up my door! I mouthed at Grandpa.

He grinned. He mouthed, *A-yup. I got the sucker.*

I pushed past them and elbowed my way into the bathroom.

Luke Remis was standing in my shower stall, naked as the day he was born but a whole lot more ... *manly.*

In a blind panic, I spun around to face my family. Threw my arms across the open doorway. Tried yelling, "Nothing to see here!"

The words came through as a whisper. My eardrums were letting sound through now but they'd added ringing bells.

Yiayia peered past me. "Is that Androniki's boy?" she whispered.

"Maybe," I whispered back at her.

"There is more of him than I remember."

Mom covered her eyes with her hands. She was only peeking a little bit.

"Mom!"

Grandpa was cackling like a loon. "Did you see that? I got that sumbitch good."

"C'mon, Mama," Mom said. "Let's let Penny deal with her ... with her ... whatever this is. Luke, my boy, come on down for lunch. When you're dressed, of course."

"Thanks, Mrs. Post," he said.

Mom giggled. The big traitor.

They all clomped out, leaving me alone with Luke and his full frontal nudity. By the time I turned around he was reaching for a towel—my towel! In my opinion, he took entirely too long wrapping it around his waist.

"See something you like?"

"Not the hole in my bathroom door, that's for sure."

His face—and only his face—hardened. "Your grandpa tried to kill me."

"The door was locked."

"Yeah, because I was showering. That's normal when you're in someone else's place."

"You aren't supposed to be in my place! Wait. How did you get in?"

That broke him out in a grin. "Cupcake, I have talents."

"A talent for being annoying, sure. Now get out."

"No can do. Your mom invited me for lunch. Didn't you hear her? Besides, I need somewhere safe to check out that video. Did you get my laptop?"

My hands were bunched up on my hips. "You can't just barge in here and use my shower and eat with my family!"

He stepped into his underwear and jeans, muscles flexing and relaxing as he went through the motions. He hung the towel on the rod. The whole time he held eye contact. I'm not proud to admit it, but I was paralyzed with lust. Which was appalling because this was Luke Remis and he was, well, Luke Remis. Trouble with a capital T. A liar with an even more capital L.

"You're a liar," I said.

His forehead scrunched. His hands poised on the jeans' button. "What did I lie about? Lunch? You were right here when your mom invited me."

"I'm not talking about lunch." My chest inflated with hot air that I intended to use to verbally blast him back into my past, where he belonged. I had grudges, damn him, and I intended to vent them—loudly and with passion. "I—"

My phone chirped. It was Chaz. He'd sent a picture of Chunky and a sad emoji face. According to him, Chunky had lost out on Best in Show because of me. Apparently I wasn't feeding him the right food when he was here, therefore his coat wasn't up to scratch.

Futility punched me in the heart. I missed Chunky. He didn't want to be a show kitty. He enjoyed sunbeams and licking his butt and sleeping on my face. I wanted my cat, and I wanted him full-time, without Chaz and his controlling loon of a mother in the picture.

Luke, damn him, noticed my change in emotional temperature.

"Hey, everything okay?"

"Nothing giving my whole life a giant enema won't fix."

"I'll fix your door."

"It's not necessary."

He wiped fake sweat off his brow. I tried not to notice his serious pecs. "Phew. Because I gotta tell you, I'm not a fan of replacing doors."

"Jerk."

"Cupcake ..."

"The name is Penny."

"I know." He pulled his t-shirt over his head in that infuriatingly sexy way some men do. I pivoted and went to my kitchen for ... for ... for whatever I could rustle up as a distraction. Water. That would have to do. I couldn't deal with Luke in my place. At thirty, he was way too much car for me to handle.

Moments later, he sauntered out, fresh and clean and looking not one bit like a man I'd soaked in pepper spray. Even the swelling in his eyes was almost gone. He sat on my couch like he belonged and grabbed his laptop.

"Wanna watch the movie with me?"

"Seen it already."

"Come watch it again. You never know if something will shake loose."

With great reluctance, and a modest flapping of butterflies in the space between my hoo-ha and lungs, I sat on the couch, leaving a respectable distance between us. He scooted the laptop across the coffee table a fraction so we could share the view.

As we watched, the Minotaur danced and died once again. This time felt different. This time around I knew the man-bull was a people-eater and a creature sent after its half-sister. Whoever had stopped its path of destruction had saved a woman and her child—at least temporarily.

Luke paused the video on the two with the Minotaur.

"Do you know them?" I asked.

"Maybe. But I can't tell from this."

"And the killer?"

He gave me a wry smile. "I know it's not me."

"I figured. Whoever killed the Minotaur is on the scrawny side, meanwhile you're built like—" I stopped.

"Like what?"

"Moving on. What now?"

Thankfully he didn't push further. He'd switched into business mode. "One of us needs to go talk to whoever shot this video. Better if I stay out of sight, so it'll have to be you."

"Me? I don't know who filmed this"

"Sure you do." He closed the laptop. "C'mon. I'm feeling all emotional about lunch."

"You mean you feel hungry."

"Starving. What's for lunch?"

"*Fakes.*"

"Does your mom still serve dessert?"

"Every meal except breakfast."

"A woman after my own heart."

"You don't have a heart."

Before I could kick or scream, he wrapped my hands in his and yanked me up off the couch. His expression softened. The brown of his eyes changed from whiskey to chocolate. "Yeah, I do. I tried to give it to you once. Remember?"

"No." Yes.

He laughed. "You remember. I get it, though. Ending a fucked up marriage with a manchild has got to be rough. You'll get there and you'll be fine. Maybe I'll be there, waiting, when you do. In the meantime ..."

His hands dropped mine. He moved closer. His body heat closed the gap between us, followed by his body, which was bigger and harder than I remembered.

"You look good." His hands slid around my waist and

dipped lower. Okay, yeah, now he was grabbing my ass. "Feel good, too."

My pulse started throwing a fit. It had ideas about how I should react. Running, screaming, pouncing, those were all valid ideas as far as my body was concerned. My stupid brain, though, it was being driven by my hormones. Those dumbass hormones, they were into this whole ass-grabbing thing Luke was doing.

When he lowered his mouth to mine, my hormones sighed. They held me in place while his hands pulled me against him and his kiss deepened. The sad—and terrifying truth—was that nobody had ever kissed me like Luke Remis. He knew when to take soft kisses deeper, hotter. And the bastard knew precisely when to pull back and leave me gasping for more.

Like now.

His hands fell away. He stepped back.

"Want some advice?"

"Huh? No."

"Don't look *them* in the eyes."

Lunch was being served. While Mom was ferrying bowls, I hacked up the sourdough loaf and loaded the slices onto a plate that I placed in the middle of the table. Everyone was in their usual places, but Mom had made room beside me for Luke. When I sat, we were way too close for comfort. He bumped me with his knee—on purpose, the delicious bastard.

"Mom, he's touching me," I said.

"Like that's a first," Dad muttered.

I pointed at my father with my spoon. "For the record, I am shocked and appalled."

Luke squeezed my thigh. My lentils wobbled off my spoon.

Across the table, Yiayia was making a face.

"What it is?" I asked her.

"This bread smells and tastes like feet."

"Yeah, I figured you for a foot licker," Grandpa said.

She scowled at him. "Who eats a foot? Nobody."

"There are people," Grandpa said. "I've seen all sorts on the internet."

Yiayia set aside her stinky foot bread. "I do not believe you."

"Oh yeah? Get a load of this."

"Dad, please, no," my father said.

"What? I'm educating the foreigner like Jesus would have wanted. Here." He thrust his phone at Yiayia. "Look at that."

Yiayia crossed herself. "I cannot believe anyone would do that to a foot. Where is his hand going?" She gasped. She crossed herself again and shot a horrified look at my mother. "Why would you give us bread that tastes like this sick and disturbed man?"

Mom rubbed her temples. Before she could pass out, I leaped in.

"Blame me for the bread. I picked it up on the way home. I didn't realize I'm the only one that likes sourdough."

Beside me, Luke was making soft snorting sounds into his lentils. I stomped on his foot.

"Penelope, my love, I thought you loved your *yiayia*," my grandmother said. "Instead you bring me this foot bread."

I dunked mine in the lentils and took a bite. "Tastes good to me."

Grandpa elbowed Yiayia. "We should introduce her to the foot man."

"I don't want to meet the foot man," I said. "I don't want to meet any man."

Yiayia leaned forward. She looked pointedly at Luke. "It is because of the baby she married. I think he does the sex with his mama."

A lentil shot down the wrong pipe. I coughed. Luke slapped me on the back until the legume dislodged itself and leaped back onto the right path.

"Chaz isn't sleeping with his mother," I said, not a hundred percent confident that was the truth.

"I never trusted him," Grandpa said.

"You loved him," Dad said.

"His eyes were too close together," Grandpa went on.

"And too far apart," Yiayia said.

I tore up another chunk of bread. "Can we not talk about my ex-husband?"

"I'm enjoying this," Luke said. "They're right about Chaz."

"Are we going on another adventure today?" Grandpa asked. "Yesterday was fun. This time I'm gonna bring some guns along, though, in case any of those homeless folks downtown try to get the jump on us."

"The homeless people aren't going to attack you," I said.

"They might."

"I want to see that dreamy man again," Yiayia said.

Luke raised his eyebrows. "There was a dreamy man?"

"Oh yes, very dreamy," Yiayia said. "He reminded me of a boy I once knew in Greece. He was a shepherd and I was a virgin."

"This story isn't going anyplace good," Dad said. "And yet I find I can't leave my seat."

"Moving on," I said quickly. "These lentils are great, Mom."

"Wait, wait, wait. I want to hear about the dreamy guy," Luke said.

"It was nobody." I gave him a pointed look and mouthed, *"Ganymede."*

He rolled his eyes. "What is it with that guy? Everyone loves him."

"Even Grandpa got all swoony."

"True story," Grandpa said. "I got some motion going below the belt. That hasn't happened since I last watched my *X-Files* videos. That gal with the red hair is a real peach."

"Grandpa," I said, remembering what Luke said earlier. "I need to buy a bazooka. Or maybe a regular gun."

Mom gasped. "What do you need a gun for?"

"My job, apparently. It was Luke's idea."

"Way to dump me in the shit," he muttered.

"If the sewer fits."

"No," Mom said. "No guns."

As soon as she left the dining room, Grandpa nudged me under the table. "Come see me in my garage after lunch."

CHAPTER 14

GRANDPA'S converted garage apartment was a tribute to his heritage. Old fishing rods. Posters featuring vintage hot rods. A neon Budweiser sign on the wall. The American flag featured heavily. Nobody loved his country harder than Grandpa. It was the people in it he took umbrage with.

"Close the door behind you," he said. "You want a gun, you've come to the right place."

"The right place is a gun shop," Luke said.

"That's what you think," Grandpa said. "You want to end up in some database somewhere?"

"We're all in databases," I said.

"Well, you ain't gonna be added to another one today."

"This seems normal," Luke said.

My grandfather gestured at him. "Why is he here anyway?"

"He just sort of followed me, like a puppy."

"The things I do for dessert," Luke said.

Grandpa grunted. He kicked back the Oregon Ducks rug in the middle of his floor, revealing what looked like a basement door, flush with the concrete. There was a combination lock.

I gave him a questioning look. "That wasn't always there, was it?"

"Heck no. I had it built when your parents went to Greece on that trip, 'bout six years ago. The whole shebang was done by the time their plane landed back in Portland."

"Does Dad know?"

"No, and he's never gonna know, is he? At least not until I'm gone. Then he can use the space however he likes. Go on now." He gestured at Luke. "You look like you know how to lift things."

Luke crouched down and pulled on the hatch, revealing a metal staircase that led down and away from the house. Lights flickered on. We all traipsed down into what turned out to be Grandpa's bunker.

The space was maybe two hundred square feet and came with a bunkbed, bathroom, kitchen, and supplies to satiate a low key prepper's fever dreams. That included tinfoil for hats, and guns. Grandpa had enough firearms to make the ATF twitchy, but I figured since he relied on Mom to drive him everywhere, he wasn't too big a danger to society.

"Wow," I said.

"Wow," Luke said, raising his eyebrows at me behind Grandpa's back. His "wow" said my grandfather was bonkers, and acquiring one of his guns was a spectacularly bad idea.

"What do you know about guns?" Grandpa asked.

"They go *bang* and kill people?" Probably not the answer he was looking for.

"And bust doors when a guy is trying to shower," Luke said.

"All right." Grandpa perused his gun collection. He selected a small one, not much bigger than my hand, and slapped it into my palm. "That there is a good girly gun. This one gives you any trouble, shoot him in the pecker."

"I hate that idea," Luke said.

"I don't hate it as much as he does," I told Grandpa.

"Atta girl. Other hand." I opened my other hand. He dumped a box of ammo in it. "Now go do some damage."

"Or don't," Luke said.

"Not unless I have to," I said. "Hopefully I'll never have to."

"You know how to use that thing?" Luke asked on the way out.

"Sure. You put the pointy metal things in and pull the squeezy thing."

"Jesus."

Luke showed me how to load the gun and avoid shooting anyone or anything that didn't require shooting. Before he left, he extricated a promise from me that I would hustle my tush to a good range so I'd have a fighting chance of hitting my target instead of my foot.

"Where are you going now?"

"Can't tell you," he said.

"For Ariadne's safety?"

"Yeah."

"What do I do if Minos's marching stick throwers come back?"

"They will. Avoid them."

He gathered up his laptop and cord and headed for the door.

"Do you need a ride?"

He hooked his finger in the neck of my shirt and kissed me hard.

"Maybe later."

"Huh."

"You want me," he said.

"Not even a speck. My legs and heart are closed to you. Wait—don't forget your house keys."

Too late. He was gone.

He'd been right about one thing, damn him. I did suspect who had shot that video of the Minotaur's murder at Waterfront Park. I stuck Grandpa's gun in the freezer and stashed the ammo in the linen closet, between the decorative towels I never used, and set out for downtown Salem.

Riverfront Park was packed again. I managed to pounce on a parking space when a family with a gaggle of kids backed out. From there, I crossed the street and railroad tracks at the pedestrian crossing. In a wide patch of sun a few feet down from the liquor store on the corner, Yellow Chucks was hanging out with one of her fashion twins. The heat didn't seem to bother them. My pits were a pair of hot tubs, even with antiperspirant, while they were a couple of cool cukes in their hoodies and jeans. The only hint that they knew about summer was their sunglasses.

With the screenshot ready to go in my pocket, I sauntered over and leaned on the wall next to Yellow Chucks.

"Nice day for a whatever it is you're doing here."

"You find out who killed your Minotaur cosplayer?"

"Nope. Not yet. But I intend to. Where are your other friends?"

"Digging a new hole."

Weird, but whatever. "They work for the county or state?"

She sighed. "What do you want?"

"Nothing much. I was moseying around Youtube the other night and found a video of that park across the street. The one with the big planet."

"Good for you."

"You got a name?"

"Yes."

"Nice to meet you, Yes. I'm Penny."

She snorted. "Go check on the hole," she told her friend. Once her friend slunk around the corner, she turned to face me. "Who did you tell about that video?"

"My coworker. Guy by the name of Luke Remis. Know him?"

She nodded. "That's not so bad. Just don't go telling anybody else. You keep your mouth shut, you hear me?"

I indicted that I'd heard her. That didn't mean I was done with my questions. "So you filmed it?"

"Maybe yes, maybe no."

"Let's pretend you captured the whole thing on your mobile potato cam. Did you recognize the people with the Minotaur?"

"Could have been anybody."

"What about the killer?"

"Could have been anybody."

"Not really. I know it wasn't Luke Remis, even though he's getting the blame for this whole thing. Wrong height. Wrong build. This was maybe a slim man or woman." I readjusted my pose and cast a longing glance at the shadier spots on the sidewalk. "Mind if we move down to the shade?"

"You can go wherever you want. I'm staying right here. I need the sunlight."

"Vitamin D deficiency, huh? I take a supplement in the

winter on account of how there's never any sun. You know, none of this is even about the cosplaying Minotaur. Not really."

"What's it about then, seeing as how you've figured it all out."

"You read any Greek mythology?"

"Nope."

"Ever hear the one about Theseus and Ariadne?"

"Do I look like I care?"

"In the story, Theseus slays the Minotaur with Ariadne's help. She's King Minos's kid. He's the one who commissioned the labyrinth in the first place. Anyway Theseus, being a love-struck dude, makes the usual promises—I'll call you in the morning, we'll be together forever, blah, blah, blah—and then he abandons her on the island of Naxos because Athena—that's the goddess—told him to leave her as a cool, fun toy for Dionysus, the god of Alcoholics Anonymous. But let's say that instead of staying behind to become a god's plaything, Ariadne went all womanpower and fled the island because she decided to be the master of her own destiny. How do you think her notoriously crabby and controlling father felt about all that?"

"Don't know. Don't care."

"See, I think you do. I don't think you're from around here, so to speak. Not if you know Luke Remis. You said your dad was a king. Which one? This world doesn't have a lot of royalty, especially not kings with daughters who hang out on a street corner in Salem, Oregon, for crying out loud."

She whipped off her sunglasses.

I froze.

Ah, crap. Not again. What was it Luke had said? Don't

look the *them* in the eye? And my dumb butt had to go and forget his advice.

When I shook off the paralysis she was gone. I walked up and down the street and didn't see any signs of Yellow Chucks, her friends, or any holes.

I drove home and flopped down on the porch next to Yiayia and Grandpa. Yiayia was stabbing colored thread through an embroidery hoop, while Grandpa was questioning our neighbor's patriotism and dedication to his lawn.

"What kind of man buys an electric mower? Nobody that takes yard work seriously uses an electric anything. A yard needs the power of gas. Probably one of them folks who don't love America."

The man across the street was a former Marine, so I was pretty sure he loved the country just fine and had swapped the gas mower for electric to save himself a whole lot of hassle now that he was in his 80s, but what did I know?

Yiayia clutched her chest. "I just remembered. That very sexy man was here earlier. I told him I want to bang him like a church door on Easter Saturday but he did not know about church or Easter."

"Luke? Yeah, I was here."

"Not him. The one with the loincloth."

Grandpa fanned himself. "That boy makes me wanna take him on a cowboy trip, like in that one movie. There was a mountain."

Oh boy. The cupbearer had done another runner already. He was slick, that one.

"Ganymede was here?"

"Ask your mother," Grandpa said.

I went inside. Mom was running the sweeper in high

heels and a face loaded with makeup. Her legs were slick and shiny, and her bodycon dress was ... mine?

"Who are you and what have you done with my mother?"

She jabbed the OFF button with her heel. "This is my new look. I want to be prepared in case he comes back."

"The cute guy in a loincloth?"

Her violently red lips curved upwards. "He's a dish."

"Nobody says that anymore."

"Well, they should because it's true."

"What would Dad say if he knew you were sniffing around after a scantily clad man?"

"Nothing, that's what. He didn't mind at all. Your friend asked if someone could give him a ride downtown and your dad took him."

"Did he say what he wanted besides transportation?"

"He wanted to see you. He said you were his new case-worker now, whatever that means."

"I am?" I asked breathlessly. My cheeks felt hot. Common sense arm-wrestled my hormones for control. "Wait—I am?"

"That's what he said." Mom unplugged the vacuum. "What kind of caseworker? It's not for drugs, is it? I swear, you're talking about buying guns and hanging out with these strange, *attractive* men." She fanned herself with her hand.

"It's not drugs," I said. "It's an immigration thing. He's not from around here."

I went upstairs and called Nikki. "Ganymede is on the loose again. My dad just gave him a ride downtown."

"When you say ride ..."

"In a car. Holy crap, I hope just the car."

"Can you—"

"Already on it."

I called Dad. "Where did you take your passenger?"

"To some shindig in the park. He said he wanted to dance. I wanted to watch, but he patted me on the cheek and ran off."

"Which park?"

"Riverfront. Last time I saw him he was heading over to the carousel." He sounded crestfallen. "Everything okay?"

"Fine. I just have to find him."

"I can help you look," he said with a disturbing amount of enthusiasm.

"Uh, no. Go home and take a cold shower."

Once more, unto the Ganymede breach. When I hoofed it my car, Yiayia and Grandpa were waiting.

And ... Mom?

"Everybody out," I said.

"It's not fair," Mom said. "Don't make me waste this nice outfit."

"Show Dad."

"He never notices me anymore."

That wasn't true. He was always grabbing her butt when he thought no one was looking.

"I have to work," I said. "Me leaving without you all is part of work."

They stared at me. Grandpa picked at his teeth.

"I'll bring him back here before I escort him, uh, home, okay?"

"Yay," Mom said.

Everyone piled out.

I drove back to Riverside Park. Now that the heat was at its peak, the families were heading home to hug their air conditioners and fans. This part of Oregon wasn't used to the hardening summers, and a whole lot of houses and apartments didn't come with A/C unless you could balance a unit on the window sill.

My inner kid experienced a small thrill as I checked out the Riverfront Carousel. The fair music made me wish I was ten again and didn't have to chase scantily clad mythological beings all over Salem. I wandered through the thin crowd, eyes wide. No sign of Ganymede.

I approached the ticket taker and asked if she'd seen anyone in a loin cloth that looked like a cross between a micro mini and an adult diaper. Her expression said I needed to be institutionalized for an extended period. Why I'd bothered asking was a mystery. If Ganymede had been flitting around here, everyone would still be swooning.

I walked around the park for fifteen minutes, hunting for any sign of the runaway cupbearer. There was no evidence of him or any imminent or upcoming musical events.

Had he lied to my family?

Unwilling to give up just yet, I wandered back to the pedestrian crossing for the second time today and waited on the little dude to turn green.

The corner was empty. No Yellow Chucks. No sign of her hole-digging compadres.

I stepped around the corner. My shoe's sole struck something sticky.

Ugh.

Not gum. Please don't be gum.

It wasn't gum. It was the weird blue blood of a mythological being, the same blue blood that had stained the ground near the big globe across the street. This was fresh, a sprawling pool of the stuff, with a bunch of gory skid marks leading into the liquor store.

My heart threw itself at the exit. It wanted me to run—

away, not in. *Not today, heart.* Sometimes—like now—my curiosity seized the wheel, and the rest of me went along with it because my curiosity had super strength once it was piqued.

The doors said PULL. I dragged one open and stepped inside. More blood. Leading to the back of the store. Past two customers, both of whom looked like they saw blood in crazy colors on the regular. The cashier glanced at me for a split second before her gaze slid away. Despite my dramatic entrance, I wouldn't be interesting to her until time came to hand over my cash.

I hurried to the whiskey section at the rear and slammed to a horrified stop as the scene seeped into my consciousness.

Three of the hoodie-clad women from the corner were piled carelessly at the back of the store. Their scalps were bleeding—or had been bleeding—and something or someone had cut off their heads and dumped them next to the bodies.

No one in the store noticed or cared, not even when one old woman with bloodshot eyes and whiskey breath toddled back to grab a bottle of Wild Turkey. Her attention skated past the massacred women without touching them at all.

The taste of cold metal filled my mouth. My gut was an ice bucket in a cheap motel. Fear galloped through my body. The weirdo corner women hadn't slipped in a puddle of Limoncello and lost their heads. This was methodical, deliberate murder.

My hand shook as I poked around in my handbag, hunting for my phone. Who could have done this? Or what? It took strength to cut off a head—a fact I was pretty sure I'd picked up on TV, not through experimenting. The average person can't easily mosey around, decapitating unsuspecting folks.

I called Nikki. Words fell out of my mouth in any old order. "They're dead. Really dead. They've lost their heads. Cleanup crew? Liquor store across from Waterfront Park? With fries. Wait—forget that last part."

"Already forgotten. Who's dead?"

"I don't know! The women who hang around this corner. One of them told me her dad is a king. I thought she was joking at the time, but I'm finding out a lot of weird, funny crap is real." I glanced at the dead women. None of them were wearing yellow Converse Chucks. "None of these women is her, though."

"Shit," Nikki said. "Medusa's girls."

My voice squeaked out. "What?"

"Did you find Ganymede yet? Is he okay?"

"No. He wasn't at the park."

"You have to find him or Zeus is going to flip out again. He does that a lot."

"Do I stay until the cleanup crew arrives?"

"Totally unnecessary."

"But they're just lying there."

"Don't worry, nobody will notice. They'll sidestep them without so much as a blip. Regular folks don't tend to see what they don't believe in. Not unless they're really high."

"This is a liquor store." I lowered my voice, way, way down. "The clientele already believe they're fine to drive."

"Good point," she said. "Stay there. If anyone notices anything, tell them it's an art installation. That's how the London office dealt with the Spinning House of Meat."

"That was real? I thought it was a Banksy about the virtues of veganism."

"Everyone mistook it for a Banksy. Alas, shredded

cyclopes. We had to give the cleanup crew a massive bonus so they wouldn't quit."

I paced and tried to make it look like I was struggling to decide between Captain Morgan Rum or a six pack of vodka coolers. My eyes kept snapping back to the dead women.

What had Nikki called them?

Medusa's girls.

They were gorgons. Or at least half-gorgons. That made a crazy kind of sense and explained the weird immobility problems I'd experienced when they were around. I wasn't having mini strokes or seizures after all. They were petrifying me, and because they weren't full gorgons, the effects were temporary. Huzzah?

Questions flitted around my head, fueled by my nervous energy.

Where was Yellow Chucks?

Ganymede?

The hole?

What was the hole?

I glanced at the women's bald and recently shaved scalps. They must have had snake hair (which explained the omnipresent hoodies) and whatever killed them cruelly shaved it off.

Had King Minos sent a fresh batch of soldiers already? Was he the king Yellow Chucks mentioned? Why would he have his men kill the half-gorgons?

For an endless ten minutes, I paced and jiggled, unanswered questions pinging around my head. I read the backs of bottles. The fronts. Boredom wanted to settle in, but the jitters refused to give it space. What was I doing here? This was a job for someone with a cast iron stomach and a six-pack, not my weak guts.

Finally, the doors flew open. A couple of women who

weren't strictly women barged in, wearing t-shirts with logos that read *Claw and Tooth Cleaning Services.*

The cleanup crew.

Who, by the way, were harpies. Human heads. Human hair. Plump, feathery bird bodies with wings tucked neatly against their sides. Their bird legs ended in a pair of feet, with talons I suspected could shred a full-sized man in seconds.

They zeroed in on me. Even though I knew we were colleagues, I shifted from side to side, nervous that I might be on their lunch menu.

"I know what you're thinking," the one on the left said. "You're wondering if we taste like chicken."

"I wasn't, I swear!"

The pair of them cawed. It took me a moment to realizing they were laughing at me.

"It's all good," the bird-woman on the left said. "We're just effing with you. Aello and Ocy." Her wing indicated she was Aello and her waving coworker was Ocy. "You Penny?" She didn't wait for an answer. "The dead girls up back? It's okay, I can smell them from here." She nudged Ocy with her wing. "Lunch is on Penny today."

I stepped aside so they could roll their cleaning supplies through.

Huh. Weird. No cleaning supplies.

"How do you clean without cleaning stuff?"

They exchanged glances. Aello extended a wing and ushered me toward the front of the store. "Uh, how about you wait there while we do our thing?"

Fine with me. I smiled in what I hoped was a "I'm still deciding" way at the cashier and then faked a call to Mom, asking if she needed anything while I was here. Over in the corner, the harpies got to work. There were a whole lot of screeching and tearing sounds, followed by nightmarish slurping that made me think the store was running a horror movie over the speaker instead of country music. Nobody else in the store was on the verge of upchucking except me. They were all oblivious.

The whole thing lasted about five minutes. The harpies clacked over to me on their man-killing talons.

"All done," Ocy said on the way past. "I'm stuffed. Those snake girls go a long way. Taste like a chicken and pork combo." She belched and they took off out the door, Aello flipping what I hoped was a harpy equivalent of a thumbs up and not the bird—pun totally intended—on the way past.

Ever so casually, I wandered back up the aisle to the rear of the store. There was nothing left. Not even a smear of blue on the floor.

Urgh.

The dead half-gorgons were harpy lunch. But I had to admit, the bird women were spectacular at their jobs.

"You need some help?" the cashier called out at last.

I plucked a bottle off the shelf. Ouzo.

Somewhere, somewhen, it was ouzito time.

CHAPTER 15

I SPENT the rest of the afternoon driving all over Salem and the surrounding areas, hunting for Ganymede. Nothing. Nobody had seen a gorgeous mythological guy in very little clothing, who danced like he was drowning in six inches of water.

Fear took a personal-sized ice pick to my gut. What if he was lying in a gutter somewhere, in a puddle of his own blue goo? What if whoever or whatever had slaughtered Medusa's girls went after him, too?

I needed to sit somewhere quiet and think. If I went home, my family would be yapping about Ganymede and the appalling sexual things they wanted to do to him. Plus I'd promised I'd bring him with me, and yet here I was, Ganymede-less. With my luck, they would revolt.

Luke's keys. They were in my bag. He'd bolted before I could return them because he was a smartass who had to get the last word in. Ha. It would serve him right if I took a break in his house.

I stopped at a Dutch Bros. and ordered a jumbo iced Cocomo—coconut mocha—and a couple of muffin tops. A pick-me-up would facilitate the thinking. So what if I was up all night because of the afternoon caffeine? Right now I needed the coffee goodness.

I pulled into Luke's driveway and helped myself to his front door. No doubt the gossip mill would start spitting out stories any minute now.

Sure enough, by the time I reached Luke's sparse living room, my phone was pinging.

Lena: *You at Luke's again??!!!*

Me: *I need somewhere quiet to think.*

Lena: *Have you been in his bedroom?*

Me: *Only by myself.*

Lena: *Are there really notches on the bedpost?*

Me: *No.*

Lena: *Sex stuff? He seems like he'd have a whole dungeon of kinky toys.*

Me: *Lena?*

Lena: *What?*

Me: *Have you been reading* 50 Shades *again?*

Lena: *No.*

Lena: *Okay, yes.*

Me: *Stop it.*

Lena: *I can't. It's wetter than late September in my pants and Matt is exhausted. He can't keep up. Poor bastard is going to suffer death by snu-snu.*

Me: *Way, way, way TMI.*

Lena: *Sorry. I can't tell what's TMI or not anymore. After all these pregnancies I feel like half of Oregon has traipsed through my ladygarden.*

Bing-bong.

Me: *Ruh-roh. Someone's at the door.*

Lena: *Probably Mrs. Remi, wondering why you're rummaging around Luke's panty drawer.*

Me: *I'm not!*

Like a fool, I went to Luke's door.

Argh! Lena had cursed me. Luke's grandmother had her malevolent eye pushed up against the wrong side of the peephole.

"I know you are in there," she said. "Everybody called me to tell me. What are you doing in my grandson's house? Stealing again? Does your grandmother know what a disappointment you are?"

I opened the door because I knew she'd find a way in anyway. Probably slither under the door or shimmy down the chimney. Thanks to my time as a goat, I already knew her helpless old woman routine was an act.

All four-foot-nothing of her glared. How she could manage a full body facial expression was beyond me, but somehow she projected scorn with every muscle and pore. Her pitch black eyes narrowed when they slid to my hand and the muffin top I was holding.

"Keep eating that *skata* and you will be too fat to carry my great-grandchildren."

"I'm not carrying your great-grandchildren!"

"Yet." She pushed past me. "Where is my grandson?"

I made a calculated guess. "Working?"

"Why are you in his house? You have been here too much lately. Are you his girlfriend? Are you using birth control? At least you are from a good Greek family, although your mother did marry that *xenos*. Do you cook? Clean? Can you do needlepoint?" She looked me up and down. "I suppose you are pretty enough." She fake-spat on me to ward away the evil eye. "*Ptou, ptou.*"

"Luke gave me his keys earlier so I could pick up his laptop. He took his laptop but forgot to take his keys. So I figured I'd, uh, drop them off."

"How will you lock his house when you leave? How will he get into his house?"

"I don't know!"

"You do not know much."

No, but I did hear something strange outside. If I had to guess, I'd say someone was rolling bowling balls down the street.

"Do you hear that?"

"I cannot hear myself *klasimo*, I am so old."

Fact: Luke's grandmother could hear the sound of a scandal bubbling a continent away. There's no way she would miss the passing of her own gas.

"Stay right there," I said. "I'm going to investigate."

I jogged out to the street.

Blinked.

Rubbed my eyes.

Holy *crap*. Nobody was bowling. The deep-throated rumble was the result of a gigantic horse rolling along the street, headed in this direction. Wooden. Crudely carved. Plans possibly drawn up by four-year-old.

I called Nikki. "We have a problem. A really big problem. Someone is rolling a Trojan Horse towards Luke's house right now."

"That is a problem," she admitted. "Can you take care of it?"

"What? How? It's a giant wooden horse! Probably it's full of soldiers. Your grandmother is in Luke's house right now. I can't do anything without making her suspicious."

"Shit," she said. "Shit, shit, shit."

"Shit," I agreed.

"They claimed it was another training exercise. I *knew* they were lying. Can you improvise until I get there?"

"I can improvise at improvising."

"Good enough. I'm on my way."

I went in one door and out another, into Luke's backyard. The garden shed contained all the usual grill accessories, including charcoal and charcoal lighter fluid. I grabbed the bottle, located a long-nozzled lighter, and trudged through the house.

Mrs. Remi pelted me with questions. "What are you doing? Are you stealing from my grandson again?"

"I'll bring it right back. I'm ... uh ... grilling a horse."

"What horse?"

"It's outside. Stay there. Maybe knit or make up some new gossip while I take care of it."

She stuck her nose in the air. "*Gamo tin putana, esai trelismeni!*"

Make sweet monkey love to the prostitute, you're crazy. The older the Greek, the stronger their ability to dig down in the sewer for insults.

The door slammed behind me.

Click.

And locked.

Fabulous. It was just me and the huge horse and Nikki, who had hung up.

I called Luke and left a message. "There's a massive Trojan horse rolling down your street. I've got a plan. It's a shitty plan, but it's the only one I've got. Also, your grandmother just locked herself in your house after calling me crazy. She's in there with my coffee and muffin tops."

The horse was moving at the speed of a live horse with two broken legs and an addiction to pain pills. None of the neighbors seemed to notice or care. I wondered what it was like for regular people. Did they see nothing—a big void where business existed as usual—or did their gazes skate away, repelled by the whack-a-doodle anomalies in their very human lives? How much mythological kookiness had I ignored over the years because my brain couldn't handle the anomaly?

I set off down the street with the bottle of starter fluid in one hand and the lighter in my pocket. I marched up to the horse and held up my free hand.

The horse shuddered to a stop. A hatch in the belly opened. A soldier stuck his head out. Another guy in Trojan regalia like the others.

"Oi! What are you doing down there?"

"Are you Trojans? Because you look like Trojans to me."

"So what if we are?"

"I thought Greeks had the big horse. There's even a saying about it. 'Beware of Greeks bearing gifts.'"

He stared at me, his face blank. "Anyway," he said finally. "We decided to keep the horse. Now shove off. You're in our way."

He vanished. The hatch closed. The giant wooden horse gave an almighty *creak* and started to move again.

Ugh. What was their problem? I was hoping a quick conversation would send them home, horse tail between their legs. Instead, they'd chosen to escalate—slowly.

Fine. We'd do this the hard way.

Keeping up with the horse was easy. I plodded alongside it, sprinkling highly flammable liquid on its wheels and up all four legs. One at a time, I touched the flame to the feet.

Whoosh!

Fire raced up the wooden horse.

"This is cozy," a voice said from inside the horse. "Smells like fall. Anyone else suddenly craving pumpkin spice?"

"That's not fall—it's fire!"

I stood back and watched as the hatch opened and about

twenty Trojan soldiers hit the ground in a tangle of swords and armor.

"Where is Diomedes?" someone called out.

"He's still in the head."

"I'm in the head," Diomedes—probably—yelled. "Got to reach the target. Save yourselves!"

As I watched, the flaming horse turned and laboriously entered Luke's driveway.

"Are you kidding me?" I screamed. I bolted past the horse and hammered on the door. "Mrs. Remi! You have to get out now! Fire! Well, not yet, but there's about to be a fire!"

"Tell us where Ariadne is!" one of the Trojans demanded. "Or the flimsy human house gets it."

"I don't know where she is!" I called out. His face said he didn't believe me.

"Onward," he yelled.

"I don't get why these people use wood," one of his brethren said. "Stones make much more sense. They're tougher and fireproof."

I called 9-1-1. "Help! There's about to be a fire!" I reeled off Luke's address.

"M'am? M'am, how do you know this?"

"I'm standing outside the house and there's a giant flaming horse rolling toward the house."

"A giant flaming ... horse?"

I'd already lost her. Not surprising. I was struggling myself.

"And there's an old woman inside and she won't come out!"

"Inside the horse?"

"The house."

The emergency dispatcher paused while she formulated

her next questions. "Is she aware of the, uh, giant flaming horse?"

"I tried to tell her but she's Greek and super stubborn! Are you sending someone?"

"To put out the horse?"

"And the house! It's—" The horse bellied up to Luke's garage. Fire leaped from the horse to the roof. "Shit! Just send the firefighters! Please! The house is on fire!"

"What about the horse?"

"Everything is on fire!" I yelled at my phone before ending the call.

Jagged red and orange flames crawled across the roof and rolled downward, gobbling mouthfuls of siding. There was no time. I had to act. With my heart clawing at the inside my chest and my bladder full of jagged ice, I charged at Luke's door.

The door held.

What to use?

The Trojans were cluttering up the sidewalk, watching Luke's house burn. I marched up to the nearest soldier and snatched his sword. When he tried to fight back, I slapped him in the face with the flat side. He dropped like a sack of potatoes.

I charged at Luke's front window and bashed the picture window with the sword. Glass blasted inwards. Using the blade, I smacked the glass away from the frame and clambered in.

"Mrs. Remi?"

Her voice wandered out from the kitchen. "There she is again, the crazy woman! Get out!"

Ha. Fat chance of that. Not when I had a rescue to perform. I stormed through the house and found her in the kitchen, eating one of my muffin tops.

"The house is on fire! I'm going to rescue you, whether you like it or not, even though you're eating my muffin top and possibly don't deserve to be saved."

"Fire? What fire?"

"The one on the roof."

She took a deep breath. "I do not smell no smoke."

Ugh. Why did old Greek women have to make everything so difficult?

I charged into the office and grabbed Luke's fireproof safe. I threw it out the window, then went back for his grandmother.

"Are you coming with me?"

Instead of answering, she drank my coffee, maintaining eye contact the whole time. Asserting dominance. Better than peeing on me, I supposed.

Fine. If she wanted to do this the hard way, we'd do it the hard way. I scooped her up in a fireman's carry and shoved through the front door. No wail of firetrucks charging to the scene. Flames everywhere. The house was about to be a goner.

"Put me down, you *trelasmeni skeela!*"

"No! And for the record, I'm the crazy bitch who's saving your life!"

I staggered to the lawn. She punched me in the boob. I slapped her on the leg.

"*Vromoskeela!* Hitting an old woman! *Ptou! Ptou!*"

I fell to my knees and let her slide off. She smacked me with my own muffin top, and then stopped.

She raised her nose in the air like an old hound and inhaled. Her raisin eyes widened. "Fire!"

I threw my hands at the sky. "That's what I've been trying to tell you!"

Coffee sloshed over me as she whacked me with the cup.

"What did you do?"

"Me? Nothing! I didn't do this."

"Lies! You burned down that hair salon!"

"No. My client did that when she lit up a cigarette. The place was full of hair spray!" I pointed. "They did it!"

"They" were scampering down the street, away from the fire. Their stupid horse had already been reduced to a black skeleton that crumbled to dust as I watched.

"Who?"

"The—" Off they went. Gone. "Oh, for crying out loud! Are you kidding me?"

In the distance—freakin' finally—sirens howled. Help was coming.

Kyria Remi hit me over the head with the sword.

"That is what you get for making fire on my grandson's house!"

———

By the time firefighters rocked up I was sporting a goose egg on my temple. Luke's grandmother really knew how to bounce a sword off a human skull. She had one foot planted in the middle of my back like I was Mt. Everest and my arm twisted up behind my head. My everything hurt.

"Here is your prisoner!" she announced to the police, who happened to show up with the firefighters.

The police had questions. Mostly about arson and whether I was a fan.

"I've never burned anything on purpose! Well, except wood in a fireplace, and I do like marshmallows charred on the outside. But that doesn't make me an arsonist!"

"You claimed a" —the police officer squinted at his notes — "horse set the fire?"

"It wasn't a regular 'neigh, neigh, clip-clop' kind of horse. It was a big horse. Huge. Like the Trojan Horse."

"A big horse nobody else saw?"

"Look, I know how it sounds but it was real."

"And it was on fire?"

"Not at first, but—"

The officer raised his brows at me. "How did the really big horsey come to be on fire?"

Crap. "I don't know?"

"Know anything about the bottle of grill starter fluid on the lawn? Or the lighter?"

"Okay, fine, I set the horse on fire, but not the house. Someone had to stop the horse and that someone had to be me!"

One cop nodded to the other. They stepped aside. Words were exchanged. Probably also judgments about my mental health—which until recently had been mostly fine, except for the usual wear-and-tear from a divorce and losing most access to my cat.

He came back. "What is your relationship to the homeowner?"

"Luke? We're ... coworkers? We've known each other since I was born, though. It's complicated and uncomplicated and weird."

"His grandmother says you've been a frequent visitor this week."

I couldn't exactly tell them Luke was trying to save a mythological figure from her mythological king dad and his henchmen. They'd lock me up in the psych ward pending an evaluation. At least I thought they might. I was hazy on Oregon's mental health laws.

"I've been helping a friend in need. How else would I have his keys? Keys that Luke Remis gave me, by the way."

I glanced back. Luke's house was half its original size now and a whole lot wetter. At least I'd managed to save his important papers. Oh, and his grandmother. Who was, I might add, playing the poor old lady card to the hilt.

Nikki's car pulled up. She angled out and sashayed over to us.

"I'm Nikki Remis, Luke Remis's cousin. What's going on?"

"Luke's house burned mostly down," I said. "The police think I did it."

"Probably she did it," the police said.

"I was trying to stop it from happening in the first place!"

Killer nails flashing, Nikki whipped out her phone. She tapped a few times, then showed off her screen. She had a link to Luke's doorbell camera and it clearly showed me trying to ward off a huge, flaming horse.

"That's a big horse," the cops said.

"Told you."

Nikki's nails clacked again, and then there I was trying to urge her grandmother out of the house, then scampering out of the house with Mrs. Remi over my shoulders.

"That's not what the old lady said happened," the police officer admitted.

"Earlier she was encouraging me to bear her great-grandchildren, so she's not exactly playing with a full deck."

I straggled home, reeking of smoke, my skin and clothes blackened with soot and soaked with coffee—my coffee. I really needed those muffin tops, but now they were languishing in the stomach of Luke's grandmother.

News had spread through the local Greek community

like a virulent and fast-moving plague. Lena left three frantic voicemails and twelve text messages. Father Gus, the priest at the local Greek Orthodox church, had called to enthusiastically suggest I show up at church tomorrow.

Sometimes life could be utter *kaka*.

The whole household was congregated in the living room, eyes glued to *Greece's Top Hoplite*, a Greek reality TV show that involved fighting with an array of fists and old-timey weapons. Dad read the subtitles to follow along. Surprisingly, Grandpa didn't care that he couldn't under-stand a word of it. He was hardcore into the fighting.

"That Effie Makri can hit me with her pointy stick and judge me any time she likes," he was saying when I slouched in and flopped down on the couch.

"She is built like a cow. A man cow," Yiayia said.

Nobody else spoke until the commercials came on. Mom kissed me on the head and disappeared into the kitchen.

Yiayia reached over and fake-smacked me on the back of the head. "My granddaughter, arrested. What will people say?"

"Lots of things, I'm sure. They usually do."

"Next time I will come with you. I could use a good adventure. Or a bad one."

Mom slid a hot chocolate in front of me like I was a kid all over again. A crowd of marshmallows slowly melted in the mug. "Penny wasn't arrested. The police questioned her, that's all."

I took a swig of the hot chocolate. The burning as it slid down my throat told me she'd laced it with something heavier than sugar. Irish whiskey.

"I don't blame them." I blew on the chocolate. "It did look bad. Luke's house is gone."

Yiayia crossed herself.

"Can I get you anything?" Mom wanted to know. "Maybe a new identity and a ticket to Greece?"

"I'm fine. I think I'm just going to drink this, go to bed and hopefully wake up next week, when there's a new scandal for everyone to get excited about."

I carried the mug upstairs to my place.

The whole thing had freaked me out. King Minos really wanted Luke's hide over this Ariadne thing. The guy was crazy, sending his horse to Luke's house. What if King Minos decided I was next on his list? The flaming Trojan Horse wasn't my first encounter with his men in connection to Luke. The whacky king had to know I existed—and if he didn't, he would. What if he rolled a Trojan Horse into my childhood home? Yes, it was stone and earthquake proof, thanks to Dad's due diligence and a whole lot of nagging on the part of our Greek relatives. But could it withstand a burning horse? What if Minos sent something bigger next time? It could happen. Greek mythology was full of giant nasties with bad tempers and pockets bulging with grudges.

I still hadn't had time to process the dead half-gorgons or the harpies who had sucked them up as if they were a pile of Happy Meals. And I was concerned about Yellow Chucks—and Ganymede, who was still shaking his money maker out in my world somewhere.

A quick check of my phone provided me with no insight. There was nothing—not even a screeching message from Luke about his house.

Was he too busy snuggling up to Ariadne? She'd sure made it sound like they knew each other in a Biblical way. Or worse: in a Greek mythological way. Greek mythology was way more pornographic, especially when Zeus stuck his wandering penis into random cracks and holes. The god of the sky wasn't the only rabid horn dog, though. Mythological Greeks had three major hobbies: fighting, bonking, and revenge.

Mom's hot chocolate worked its magic. The whiskey melted my muscles and bones, and I curled up on the couch, intending to do more reading.

The road to hell, and all that.

CHAPTER 16

I woke up with my face stuck to a book and several dead things in my mouth, battling to be the biggest stink. It was 4:00 AM. Stupid o'clock. No matter how hard I tried to bury myself back in my dreams, my brain kept dragging me by the leg down old, embarrassing memories' lane. The ghosts of screw-ups' past rattled their chains at me. Perfect comebacks arrived years and months late.

Dumbass, the ghosts howled. *Shame.*

I hauled myself to the shower and stood under scalding water until the stench of Luke's burning house vanished down the drain. The day was supposed to reach a blistering 95F, but at 4:30 AM the temperature was hovering at a cool 53F. I pulled on faded jeans with holes I'd paid for, much to my mother's horror ("*Po-po!* They should charge less since you're getting less fabric! Everybody is a criminal today!") and Yiayia's ("Come, let me stitch the holes for you.") I threw on a fitted t-shirt and slipped an ancient OSU sweatshirt over my head. Coffee was next. The caffeine buzzed my brain hard enough that all my problems came flooding back.

Today was Sunday. Luke wouldn't—couldn't—show up to escort Mrs. Remi to church. Which meant his grandmother would flip out. We'd all be hearing about how Luke abandoned her—which he would never do unless he was in grave danger. She'd call the police, probably point them in my direction, and maybe this time I wouldn't be so lucky, seeing as how I was already smothered in a cloud of suspicion.

Probably I should do as Father Gus asked and show up to church today for the first time in ages. During our marriage, Chaz insisted that we go to his church with his mother because the Greek Orthodox church wasn't a real American church in his mommy's eyes. Not enough snakes in bags or hand-laying for her liking. To her, babbling in tongues was only acceptable if it was a completely made up language and not the liturgical Koine Greek. I'd gone along with the exhausting and traumatic routine because it enabled me to avoid Luke Remis for years.

I opened the windows to let the cool air in. I carried my coffee out to the rear balcony that overlooked the yard.

Dark.

Amorphous and loaded with potential.

My parents' yard was fenced and gated and felt safe. Here, darkness could be anything, which I used to find soothing.

This morning, not so much. This darkness felt menacing, as though something was out there, watching me staring into the abyss.

Given that it was summer in Oregon, where dawn would show up flinging sunlight in less than an hour, the darkness was starting to diminish in places. In those thin patches, things moved. Waving. Laughing at me.

I jumped up and flipped on the yard lights. *There, you creeps. You can't hide from light.*

Nothing.

No oogie boogies from Greek mythology or anyplace else. The yard was completely empty except for the normal tables and chairs and grills and garden beds. The shed was just a shed.

Over in the far corner there was one dark spot, like a hole. Maybe two, three feet in diameter. Probably an optical illusion. Mom was most likely trying out a compost heap again. Last time the pile of old peelings had wound up as a communal litter box for the neighborhood cats.

There was a *pop* followed by a *hiss* as the sprinklers woke up to blast faux rain over the grass. The average rainfall in Salem is zero during the summer months, so sprinklers are a necessity unless you want to live in a bowl of dust and dirt.

Water misted across the grass and flower beds. Birds started to stir.

The hole moved. Or rather, something in the hole dragged itself out of the hole and flopped facedown on the wet grass.

Sirens went off in my head. My heart began flailing in my chest, throwing me off balance. I felt as though I was encased in viscous liquid in the moments before it reached the boil. Yellow Chucks was sprawled out on my grass, head bald and bleeding. She'd lost her hoodie and was left in jeans and a torn and muddy tank top.

I threw open the linen closet and located towels. I raced down the stairs barefoot in strange silence. The pounding in my veins had dampened all ambient sound. I fell onto the ground alongside her and covered her with towels and compressed her wounds. By the looks of things, someone had tried to fillet her.

Should I call an ambulance? Did they know what to do with a daughter of a gorgon and who knows what? Probably not. Her blue blood would only be the first problem.

I clawed at my phone and managed to dial work's number. "Help," I told the voice on the other end. It wasn't Nikki, I recognized that much. "There's a maybe dead half-gorgon in my backyard." Wedging the phone between my ear and shoulder, I felt around for a pulse. A small hammer tapped on my fingers. "She's alive—for now. I don't know what to do. I can't call a real ambulance. Do something, please."

I stuffed the phone back in my pocket and rolled Yellow Chucks over. Her eyelids were closed tight and she was unresponsive. I couldn't leave her here under the sprinkler. I didn't care that my family would be rolling out of their beds soon and taking in a view of a mythological being who'd been stuffed in a hole and crawled out to die on the lawn. I only wanted her to be okay.

"Yellow Chucks? Oh heck, I don't even know your real name! Whatever your name is, I'm sorry I can't move you. There's too much blood and you're all chopped up and I don't know what to do. I think there's help coming—at least I hope there is."

Not even a flicker. Wherever she was, I hoped it was someplace nice where she wasn't in pain and the rest of her family wasn't dead in a harpy's belly. If Harpies had bellies. Their biology was a mystery to me.

I pressed down on her wounds with the towels.

The sprinklers hushed and sank down into the ground. Others in different section of the yard popped up. The previously dark sky was fading to a bruised gray with a hint of lavender. The sun was a rapidly approaching threat.

Somebody spoke my name. It didn't register at first. I

was too busy trying to keep Yellow Chucks from losing what blue blood was left. When the man knelt down beside me, that's when it clicked that I wasn't alone. Golden hair buzzed close to the scalp. Bright green eyes. Clean-shaven. Prominent nose. He wore scrubs and Crocs and carried a big stick with a live snaked wrapped around the wood. The snake was brown and black and appeared to be okay with hugging its stick. The new arrival got to work straight away, helping me compress the half-gorgon's wounds.

"Asclepius."

"Penny. Is she going to be okay?"

"She's lost a lot of blood." He scooped her up in his arms, towels and all.

"Wait—are you supposed to move her? Won't she bleed more? Are you even a doctor?"

The snake laughed. He spoke with a deep baritone. "Is he a doctor? Are you kidding me? Asclepius is the OG doctor."

"I don't know what that means," I said. "Is that a mythology thing?"

"He's the original, baby. The biggest and the brightest. The god of medicine. Son of Apollo and some mortal chick."

"Coronis," Asclepius said. "Mom's name is Coronis."

"Student of the centaur himself, Chiron," the snake went on. "As for me, you can call me Rod."

"Is that your name or job description?"

"Yes."

"You're lucky you caught me between slayings," Asclepius said. "Zeus is scheduled to kill me again any day now."

"I hate it when we die," Rod said. "It stings. But Zeus gonna Zeus. He's worried my man here will turn everyone immortal."

"I can't turn anyone immortal," Asclepius told me.

"That's what he wants you to think," Rod said.

"Where are you taking her?" I asked.

"To my clinic, of course," the god of medicine told me. "Want to come with?"

I glanced down at myself. Clean clothes drenched in blue blood. That couldn't be sterile. "Do I need to change?"

"No time," he said.

A slit opened in the air. Asclepius stepped through. His staff poked through the rift. "Touch my wood," Rod said. "Go on, you know you want to."

"Pervert."

"I try."

Curiosity and concern overwhelmed my self preservation. I grabbed the rod—avoiding the snake—and stepped into the rift.

Shock of shocks, the rift opened into the labyrinth. Asclepius was several steps ahead of me, Yellow Chucks draped over his arms. As we walked, the labyrinth changed form around us. The ancient stone transformed into institutional beiges with the occasional piece of generic art hanging on the walls. The god of medicine stopped in front of a set of swinging double doors, the kind you see in hospitals, and pushed through using his back. I caught the door and slipped through behind him, into a fancy consultation room.

"You can wait over there," he told me.

I sat in a chair that was more comfortable than it looked, and waited nervously. At some point, the door opened and a woman in a head scarf entered. The chair farted as she sat down beside me. At least I hoped it was the chair.

"Don't look at me," she said.

That was weird, but weird had less meaning now. Or was

it more? I had to keep recalibrating the definition of *weird*, establishing a new baseline.

"Okay."

"What happened?" the woman asked.

I told her the truth, including the bit where Yellow Chucks hauled herself out of the hole in the ground when the sprinklers came on, and that I didn't know her name.

"Ivy. Her name is Ivy."

I almost glanced over in surprise. "You know her?"

"I told her not to stray into the other world, not to follow her sisters. But did she listen?"

"No?"

"No. That place is not for us. You die there, you don't always come back. I don't even know if her sisters will make it back to me."

"You're Ivy's mother?"

"Who else?"

Fear sent a tremor through my body. I squashed it with a pound of logic. The gorgon explicitly said not to look at her. If she'd wanted to turn me into a garden gnome, she wouldn't have dispensed that particular life pro tip.

"I'm sorry about your daughters."

Her hand reached for mine. Squeezed. It looked human enough, although now I was starting to wonder about gorgon body hair. Was it snakes, too? As a one hundred percent human woman with longish hair, I regularly had to fish a stray hair out of my undercarriage. What happened when a gorgon shed? Was it a snakes-in-the-underwear situation?

"Find who did this and send them to my hole. I want to deal with them myself. I could use a new statue."

"Your ...?"

"Hole."

"Where is your, uh, hole?"

"In the ground. Where else would it be?"

"I thought it might be like a Hobbit hole with a cute round door and a massive pantry."

Medusa stared at the side of my head. I could feel her petrifying gaze trying to make a patio out of my cheek. "Hobbits are not real. Recently I did move, though, so I have a good-sized pantry now. I hang my prey there."

I was afraid to ask about a gorgon's diet. I was being risky asking about their accommodations as it was. "So gorgons live in holes?"

"Where else would we live?"

Must be because of the snakes. Although now she had sparked more questions. Did Ivy dig the hole in my parents' yard before or after she was attacked? Why our yard? Why not knock on my door and ask to crash in my spare room?

"I don't know."

"It's the snakes," she said in a sad voice. "They need holes and heat, and they nap all winter. The only time I ever have straight hair is in the winter months, when they are hibernating. And then they want me to wear a hat so they don't freeze."

A throat cleared. The boss—AKA: Daedalus—interrupted my gorgon biology lesson. "See me in my lab, Agent whatever your name is. Girly."

"Are you talking to me?" I asked.

"Who else?"

"The whole thing where you don't know my name makes it confusing. You could be talking to anyone."

"I mean you." His voice had a definite irritated edge to it. I guess I had that effect on him.

"How do I get there from here?"

The disembodied voice of Daedalus strung a bunch of words together that made Asclepius's snake cackle.

"What do you say?" the snake said to the gorgon beside me. "How's about you and your snakes and me and my snake?"

"Zip it," Asclepius told him.

"I'll walk you through it," Daedalus said. "If I can. The labyrinth can be a bit unpredictable."

I made Asclepius promise to keep me up to date on Ivy's condition, then I said goodbye to her mother without making eye contact.

I pushed through the double doors. The clean, soulless institutional look was gone. Now I was in a marketplace, somewhere in what looked like the Middle East, probably before anyone called it the Middle East. Everything had an Aladdin feel, which made me think this was something the labyrinth pulled out of its own imagination rather than any actual location, present or past.

Heat beat me from all angles. Sweat bubbled out of my pores. I hauled off my sweatshirt and tied it around my waist. Trinkets crowded together on tables. Sun glinted off knick-knacks, stabbing me in the eyes. A rainbow of cool, diaphanous robes and dresses hung from racks.

"Can I just—"

"Nope," Daedalus said. "Don't touch anything."

"Why not?"

"Too risky. The labyrinth can be temperamental. You could lose a hand. Or a head."

"I don't want to lose either of those."

"Then keep your mitts to yourself. Turn right."

I wandered for another five minutes before he directed me down an airless and oppressive alley, where the walls rose forever and the end never seemed to come any closer.

Until finally it did, all at once. A door leaped out in front of me. Purple and gold and definitely out of place in the sand-colored wall that towered over me.

I opened the door and stepped inside.

Bam.

Back in Daedalus's lab, with his smug head smirking at me.

"Do you ever think about getting some decorations for that tank? Maybe one of those bubbling deep sea divers? A treasure chest? What about some fish to keep you company? Neon tetras would be cool. You could get a black light and watch them glow."

"You have failed in your task," he said matter-of-factly. "Please see the girl at the front desk to collect a small severance fee."

"Nikki. Her name is Nikki, not 'the girl'. And ... what the heck? You're firing me?"

"No. I believe the correct term is 'letting you go.'"

"Letting someone go is firing them."

"Oh, is it? My mistake. Then yes, we're firing you."

"'We' who?"

"The royal We. You have failed to bring in Luke Remis, therefore another agent will be assigned to the task. Feel free to go back to whatever it was you were doing before all this. Doing hair. Being irritating."

Gut punch.

As recently as two years ago, I would have slunk away, probably without collecting his so-called small severance fee. That was before the courts dragged me around and spat me out the other end. To heck with this. I survived Chaz and his mother; I could deal with a brain in a fish tank.

"If I failed, it's because Luke didn't kill the Minotaur! Why would I drag an innocent person here to be tortured by

King Minos if he didn't do anything? Anyway, none of this is even about the Minotaur. I bet ten of whatever currency Greek mythological peeps use that King Minos doesn't give a crap about his half-bull kid. In the stories, he considered it a monstrosity and stuck it in this labyrinth. You don't do that to someone you love!"

"You don't have to tell me the story," Daedalus snapped. "I was there!"

"Then you probably also know what King Minos really wants: his daughter. He sent the Minotaur to kill its half-sister or drag her home. When someone killed his man-cow flunky, he sent soldiers, followed by more soldiers and a Trojan Horse, that burned down Luke's house. And now he'll send something else, all to get to his daughter, who just wants to start over, far away from her vindictive and crazy dad."

"Get out. Do not pass go. Do not collect two hundred dollars."

"Keep your stupid money!"

I flipped him off Greek-style (same as American, but with more passion) and stomped out, this time into what appeared to be an empty IKEA store.

Great. This was going to take forever.

After about thirty minutes of wandering through bathroom and kitchen displays, a door appeared and I was back in the corridor. One more door later, I fell into the office. Nikki was arranging files in the filing cabinet.

"The boss had a hissy fit and fired me."

"For crying out loud," she said. "Daedalus, what's your problem?"

"She's my problem!" he said. "The job was simple and now it's a disaster!"

"Let me see what I can do," Nikki mouthed.

"Nothing. That's what you can do," my former boss said. "And before you ask, I can read lips and about five thousand languages."

"Are there five thousand languages?" I asked.

"About six thousand, five hundred spoken today," Nikki said. "That's not counting those old timey languages we've forgotten."

"I haven't forgotten them," Daedalus said in a petulant yet somehow know-it-all tone.

"You know what?" I said. "I think you're in Minos's pocket! Why else would you sacrifice Luke?"

With a gasp, Nikki crossed herself.

Daedalus sucked in a deep breath—really, without lungs how was that even possible?—and unleashed an almighty roar. "Get out!"

I skedaddled.

CHAPTER 17

THEY WEREN'T my problem anymore. Not Daedalus, not Luke, not Ariadne and her daughter. Not Ivy—although I was experiencing serious pangs of concern for the half-gorgon woman.

I straggled home, stopping at a drive-through for an obscenely huge Frappuccino, roughly the size of my head. By the time I pulled into my parents' driveway, I was bloated and high on sugar. I popped the button on my jeans and slouched to the porch, where I plopped down on one of the three steps, next to a stone lion.

"Great job warding off evil, dude," I told the lion.

For a split second I wondered if he and his opposing compadre had started out as real lions and screwed up in a full-frontal experience with a gorgon.

Yipes!

I jumped up as if I'd been bitten on the butt. The back-yard was still the scene of a crime, and if my family hadn't spotted Ivy's hole and blue blood yet, they would soon. Without the agency behind me, probably I'd be filling in the hole alone and pretending Ivy's blue blood was the result of a mid-air dump from a passing airplane.

I rounded the side of the house and made a beeline for the backyard instead of heading upstairs to my place. From this vantage point I couldn't see the hole.

I kept going.

Nope.

No hole.

While I was gone, the hole had been filled in, the sod replaced, and every last speck of blue blood had vanished. There was a piece of cardboard folded in a V and placed upside down on the patch where the hole had been. I plucked it up off the ground. Calling card from the harpy cleaning duo at *Claw and Tooth Cleaning Services*. They'd left a number and an incantation in case I needed a cleaning crew. Nice to know I wasn't completely alone.

I carried the calling card upstairs, stuck it to the fridge with a cat butt magnet. Exhausted and sad, I flopped down on my couch and let the cushions and pillows hug me. Only thing missing was a big blanket. One oversized comforter and my protective fort would be complete. The monsters would never find me there. This was the perfect place to wallow and indulge in self pity.

Chaz was right. I was a loser who couldn't keep a job. I'd juggled several at a time consistently throughout our marriage, struggling to pay the bills while he finished college. When I got fired from one because I couldn't keep up, I'd find another.

Now I couldn't hold on to one stupid job.

My Greek Orthodox guilt kicked in. Maybe I needed to spend some time convening with the big guy upstairs and drop a few dollars in his earthly representative's collection box. I could ask for a few favors. A full recovery for Ivy. Safe, free lives for Ariadne and Stella. No hassles for Luke from his home owner's insurance company. A stable job for me, and Chunky back on the big cat tree in my living room, where he belonged.

I slid bonelessly off the couch and landed in a puddle on the rug. Going to church with my family meant church clothes. I'd have to rustle up something clean and not too tight around my waist. Thanks, giant Frappuccino.

For the second time in twelve hours, I watched blue blood circle the shower drain. I washed my hair. I showed my legs and pits a razor. I spent time with the hair dryer and a hot air brush until my hair had more bounce than a trampoline and more shine than a stripper's chest. Chaz and his looney "mommy" always insisted I dress for church in outfits normally not seen outside of Amish communities. The Greek Orthodox church didn't care. Church was the place to see and be seen, especially on holidays. The old guard dressed for the 1910s, but young people flashed their wares and bling. I settled for a look that wouldn't have anyone mistaking me for a budget sex worker or a nun: a cute, floral dress with cap sleeves and a smocked waist that didn't squash my iced coffee. I rustled up earrings—tiny hoops—and shoved my feet into slingback wedges with a closed toe.

Voila! Ready to go and beg any attentive holy ears for assistance and a miracle or two.

Downstairs, my family were flapping around like a bunch of wet hens. They all stopped to gawk at me.

"Are you ... coming to church?" Mom asked with a dazed look.

"Thinking about it."

Yiayia crossed herself, kissed her fingertips, and shook her hands at the ceiling. "*Panayia mou*, it is a miracle!"

"As far as miracles go, me attending church is pretty lame. A miracle would be if it started raining chocolate." We all looked up at the ceiling. No chocolate. Life could be rough sometimes. I sat on the edge of the couch to adjust my shoe's buckle. "I figured I'd go, and not just because Father Gus called to suggest I return to the flock. I guess he wants another shot at saving my soul."

Grandpa snorted. "More like saving his bank account."

Father Gus did sport some fancy robes. He was a theatrical character who put serious acting skills into his services. But a money grubber? I'd have to go with *no*. He lived over on the east side of Salem in a grungy apartment building because he felt that's where he could do the most good.

We piled into the minivan with me wedged between my grandparents, the assigned peacekeeper. I was responsible for keeping them from slapping and pinching each other and complaining about who was breathing on who. I couldn't stop them from farting, but I could elbow them if the stink got too bad. Things eased up when we dropped Grandpa off at the bus stop for his weekly jaunt to his own church.

Saint John the Baptist is Salem's other Greek church. It's small but it does its best to cram as much gold as humanly possible into a building the size of a Starbucks. The back wall, behind the altar, is basically one giant painting of the Virgin Mary, holding up Jesus like Simba. This particular Jesus was a toddler with a grown man's face. Like most Greek Orthodox churches, Saint John the Baptist divided us according to sex so the boy and girl cooties wouldn't mingle. Women on the left—probably because it was the devil's side —men on the right. Seating was sparse and reserved for the oldest or illest members of the congregation, or whoever had the deadliest elbows.

One at a time, we kissed the icons, crossed ourselves, and moved to our respective sides.

My gaze roamed the church while my mouth went on autopilot, performing the usual greetings.

One of Yiayia's friend's daughters sidled up to me. She wanted answers, damn it, and she was wearing her best mastiff expression along with her dowdy blue dress.

"*Po-po-po*, here she is! Welcome! You have not come to see us in so long. Was the other church better? Did it have more gold?"

"More seating," I said.

She forged on, undeterred. "I heard you got a divorce."

"Everyone should get at least one. I figured I'd get my first out of the way early, you know, for the experience."

"And you moved back in with your family, of course."

Yiayia looped her arm through mine. "Where else would she go, eh?"

The snoop pressed onwards. No shame. "People are saying that now you will get married to Luke Remis. His grandmother is telling everybody that you will give her great-grandchildren. Of course, that was before you stole his computer and burned his house down."

"That's not true! Any of it!"

"People are saying," she said in a knowing voice.

"People say your husband stuck his *poutsa* in a donkey once," Yiayia said. "Or was it two times?"

"I heard three," I said.

The snoop sniffed and scampered away. She and several other hens put their heads together and shot glances at me.

"This was a mistake," I said.

"Life is one mistake after another," Yiayia said. "I

married your grandfather by mistake because I thought he was his brother. I had my children by mistake—"

"Yiayia!" I said.

"—because in those days birth control was saying '*Oxi!*' or rolling over, and I did not like either of those things. So you made some mistakes ... okay. You will make more." She patted me on the arm, completely confident that I was a screw-up, but in a good way.

Too bad I didn't have her confidence. I was hoping for fewer mistakes, not more to add to the string.

I scanned the crowd for Mrs. Remi. Which was silly, really. She always claimed one of the few seats near the front. Sure enough, there she was, holding court with a gaggle of her peers. She glanced over, her black eye raisins boring into my face.

Yipes.

My gaze skittered away. I tried to look cool in my pretty dress, while in reality I was starting to sweat. Was it hot in here or was it just me? The heat, the lack of air conditioning, the incense competing with the damp, heavy clouds of vintage fragrances: Poison, Shalimar, Opium, Chanel No. 5.

The service started. More incense infiltrated the air, swung in a thurible. I had to hand it to Father Gus: he made the barely comprehensible Koine Greek entertaining. I couldn't understand what he was verbalizing, for the most part, but I liked the way the words warbled out. Ten out of ten for enthusiasm. Did I feel like my soul was on more solid ground? No. But had my prayers been answered? Also no. Didn't matter. Right now I was caught up in his hand waving, head bobbing interpretive dance.

Then my peripheral vision snagged on something. Someone was watching me. *Staring.*

Luke Remis was here. At church. When he was

supposed to be on the run or hiding or whatever it was he was doing. Evading Minos's heavies while protecting Ariadne and Stella. Instead, he was dressed in dark slacks and a crisp shirt, his gaze steady and fixed on me.

I turned my head and raised my eyebrows at him, like "What?"

He nodded once, then turned around to focus on the service.

Whatever. We weren't friends, and now we weren't coworkers either. Our relationship had been severed in every way, as nature intended.

I went back to staring straight ahead at the Father Gus, who was doing spectacular spirit fingers in time with his sing-chant. He really brought the razzamatazz. Why I'd caved to Chaz's wishes, I didn't know. This was so much better than his mother's dour church.

Eyes were on me. Did they know I was having my own one-sided conversation with—hopefully God or one of His personal note-taking assistants? My list wasn't long but it was specific.

Those same eyes flicked to Luke, then back to me.

Ha. I wouldn't give them the satisfaction of acknowledging his existence beyond our initial cursory non-greeting.

Yiayia tilted her head toward me. "The Remis boy is staring at you. If he looks any harder you will have to get married."

"Not going to happen."

She shrugged. "We will see. Last time a man stared at me like that I ended up pregnant."

"I'm on the pill."

"That kind of staring does not care about pills. His *poutsa* will smack it out of the way like a football."

I swallowed a laugh. Eyes zeroed in on my quirking lips. What was I trying to hide, eh? What? They desperately, hungrily wanted to know. I fixed a serene, bland expression on my face and hid behind it for the next half hour.

The service ended without incident. Everyone stampeded the exit before they drowned in their own sweat. Slowly, the BO cloud lifted. Hooray, I wasn't going to suffocate in the stench of boiling pits. At least one prayer had been answered.

Luke caught up with me outside. Before I realized what was happening, he had me by the elbow, steering me off to the side. Wow, like that would help the gossip situation. Now we'd be even more suspect.

"You burned my house down, you kook!"

"No—King Minos's flunkies and their stupid giant horse burned your house down. All I did was set the horse on fire."

"Why?"

"So they'd stop!"

"Next time stick a wedge under the wheels!"

"You didn't have a wedge in your shed! I had to improvise."

We were nose to nose, hissing at each other. Every eye was on us, although Yiayia made an attempt to distract them by hiking up her skirt and trying to start a *sirtaki*.

Mrs. Remi elbowed her way through the crowd and planted herself alongside her grandson. "Come, Lukaki. Take me home. I have to cook. Not the goat I planned to cook, but something you will like anyway."

Yiayia was next to arrive on the scene. "Why are you interfering? Can you not see they were trying to talk? Let them."

"We're not trying to talk," Luke said. "I want Penny to know she's insane."

I slapped my forehead. "Because you make people crazy! That's what you do! You're like meth. Walking, talking meth!"

That set him back on his heels. "Are you saying you're addicted to me?"

"Addicted to you? Excuse me? I don't care if I never see you again! You were never habit-forming! I'd rather shoot heroin into my eyeballs!"

"Did you hear that?" Mrs. Remi said, appealing to the now-sizable audience. "Penelopi's granddaughter wants to do the drugs."

"This was a terrible idea," I said to no one in particular. Without excusing myself or saying farewell, I stomped toward the parking lot before remembering that I'd been the meat in a Yiayia and Grandpa souvlaki on the way over. Which meant I'd have to call for a cab or wait.

Given that I was freshly fired, yet again, I decided to keep what little money I had and wait. Over at the church, Yiayia and Luke's grandmother were arguing. Father Gus and Luke were between them, doing their best to prevent all-out war. I rolled my eyes, and as I did, they snagged on something up in the sky. A black cloud, moving in this direction. Except it was moving too fast to be a cloud. Erratic, too. Pieces of the cloud were out of sync with the whole. Using my hand as a visor, I squinted through my sunglasses and tried to make sense of the oncoming cloud.

Canada geese? Too silent. Wrong season.

Air Force shenanigans?

Sentient pollution?

"Get in the car," Luke yelled. He was looking up, too.

"Huh?"

"Just get in the car!"

He started running in my direction.

"Don't give me orders! You're not the boss of me!"

"For fuck's sake." He grabbed my hand and jerked me away from the minivan. Together we ran over to a mid-size SUV I didn't recognize. He unlocked the doors with the fob and shoved me inside before coming around to the driver's side. He jammed the key in the ignition. The engine roared to life.

Everyone at the church was watching Luke practically abduct me. Great. More gossip fodder.

"Are you crazy?" I yelled at him as he peeled out of the parking lot.

"Crazier than I was before you came crashing back into my life," he muttered. "We've got to get out of here."

"What? Why? Is this about that cloud."

"Not a cloud. Ever heard of Stymphalian birds?"

"Bronze beaks? People eaters? Most of them were killed off by Heracles."

"Most, but not all."

"Wait—those are Stymphalian birds?" I glanced in my side mirror to see the cloud gaining on us. It was lower now, and maybe a city block away.

"Not exactly." He adjusted the mirrors. "Shit, they're fast. The original Stymphalian birds live on an island in the Euxine Sea—that's what we call the Black Sea nowadays. These are replicas. Man-made replicas. They're automatons."

"Evil robot birds?"

He winced. "When you put it like that ..."

The evil robot birds caught up to us. One of the little jerks pecked the SUV's rear window with its metal beak. It made a dull thud. A second bird struck. Then a third.

Soon they were all around us, pecking and tearing at the SUV.

Luke swerved and drove us under a bridge. Metal exploded behind us as some of the birds failed to dodge the concrete slabs.

"They really hate you," I told Luke. "What did you do? Steal their WD40?"

"They're not after me." He threw a fast u-turn and sent us flying back under the bridge again. That shaved off more birds. They hit the ground and exploded to nothing. "They're not under Minos's control. They couldn't care less about Ariadne or the dead Minotaur. They want you."

"Me? What? Why?"

"You tell me."

"Daedalus fired me?"

He did a double take. "He what?"

Birds swooped the SUV. Several of their metal beaks tore through the roof.

"Tell me there's a way to stop these things," I said. "Isn't it in the handbook or something?"

"Nope. I'm all out of rattles from Athena and arrows dipped in Hydra blood."

I tried to think—hard to do when you're being swarmed by the equivalent of tiny fighter jets. "They're automatons. Teeny tiny robots?"

He glanced in the rearview mirror, then tapped the brakes. A handful of the birds slammed into the truck ahead of us, scattering bits of debris on the road. They exploded soundlessly in puffs of colorful smoke.

"Yeah."

"With all the frailties and weaknesses of their kind?"

"Tell me what you're thinking, and make it fast."

"Got any quarters?"

"Just bought this," he said. "Didn't stop to check the glovebox."

"Well, we're in luck because I happen to keep a roll of them in my purse."

"For what? Throwing at automatons?"

"For library parking." Which was true, although recently the Salem Public Library had renovated their building and revamped parking, so the quarters were rarely necessary. Still, one never knew when one might need a roll of quarters. Case in point: now. "Car wash. The do-it-yourself kind. Is there one around here?"

Luke hit the gas. With birds pecking holes in the roof and doing their best to smash the windows, he sped us up into north Salem. The rear window cracked like it had been struck with a fast-moving rock. He jagged left and gave it more gas. The birds went one way, we went the other, buying us a few seconds.

The SUV bumped into the driveway. Luke pulled into the closest open bay.

I cracked open the roll of quarters and dumped half in his hand. "On the count of three."

We leaped out of the SUV. Luke ran to the next bay. I seized the sprayer wand and shoved quarters into the slot as fast as I could and went straight to power spray.

The birds rocketed towards us on their sharp metal wings. As soon as the spray smacked them, they short circuited, shooting low level fireworks as they struck the pavement. We used the sprayers like flame throwers, knocking the automatons down before they could peck us.

Finally, they quit coming.

The sprayers kicked off.

Luke stood next to me, hands on hips, checking out his recently acquired SUV. The paint job had been massacred.

The windows were cracked and the body had more holes than the average colander.

"At least they didn't poop all over it," I said, trying to fill the awkward void with cheerful sound.

He shoved both hands through his hair. "My house is ruined, and now my SUV. What next?"

"I saved your fireproof safe, so it's not all bad. And your grandmother."

He reached for his phone and stabbed some numbers.

"Calling for backup?"

"Cab."

"Where are we going?"

"You're going home. The boss fired you. Go home and stay there."

"But you said the robot birds were after me."

"They won't be after it gets out that you were let go. Probably."

That was reassuring. Not. "Who sent them after me?"

"I don't know."

"Why did they send them? How do you know they were after me? It's not like they were wearing I Hate Penny t-shirts."

"The birds like me."

"They *like* you?"

"Sometimes I feed them."

"You *feed* them? What, exactly, do you feed killer robot birds?"

"When I do an oil change they get the oil."

I stared at him. My brain stuttered. I tried to imagine Luke Remis feeding the automatons bowls of dirty engine oil. Nope. Couldn't do it.

"I don't know why they were after me! I spent yesterday looking for Ganymede again, then discovered the half-gorgons had been killed. Then in the wee hours of this morning I found the last remaining half-gorgon injured in my yard."

"They're dead?"

"All except Ivy."

"Where is she?"

"Asclepius took her back to his clinic in the labyrinth."

He blew out a sigh. "At least she's in good hands. Okay, you need to go home and stay there. Go do something safe. Wait tables. Whatever. Go back to school. Finish your education. Stay away from Greek mythology."

"Go back to school?"

"Sure, why not? You dropped out to support whatshis-name, didn't you? Now you can focus on yourself."

"Have you been keeping tabs on me?"

"Hard not to in our community. Everyone talks."

The cab pulled up. Luke opened the back door.

"Go and be even more amazing—and alive."

He slammed the door and the cab pulled away. Last thing I saw was Luke angling up into what was left of his SUV.

CHAPTER 18

As soon as I hit the porch I was on the grill.

Yiayia: "Where did you go? Who did you see?"

Grandpa: "Forget that. Why do you look like you was dragged through a river?"

"I helped Luke Remis wash his car," I said.

"Must have needed it bad," Grandpa said. "I heard you two left like your asses were on fire."

"It was pretty grubby."

I went inside to see if Mom had any comfort food for a person who'd just been attacked by robot birds. She was putting the finishing touches on a coconut cake. Without a word, she cut a hefty slice, dumped it on a plate, handed it to me.

I grabbed two forks and gave her one. We attacked the cake like it was the last cake on Earth.

"I like Luke," she said.

"That makes one of us."

"Why so sassy?"

"It's complicated."

"You two used to be close. You did everything together."

"Until I grew boobs."

"Seems to me like you spent time together then, too."

For this conversation I needed more cake. Mom was happy to oblige. "I should do this more often," she said. "Dessert is better before a meal."

"I got fired again, and Luke told me I should go back and finish college."

"Now I like him even more."

"Did you miss the part where I got fired?"

"Obviously they're losers who don't deserve you."

"Thanks, Mom. But to be honest, I liked the work." Was it weird? Yes. But it was fun and interesting. Never the same thing two days in a row. "Luke thinks I should do something safer."

"What do you think?"

"I don't know. Yet. In the meantime I need to start looking for something else. Chunky's support won't pay itself."

"What are you going to do about Luke?"

"Nothing. We're no longer working together. I won't be seeing him again, thankfully."

All this time, Lena had been blowing up my phone. Bloated with coconut cake, I flopped out on my couch and returned her bazillion calls.

"Oh my God," she said. "Sorry, God." I felt rather than heard her crossing herself. "Everyone is talking about you and Luke running away from the church together. Spill. Everything. Now."

"Did you hear about anything weird in the sky when we left?"

"Weird how?"

That was a no. If anyone else had even caught a glimpse of the killer robot bird cloud, the news would be all over the Greek community. Robot birds tended to leave an impression and a whole lot of dents.

"Never mind. Luke wanted to yell at me about his house burning down, so I figured letting him was the least I could do. Venting is good for mental health."

"He just yelled at you? That's it?" Disappointment hammered her question into a flat line.

"Pretty much. And also he told me to go back to school."

That confused her. "Like, as an insult?"

"No. More like career advice."

"It's a great idea."

"That's what Mom said."

"He likes you," she said with concrete certainty. "Probably he wants to get in your pants again."

I shivered at the thought, and it wasn't entirely repulsion.

"Fat chance," I said. "That ship sailed and sank at sea."

"You say that now, but wait until you're riding the Remis penis pony again."

"Never. My big plan is to move to a desert island—with WiFi and electricity, preferably somewhere that gets regular deliveries—and avoid men forever."

"If you can wait until I deliver this bucking, kicking watermelon, I'm coming with you. No men or kids allowed, right?"

"None."

"So you really didn't have sex in his SUV like everyone is saying?"

"What? No! It was the opposite of sex."

"Don't hate me, but he's right about you going back to

school. You gave up everything for fuckface Chaz. Have I mentioned lately that's he's a life support system for a sphincter?"

"Once or twice."

"Next time you're in the mood to burn down a house, call me and we'll go do Chaz's. We'll snatch Chunky and run."

"Deal."

"Love you." She blew me a kiss, I blew one back, and we ended our call.

What galled me was that Luke was right. Where did he get off giving me excellent advice?

I rolled over in the couch's pillows. I'd been awake since insane-o-clock, and Hypnos, the Greek god of sleep, was stalking me. Possibly literally. Anything was possible.

Except not for me. Not really. Not now that Daedalus had given me the figurative axe. Losing jobs before wasn't that big a deal, except for the financial hit and the friendships formed. The work itself was always meh; drudgery I had to perform to pay my share of the bills—which was all of them. But this was different. I liked my work at Labyrinth. In time, if I'd survived, I would have loved dodging soldiers and avoiding transformations into various farm animals. Even the birds could be survivable, if I carried a Super Soaker.

Sleep dropped over me, warm and heavy. I sank down into its cozy arms.

Then I woke up in a freak show.

CHAPTER 19

"Good job, Morpheus." The voice was male, deep in the way that the Mariana Trench was deep and also terrifying to people who aren't James Cameron. "Let's rough her up a bit for fun."

Wait, what?

My consciousness surfaced. Or maybe it was my unconsciousness doing the heavy lifting. Whichever it was, I became aware that I was no longer in my apartment on the top floor of Mom and Dad's house. Color flickered around me, a constantly shifting kaleidoscope that stopped, one element at a time. Great—I was stuck in a Vegas slot machine.

First came the mountain, the nearby cave, the passel of scantily clad youthful men dancing around a marble fire pit. The sky was full of crows—or ravens, maybe. It was hard to tell without any of them going "Nevermore!" Perched around me were a slew of creatures that didn't make sense. Too many heads. Too many eyes. A disturbing overabundance of arms. Perfect for a career in envelope stuffing.

And then there was the owner of the voice. He was

human-sized, but he gave off the aura of a bulging piece of luggage. Picture a skyscraper stuffed and crammed into a buff, solid body and then sat on so someone could get the zipper. He wore short shorts and his hair was cut in a shag. With the addition of a *Magnum P.I.* mustache, he was obviously a casualty of the 1980s.

The other guy—Morpheus, perhaps?—was a clippy cloppy demon dude with huge wings and the face of an abstract painting. I couldn't focus on any one feature because the whole mess kept swirling.

"First of all," I said, "nobody is roughing me up. Second of all ..." I screamed until my lungs ran out of air. Then I screamed some more in case the first scream hadn't registered.

Mr. 1980s raised his caterpillar-esque brows. "Feel better?"

"No."

"Okay. So down to business then."

I held up a hand. Or what was supposed to be my hand. When I raised the appendage, it was a chicken drumstick.

"Sorry about that," Morpheus said in a voice like a nail grinder. "Hazard of the dream experience, I'm afraid. Your real arms are just fine on your couch, I promise."

"What does the rest of me look like?"

Both men winced. At least I think Morpheus winced. It was hard to say with all the abstract face going on.

"Moving on," the other guy said. "This isn't about you, it's about me."

"It usually is," Morpheus said. Both men laughed.

One of the youths dancing around the fire stopped. He looked exhausted and sweaty.

"Keep dancing!" Mr. 1980s boomed.

"Can't ... tired ... my feet ..."

The guy who wasn't Morpheus waved a hand that looked like it could crush brazil nuts without straining. A lightning bolt shot out of the sky and zapped the exhausted dancer out of existence.

Although I was terrified, I found myself rolling my eyes.

"You're Zeus," I said.

He looked delighted. "You've heard of me!"

I held up one of my chicken drumsticks. "Little bit. You golden-coin showered me the other day."

"Then you know what I want."

The scenery shifted into something new. Everything beneath us dissolved. Now we were on a cloud. My hands had claws and an unnatural amount of hair, even for a half-Greek woman.

"Love, stability, and a gallon of ice cream?"

He threw back his head. Everything shook. Then, like whiplash, he stopped. "No."

"A hint would be nice."

Morpheus folded his arms and wings. "Rhymes with schmanymede," he muttered out of the corner of his mouths.

"Ganymede?" I said. "You want Ganymede?"

"I have nobody to pour my nectar," Zeus lamented. "Do you know how difficult it is to be me right now?"

"Can't you pour it yourself?"

His head tilted. He stared at me like I'd suggested eating out of a truck stop toilet in the backwaters of Idaho. "Huh?"

I demonstrated filling a cup as best as I could with these claws.

He shook his head slightly. "I don't understand. Pour my own nectar? Then why do I have servants that I have manipulated and be-spelled into doing my biding?"

"I really want to wake up," I muttered.

"Not yet," Morpheus said.

"Daddy needs his cupbearer," Zeus said. "Find him."

"Uh, no?"

His face purpled. Sparks shot out of his fingertips.

"Ruh-roh," Morpheus said. "Bad answer. It's not too late to change it."

"This is just a dream, right? If he zaps dream me, I'll be fine in the real world."

Palm down, Morpheus rocked his hand side to side. "Eh ..."

"Look," I said, appealing to the mythological dad of the gods and all-around pervert. "I don't work for Daedalus anymore. He fired me. I'm off the payroll. As soon as I wake up from this nap I have to start looking for a new job—one that pays. I have a cat to support."

He stared at me.

"And an ex-husband with mommy issues."

"Oooh," they both said like they knew.

"So I can't just run around Salem looking for a gorgeous and strangely androgynous cupbearer who loves to dance but who apparently sucks at it."

Zeus peered over the cloud. "Nice house you live in. The lions are an attractive, homey touch. Be a shame if somegod happened to it."

I gulped. "Are you threatening my family?"

"Yes. Maybe I will spare your mother, though, because she has a good *kolos*."

He had me. Nothing mattered more to me than my family. The last thing I wanted was for them to fry, just because Zeus was having to pour his own drinks.

What a giant, spoiled man-baby, by the way. He and Chaz could compete for World's Biggest Infant together.

"What's in it for me?"

"Your family gets to live."

"Okay ..."

He rubbed his hands together. Sparks flew. "Great!"

"But I need help. I couldn't find him before. Any ideas where I should look?"

Zeus scratched his shag 'do. "Ganymede enjoys two things: music and serving my drinks."

"I was hoping for a little more specificity."

"He enjoys taking it up the—"

"Don't finish that. Never finish that."

"The music," Morpheus said quickly. "He loves *C+C Music Factory*. Play it and he might come."

"I know he makes me come," Zeus said.

"For crying out loud," I said. "Somebody wake me up."

Morpheus snapped his fingers.

My face was stuck to a pillow with a serious amount of my own saliva. The good news was that my hands were hands again. No claws. No chicken drumsticks. The bad news was that now Zeus himself expected me to find his honeybun and cupbearer

Yikes. What if Hera found out I was working for Zeus? Although was it really working if I wasn't getting paid? Yes, technically he was going to pay me in "not killing my family," but that didn't cover my costs of living. It wasn't taxable, spendable income.

Better work fast. The sooner I found and returned Ganymede, the sooner I'd be out from under Zeus's sketchy thumb.

I unstuck my face and went to perform a hasty cleanup with the help of the bathroom mirror.

Yikes. Not only was my face caked with dried spit, but my mascara had radiated outwards from my lashes. I looked like I'd slept with the whole band. I got to work with makeup remover until I was presentable again. I threw on some lip gloss, then immediately tied my hair up in a sock bun because I didn't want to spent the next however long peeling hair off my lips. Outside was a dry sauna, so I scrounged up gym shorts and a t-shirt in an attempt to beat the heat.

"Looks like someone threw Jell-O at your mouth and you forgot to catch it," Grandpa said when I stopped by the main house to make sure Zeus hadn't jumped the gun and smote my family. Everyone was alive, even my father, who was spending Sunday passed out on the couch.

"Virgin Mary!" Mom said.

Grandpa looked at us one at a time. "What? Am I right or am I right?"

Yiayia jabbed him with her crochet hook. "*Se hezo,*" she said in Greek.

"Don't know what that means, but it sounds good," Grandpa said.

My grandmother jabbed him again. "It means I shit on you."

Grandpa inched sideways. "Not my style, you old bag."

"Job hunting already?" Mom asked, her eye twitching.

"Atta girl," Grandpa said. "Get right back on the horse. Tug on those bootstraps good and hard."

I patted my pockets and purse again to make sure I had everything. "Less job, more hunting."

The mention of hunting lit Grandpa up. "I know everything there is to know about hunting. What's your prey? Deer? Something bigger? I know where you can get gallons of urine if you need it."

"He keeps it in his underpants," Yiayia said.

I kissed everyone goodbye and set out to find the missing cupbearer. Morpheus's advice ringing in my ears, I cobbled together a *C+C Music Factory* playlist. They were from before my time, but undeniably catchy. I had no idea where I was going, only that I was going there. With the windows down, blasting pop music, I cruised up the highway to Woodburn and back again, this time cutting through Keizer.

If I couldn't find Ganymede, maybe he'd find me.

Hopefully.

Otherwise I'd have to pull another plan out of my butt, and my butt wasn't used to being a plan receptacle. All it really knew was sitting and walking and the occasional squats. Giving up was unthinkable. Zeus would fry my whole family, and possibly enslave my mom, probably tricking her into his god-cave by pretending to be a cake. We Post women were easily bought with excellent baked goods.

I cruised through the main streets of Salem for a couple of hours, music blaring.

Where was he?

With the windows down, I pulled off to the side to check local online groups. Surely someone had seen a pretty man dancing badly in almost no clothes. This was a town where people sat at their windows with their phones, reporting everyone else for engaging in suspicious behaviors like walking.

Nothing about loincloths or men wearing them.

I got a potential lead when someone mentioned a naked dancer in a nearby supermarket. Apparently the police had suggested he exit the premises and find some clothes, mostly in case of sunburn. Nobody wanted a sun-scorched sausage. Public nudity was perfectly fine in this neck of the woods, provided onlookers weren't openly "enjoying" the view in a physical way. Because Ganymede was irresistible to all who gazed upon him, I couldn't imagine the local police were too popular right now. The man was a snack.

I drove to the supermarket and scouted the area with *C+C Music Factory* singing about a variety of sketchy activities that make a person go "Hmm ..."

Nothing. No sign of Ganymede or his absent duds.

Huh. So maybe that's what Sibyl meant about the lost loincloth. But what did it mean, other than he was prowling around my city, bare ass naked?

If Nikki was right, I was searching for meaning in a pile of gibberish.

Sibyl had mentioned birds, though. They weren't what they seemed.

Suddenly my passenger door flew open. Ganymede threw himself in beside me. "Drive," he said, panting.

"What?" Despite trying not to let my gaze drop, it fell like a rock to his crotch. Ganymede was sporting a massive bush and not much else. Huh. So the statues weren't entirely inaccurate. They'd just had more pruning. "Sorry," I said, dragging my gaze up. "What are we doing?"

"I want to go back," he said. "There are soldiers looking for me!"

Alarm crackled through me. "What soldiers? Trojans?"

"No—soldiers from your world. They wear dark blue clothes all over their body. Tight and restrictive. How can they fight and love in those strange clothes?"

The police. He meant the police. "I don't think they do a lot of loving in those clothes. Mostly they keep order." I pulled out of the parking lot. "What happened?"

"I followed the music, just like I followed the music just now and found you."

"What happened to your, uh, clothes?"

"Some metal birds took them. Does it bother you?"

"No."

"Because everyone is naked under their clothes."

"Yes, I'm aware of this." I headed east, back to the scene of my firing. My goal was to stay in the parking lot and make sure Ganymede went inside, then I'd leave. Hopefully he and Zeus would be reunited and I'd be off the hook. "I've been looking for you since you came back. My father said he dropped you off at Riverside Park. I went there and—" Waves of nausea crashed against me as I remembered the slaughtered half-gorgons.

He touched my arm. My skin tingled. "What is it?"

"When I went looking for you, I stumbled across a crime scene. Some women were murdered."

"Is that bad?"

"Yes, it's bad! Maybe murder is a way of life where you're from, but here it's a crime. They were from your world, you know. The women."

"Those of us who come from mythology are accustomed to such things. All I know are callous gods and their vicious emissaries. Such things are games in my world."

"Well, not here. Not unless you're a psychopath." I pulled into the strip mall and parked outside the Thai restaurant. "Zeus wants you back. He had Morpheus hijack my dream. If he doesn't get a drink refill soon, he's going to destroy my house, kill my family, and molest my mother after pretending to be a cake."

"Then I had better go." He lifted my hand and kissed the palm. Heat rippled up my arm. He was so dreamy. "I am sorry about the dead half-gorgons. Perhaps they will return."

Clouds were amassing overhead. This time they were real, not scores of robot birds. They triggered a memory.

"Wait—you said your outfit was stolen by birds?"

"Daedalus's automatons. Spiteful creatures. Perhaps they did not care for my dancing. Or perhaps they wanted to see me naked." He winked and got out of my car, tight buns flexing as he padded toward the Labyrinth Agency's storefront. The door open and he vanished.

I waited until the storm clouds faded, leaving clear skies in their place. Everything was normal again.

Zeus got his refill. My family was safe.

I didn't leave. Not at first. Something felt ... *off*. Like the situation had a splinter stuck under its skin. I twisted the pieces around, hoping to dislodge the foreign body. At that point, I'd be flooded with enlightenment.

Nope. No pop. No blinding, revelatory light.

When the sun clawed its way further west, leaving dust and dehydration in its path for yet another day, I started the engine and headed south, toward home. My family were all cloistered inside, chilling in the air conditioner's fake climate. I jogged upstairs, brain still gnawing on whatever was bothering it. Yes, I was jobless—again—but I'd saved my family. A sane person would be content with that.

Right?

My gaze was pulled towards that spot on the lawn again where Ivy had dug her hole. I felt a tingle of terror. Had she been attacked elsewhere and dragged herself here to hide? Or had her assailant followed her here? Or—worst possible scenario—what if her attacker was here all along? A lump of fear formed in my throat. Cold tendrils radiated outwards. I glanced over my shoulder. There was nobody around, except our next door neighbor, Carol. I waved. She waved back and kept on watering her plants.

If there was a boogeyman lying in wait, I couldn't see them. And yet my imagination had seized the reins and was off and running, imagining bushes filled with eyes, and creatures to go with those eyes. Or one horrifying creature. Which was worse, I wasn't sure. Rationality wasn't exactly my thing right now. Not after today.

I fumbled with my keys, dropping them twice. Finally I managed to get the house key in the lock.

The door was already unlocked.

My heart stopped. Time stood still. Someone was in my place. Or they had been. Both options were equally hair-raising. At this exact moment I could sense every patch I'd missed while shaving.

I poked around in my handbag and found the pepper spray. If only I'd been brave enough—or dumb enough—to take Grandpa's gun with me instead of separating it from its ammo and hiding the parts. In the other hand, I held the dagger-sword in what I hoped was a menacing and useful grip.

I nudged the door with my toe. It swung open and into Luke Remis's face.

He yelped.

"Sorry, sorry, sorry. Wait—not sorry."

"I was coming to get the door for you," he said, clutching his face. "I heard you pull up."

"Are you crazy? I could have stabbed you!"

"With that? Doubt it."

"Size doesn't matter."

He smirked. "Put your nail file away. Come help me cook."

"You cook?"

"How else is a single guy supposed to eat?"

"Why are you cooking in my kitchen?"

"Mine burned down."

Guilt settled around my shoulders like a weighted blanket. That didn't stop me from popping off at the mouth. "Ever hear of a drive-thru, Remis?"

"Cut me some slack." He returned to the kitchen. "My grandmother served *revithia* for lunch."

I made a face. When we were kids we'd shared a common hatred for the popular Greek chickpea soup. I couldn't fault the man for not wanting to eat his grandmother's slop, although I was certain he'd eaten two servings to keep her happy anyway. It was that or hear about the time he didn't appreciate her cooking forever and ever, until one of them died. And Luke was, at heart, a Good Greek Boy. Whatever he was making, it was a palate cleanser.

"Okay." I put my battle gear away and dropped everything on the entry stand. "What are we having?" I called out.

"Pizza."

Okay, that didn't suck.

I went to change clothes. My gaze snagged on my bathroom door which was now one solid piece. No splinters. No hole.

"You fixed my door," I called out.

"You're welcome," Luke said. "I wouldn't replace a door for just anyone."

How was I supposed to feel about that? On an empty stomach, I was undecided.

In my kitchen, there was definitely a pizza in progress. A lump of dough was rising in the mixer and Luke was busy chopping ingredients—ingredients he must have bought—

into piles. Olives, ham, salami, chunks of real mozzarella, not the shreds, peppers, mushrooms, onions.

I perused the ingredients while I washed my hands. "Is there ..."

He presented me with a can of pineapple. "Of course."

"You remembered."

"That you're a freak who loves fruit on her pizza?" He grinned in a thoroughly devastating and therefore completely inappropriate way that stirred old, cold coals. "How could I forget?"

"Pineapple on pizza creates the perfect harmony of sweetness and salt. Like salted caramel."

He shook his head, laughing softly.

"Fine." I grabbed a second chopping board and knife and got to work slicing onions. We worked together seamlessly until the dough was ready and Luke stretched it out on the peel. He decorated my side with loads of ham, pineapple, and thick slices of fresh mozzarella.

"I think I'm going to build an outdoor pizza oven," he said after he slid the whole shebang onto the hot stone.

"Shouldn't you build a house first?"

Luke busted out laughing. His laughing triggered mine. We stood in my kitchen, holding onto the counter, wheezing and tearing from the insanity of it all.

"A Trojan Horse burned your house down," I said through the guffaws.

"You set the horse on fire," he managed.

"With your grill lighter fluid."

"And now I don't have a house."

The laughter ran out. We slumped against the counter, waiting in a companionable silence for the pizza to bubble and puff.

"Where have you been all afternoon?" he said casually. "I figured you'd be here, hunting for a new job."

"Working for Zeus. He had Morpheus hijack my nap dream so he could threaten my family and be a dick. Does he really get the ladies, men, and non-humanoid creatures with that bad hair and 80s porn-stache?"

"Wait—Zeus abducted you?"

"Just dream me. My body was on the couch. Why?"

"What did he want?"

"Ganymede. Apparently he needed a refill and he was pissed his servant wasn't around to pour his god cola. He figured threatening to kill my family and turn my mom into a weird sex slave was great incentive. He was right."

"You found Ganymede?"

"He caused a kerfuffle dancing naked in a supermarket, but yeah, I found him and returned him to his kooky, over-bearing lord and master."

Luke checked the pizza. He lined up plates, shoved the peel back into the oven, and pulled out a pizza lover's dream, all puffy golden crust and oozing cheese. "Get the drinks?"

I opened the fridge to discover Luke had stocked that, too. He'd bought beer and a couple of bottles of wine— retsina and mavrodaphne. The later was on the counter. After today's gut-wrenching shenanigans, I needed a hit of piney retsina, so I poured two glasses of chilled wine and took both to the table. The table, I might add, that Luke had already set. Not in a romantic, presumptuous candlelit way, but in the simple and casual "we eat together all the time" way, which was somehow worse.

Luke carried our plates to the table.

"I've got a proposition for you," he said.

"No, I won't have sex with you. Again."

"I wasn't offering."

"Good, because I wasn't going to accept. Now let me eat this pizza in peace."

We ate in silence for the first few minutes. The retsina tasted like licking the inside of a pine barrel, but I appreciated the way it turned my muscles to warm liquid. It was like getting a top notch massage from the inside.

"Okay," I said. "What do you want?"

He set down his slice and leaned back. "The whole Minotaur thing was a ruse, which we both know. Minos is after his daughter, and he knows I know where they are, so he plans to do whatever it takes to get their location out of me. Which I won't do. But what I can do is call his bluff."

"How?"

"King Minos hired a myth agent to catch the Minotaur's killer. If I give him that assassin, he has no choice but to sit up, shut up, and accept it. Otherwise he risks destroying the treaty between our worlds."

"I don't get it."

"Sending bounty hunters and assassins to our world from the other side is strictly against the treaty. That's what the agency is for. We bring back anyone who is unauthorized to be here so they can be dealt with in their own world. Minos only got a pass because he claimed the Minotaur snuck in without his permission. He never said the Minotaur was here to abduct or kill Ariadne in the first place. He'll lose face and risk war if give him the Minotaur's assassin and he sends someone else to get me."

"What about the Trojans and the horse?"

"He claimed they were here for a training mission."

"And the killer robot birds? Who is responsible for those?"

He sipped his wine before answering. "Don't know. Don't like that I don't know."

"Where do I come into this, given that we're no longer coworkers."

"If this works, the boss will get over his hissy fit. He usually does. Do you know how many times he's fired me? About a dozen."

"And if it doesn't work—whatever *it* is."

He raised his glass. "Then we'll all be dead: you, me, Ariadne, Stella. But it'll work."

I threw my hands up at the ceiling. "What? What will work?"

Big grin. "I need you to be bait."

CHAPTER 20

BEING bait sounded like the opposite of safe and fun, and I told Luke so.

"Sugar buns, none of us are going to be safe until this is over, and this is the only way to put a stop to King Minos's current tantrum."

"Current?" Sounded ominous. Current suggested past—and worse—future tantrums. Dealing with more of Minos's murderous mythological flunkies at a later date wasn't my idea of security.

However, Luke was onto something and he knew it. I wanted back in the Labyrinth Agency fold. The money was spectacular and the work was heart-racing. Not only could I pay Chaz regular cat support, but if I scraped together enough cash I could hire a lawyer—a good one this time—and get Chunky back. And I could see about reenrolling in college.

This was the best way forward.

If I survived.

"Tell me your oh-so-brilliant plan where I'm probably going end up dead."

He served us more pizza, while I refilled the wine. Way too harmonious and normal for my comfort. Chaz had expected me to wait on him the way "mommy" did.

Luke bit the end off the triangle slice. He dropped the remainder on the plate.

"I'm going to put the word out that the Minotaur's murder didn't stick and that it was last seen at The Bread Basket."

Ariadne's bakery. "That's it?"

"You'll be there pretending to be her."

"And Stella?"

"There will be *a* Stella."

"You're going to put a child in harm's way?"

"Trust me."

"The last time a man told me to trust him it was—oh wait, it was you! You fed me that bullshit story about being chained to a rock for six months, and you came back with a spectacular tan and a snake tattoo."

He winced. "That was the job. I couldn't exactly tell you the whole truth. What would you have done if I'd said, 'Hey, baby, I got chained to a rock and had my liver pecked out every day for six months because I pissed off the wrong god.'"

"Zeus chained you to the rock like Prometheus?"

"Technically he put our rocks next to each other. Asclepius gave me the tattoo to cover up the scar afterwards. He does that with scarring. Sort of his trademark."

"I figured it was some trashy ho in Juarez."

"No trashy ho in Juarez." A wicked light flashed in his deep, dark eyes. "Just you."

I kicked him under the table. "Well, I didn't trust you then and I don't trust you now, but I'll go along with this flimsy and bound-to-fail plan. King Minos strikes me as a lunatic psychopath, but you don't get to be king and stay that way unless you've got some smarts."

Luke laughed. "Lady, have you even met kings?"

"Not lately. Or ever."

"Kings get to be kings through bloodlines and bloodshed. Neither of those takes a functioning brain. Minos is cunning, but he's a brick. Because people have been blowing smoke up his ass his whole life, he's under the illusion that he's brilliant. He's not. He's just another asshole who managed to fail upwards. This will work."

Confidence, thy name is Luke Remis. He made me want to believe, but experience and a flaming wooden horse in my recent past made me twitchy.

"Okay, fine. But if I get killed, I'm going to make sure everyone knows it's your fault."

"Deal."

Luke strolled in at 6:00 A.M. with a Walmart bag and two coffees from Dutch Bros. He looked mildly disappointed that he didn't have to drag me out of bed. The joke was on him; I'd spent the night tossing and turning, fretting about Morpheus hijacking my dreams again. Finally, I'd abandoned the idea of sleep and schlepped out to the living room to tackle the pile of books Luke had insisted I check out from the library. I was nose-deep in Percy Jackson when he dropped the bag on the couch.

"How do you keep getting in?"

"I'm magic, baby."

I raised an eyebrow at him.

"Key."

"Where did you get a key?"

"John."

Ugh. Of course. I should have known my brother ponied up the keys to his bachelor pad, way back before he went legit as a human being.

I held my hand out. "Gimme."

Luke laughed. "Forget it, cupcake. The key is mine. Besides, you never know when I might have to save your hide."

"My hide is fine."

"Yeah, I remember."

"Don't talk like you know about my hide."

"Cupcake, my memory is long and detail-oriented. I remember every blemish. The freckle on your ass. The tramp stamp of a marching band—"

"What? That wasn't me!"

"Huh." He rubbed his chin. "Must have mixed you up with someone else."

I glared at him like a Greek woman of a certain age, the one where they're over all the bullshit. He laughed and chucked the bag at me.

"Get dressed. Bakery life starts early."

———

A lot of work went into being Ariadne. For starters, I needed to start dieting months ago and return to my childhood for growth boosters. Neither of those cities could be built in a fifteen minute window, so I did the best with my alternate resources. Luke had brought me a wig and some of Ariadne's clothes. From the waist up I was doing okay. From the waist down I improvised with my own long, flowing skirt and platform wedges that boosted me from shrimp to prawn. I faked her perfect, glowing skin with mineral powdered foundation, and piled on the kohl liner. There. That would have to do.

"Good enough," Luke said.

"What about the fake Stella?"

"Meeting us there."

The plan was simple. I would take over running the bakery as Ariadne, while Luke hid out of sight, waiting for the Minotaur's assassin to show up.

"Wait—how do you know it'll be the one that killed the man-bull?"

He booped me on the nose. "You'll see.

That sounded ominous.

To add another layer of authenticity to the deception, Luke had commandeered Ariadne's Mercedes. He had me drive the car to work and park in her usual spot.

The Stella lookalike was waiting for us inside. He looked nothing like Ariadne's cheerful daughter. His wig was lopsided for starters, and he had a five o'clock shadow.

I pulled Luke aside. "What the heck?"

"That's Geranos—"

"Call me Gerry," the little guy called out.

"He's a pygmy."

"From here or there?"

"Mythology," Luke said. "Watch out for birds. Like all of his kind, Gerry hates them."

"Especially cranes," Gerry said. "They're our mortal enemies. Fucking long-legged shit-heads. There's no trusting anything with legs that long. Did you know that harridan Hera turned our queen into a crane?"

"Hera turned me into a goat," I told him.

We fist-bumped in solidarity.

"Hera also turned Luke into something but he won't say what," I told Gerry.

Luke shoved his hands in the pockets of his black cargo pants. He looked distinctly uncomfortable.

"I'll be close by," he said.

"Wait," I said. "I still don't understand—"

On the far side of the back door, something bellowed. My gut turned to liquidy, goopy lava. My heart made noises about getting the hell out of Dodge.

"It's okay," Luke said. He opened the rear door that lead to the outside.

I'd only seen the Minotaur captured on video and as a corpse in Daedalus's lab. Both had hinted at its size—huge —but neither prepared me for the walking, snorting Minotaur that paused at the door and performed a crouch and twist to maneuver through the door way.

"Are you crazy?" I hissed at Luke.

"Relax," he said.

"Not helping!"

"He's on our side, aren't you, man?"

Huh? My body and nerves didn't care about the reassurances rolling out of Luke's mouth. If anything, my body was sure Luke Remis had lost his mind.

"It's okay," the Minotaur said, his voice low and steeped in futility. "I'm used to it. Everyone thinks I'm the big bad bull in a china shop because I'm so, well, big. But really I'm just like everyone else, except I'm a bull on top. I like eating people, grass, collecting apples, and dancing—dancing is my life. Nobody wants to dance with me though. Every time I pull out my sweet moves, they mistake it for fighting."

Was it just me or was the Minotaur ... depressed?

"I've seen you dance," I said. "You were pretty good."

That perked him up a bit. "Really? Thanks."

Luke leaned on the counter. His forearms flexed. I refused to make eye contact with those, tan, alluring muscles. Bad things happened when I did. Naked, sweaty things. "Minotaur is on our side."

Color me confused. "Wait—I thought he was the bad guy."

"Everybody assumes that," the man-bull said glumly. "And it used to be true, until I discovered healthier outlets for my frustration. I know, you're probably wondering what a guy like me has to be frustrated about. Shirts. It's shirts. You just can't get one in my size. Even at home they don't make chitons big enough to cover all this. It's the head hole," he lowed. "It's too small."

"Have you tried ponchos?" I said, trying to be helpful.

"Ponchos?"

"If we survive this, I'll teach you about ponchos."

Luke looked at us all in turn. "Minotaur was originally sent here by King Minos to find Ariadne and drag her back home to the palace, or kill her if she refused to comply. But Minos didn't count on the siblings reconnecting and teaming up to protect her and her daughter. So we think he sent someone else here to take out the Minotaur. We're going to get that person."

"His own son," the Minotaur said. "Can you believe it?"

Sadly, I also lived in a world where parents were occasionally monsters, so I had no trouble believing that King Minos was a shitty father. Probably a textbook narcissist, too.

"King Minos is a prick," Gerry said. "Most of Zeus's kids are assholes. And his wife. That crazy crane-loving *mouni*."

The Minotaur wasn't the bad guy at all. Not now, anyway. A thought popped into my head.

"The two people the manager at BOGO burger saw with you, was that Ariadne and Stella?"

The Minotaur snorted hot bull breath over us. "My sister

heard I was in town, so she found me before I ate any more people. Once she started talking about our father and what a *malakas* he is, I saw the light. No more people-eating. Not people here in your world, anyway." His damp, brown eyes blinked at us. "They're so delicious, like potato chips. I can't quit completely."

"They were there at Waterfront Park with you, too, weren't they?" I asked.

He bowed his head in what I assumed was a nod. "We were sightseeing. Where I come from, we believe the earth is flat. My sister wanted to show me it's round, like a human head. A delicious human head. They went back to the car because my sister forgot her phone. While they were gone, one of Minos's assassins killed me. But I came back. I always do. This one"—he slung his huge head toward Luke— "tells me I can help my sister and, as he put it, stick it to our father."

Luke's gaze met mine. He shrugged.

"So I'm bait, he's bait, and he's bait." I pointed at everyone at except Luke. "And you're not bait." This time I pointed to Luke.

Not-bait said, "I'll be watching and listening."

"Bug?"

"In the wig."

Luke bailed and left us to the bread-selling. The Minotaur sat at a small table and even smaller chair in the corner. Miraculously, it didn't collapse. The cabinets were filled with bread. According to Luke, Ariadne had spent the night baking and he'd filled the shop before swinging by my place. The stage was set. All we needed to do was sell bread and wait for the murders to begin.

Or, preferably not. Hopefully Luke would arrive on the scene in time and save us all.

Luke had put the word out that Ariadne was back in town and slinging bread, along with her daughter and half-brother, the Minotaur. He was relying on the Greek mythology grapevine to perform the heavy lifting. If it was anything like the regular Greek community, the assassin was already sharpening his or her blades, ready to chop off heads.

Because I'd put in my fair share of time being paid peanuts and getting yelled at in retail, selling bread while pretending to be the boss was a breeze. The Minotaur did a lot of sighing and bellowing in the corner, talking about his woes. Every so often someone wanted to pose with him for a selfie. Occasionally a song came on the radio and he'd leave the chair to bust a few moves.

I tried not to gawk because my mother had raised me better than that. Something that size shouldn't be able to shimmy and shake like a *Solid Gold* dancer. When I mentioned it to Gerry, he laughed.

"Everything in your world is constrained by rules. Laws of physics, laws of nature, an absence of magic. When was the last time anyone in your world was turned into a crane?"

"Never?"

"Exactly." Gerry pointed a baguette at me. "Rules. That's why I like it here. All the rules."

The day slid by without incident. Nobody came to kill us. At knock-off time, I locked up the shop, pocketed the key until tomorrow, and said goodbye to my new pals. The sun was on its way down. Full dark would be here soon.

"Anyone need a ride?"

"I'm good," Gerry said. "I sleep at the park down the street when I'm in town. It's close to the shops."

My eyes cut to the Minotaur. He blinked at me. My eyes

swung to the car. The Mercedes was roomy but it wasn't man-bull generous in the size department.

"It's fine," he said, head hanging to chest level. "It's fine. I'll just bunk down at a farm. Plenty of good grass around here. The lady cows are friendly, too."

Given that Woodburn was surrounded by farmland, I figured he was right.

I climbed into Ariadne's Mercedes and started the engine. Pop music blasted from the sound system. Because I'd been marinating in sound and music all day, I switched it off and took off toward home, merging with traffic on I-5. After hours of waiting to be attacked, adrenalin was coursing through my body, giving me jitters that wouldn't quit. I didn't want to go home—not yet. Which was how I wound up in the parking lot outside the Labyrinth Agency. Windows shut. Lights off.

What I was waiting for, I wasn't sure.

My phone rang.

Luke said, "What are you doing?"

"Taking a detour before I go home."

"You okay?"

"Peachy."

I ended the call before he could get chummy. The door was opening. Ivy stepped through, hoodie up, glasses on, even though the temperature hadn't started to fall yet. Relief coursed through me.

I jumped out. "Ivy?"

She jerked to a stop, looking shocked to see me. I remembered the disguise and yanked the wig off.

"It's me. Penny."

The muscles at the side of her eyes tightened. "What are you doing here?"

"I came to check on you. How are you?"

"What do you care?"

Wow, okay. Someone was salty. "Well, excuse me. I figured since you dug a hole in my yard to hide in, I should at least make sure you're doing okay. Especially since the last time I saw you you were bleeding blue blood all over Asclepius."

She shuffled side to side. "I got to get out of here. You should, too. It's not safe."

I gestured at Ariadne's wheels. "You need a ride? A place to stay? Somewhere to dig another hole? The harpies filled in the last one, but there's a spot in the corner you can have."

"You best take those clothes off, return that car, and go home. You don't know what you're messing with."

"Who was it, Ivy? Who hurt you? Who killed the others?"

She shook her head. Under the hood, things moved. Snakes, probably. "Nuh-uh. I'm not saying anything."

"I can help you if you do. We can catch them."

"You think anyone is gonna care about a half-gorgon? We're not even the real, full-blooded deal. We're useless in our world. Not even a prize worth killing. A real gorgon's head is worth something in a battle, a kill a hero can be proud of and use to intimidate their enemies. You think I'm going scare anything with these?"

She drew back her hoodie.

Ivy's hair wasn't all that freaky. The parts that were hair —most of it—were a pretty strawberry blonde. The wiggly green snakes were more like highlights.

"Aww, they're adorable!"

Not the right answer, judging from the way she hoisted up the hood and marched out of the parking lot, hands in her pockets.

"I'm sorry!" I called out.

She flipped me off with both hands. Very human of her.

I returned to Ariadne's Mercedes, but before I could yank the door open, something stayed my hand. I'd purposely turned off the radio earlier. Now it was on—low but definitely pumping out pop music. Reaching for a weapon was out of the question; my bag was on the passenger seat.

I stepped back.

The driver's side door swung open, revealing Ganymede, who had found his loincloth, thank the Virgin Mary.

"Come in! The music is delightful!"

Relieved that I wasn't about to be beheaded by some music-loving kook from mythology—or Salem—I angled behind the steering wheel. Ganymede tilted his head at me.

"What?"

"You don't look like you," he said.

I wagged a finger at him. "Has someone been a bad, bad cupbearer again?"

He leaned his head against the headrest. "I can't take it anymore. 'Ganymede, bring my nectar.' 'Gaymede, tickle my balls with your tongue.' 'Ganymede, Hera is coming, so now you're a pig.'"

"That does sound annoying."

He threw up his hands. "That's what I said. So I'm back again, for however long that lasts. Do you think" —his eyelashes fluttered— "I could sleep at your accommodations for now?"

I had a second bedroom that was currently functioning as a home office for a job I didn't have. But I was hopeful. And I did have a spare bed. Actually, it was my old childhood bed that Mom and Dad were storing because Mom turned my old bedroom into a craft room. I couldn't really see Ganymede bunking down on my old princess bed.

"You can have my couch for a couple of nights," I said. What about Zeus? Would he come after my family again?

He took my hand and kissed the palm. "I would be forever in your debt."

A shiver of revulsion started in my throat and rolled down through my body. What was that about? Up until now, even the sight of Ganymede had my heart turning to thoughts of springtime and fornication.

"You know what—"

"Please," he said.

Threads of fear spooled around my guts. "Now that I think about it, the couch might already be spoken for. But there's plenty of motels around town. I could find you—"

In an instant, the cupbearer's face transitioned from pretty to cruel. His hand shot out, grabbed a chunk of my hair. "Where is she?"

The world slowed down, or at least it felt that way. My breaths were loud, my heartbeat frantic. Outside, a storm was barging toward Salem, banging its drums and throwing bolts. Weird for July when rain was a couple of months away.

Zeus. Furious that his man-toy was missing—again. And his storm was coming right for me.

"Who?"

"King Minos's bitch daughter."

"Can you not use that word? It's super misogynistic."

I winced as he shook me by the hair. Tears leaked out of my eyes. Part pain, part fear. But there was another part of me that was calmly taking notes and plotting. That part of me remembered that Luke had bugged my wig. Hopefully he was still tuning in and on his way here.

"Why do you care where she is?"

"Are you that stupid?"

"Let's assume yes."

Sheet lightning lit up the parking lot. Thunder rolled, so close and so loud my insides shook.

"Because I'm going to kill her, but the dumb bitch is hiding from me because you people keep helping her!"

"I don't know where she is!"

"You lie."

"No, really, I don't know!"

"You have her car and her clothes and her hair." He banged my head against the headrest. My fingers felt around for my bag but he'd shoved it into the footwell. Reaching it from here was impossible. I couldn't even kick him from this position.

"I don't work for Labyrinth anymore. You're asking the wrong person."

His fingers tightened in my hair. "Are you scared?"

Terrified. Probably I was going to die at the hands of a mythological figure. "Yes."

"Good. I like you like this. The fear makes you smell good. It's not every day I get to touch a woman."

"That's the bread and perfume, asshole."

He slapped me. My head bounced off the headrest. Blazing heat spread across my face. My ear alternated ringing with a stabbing sensation.

I struggled but his grip was too strong. He wasn't a mortal with a mortal's limited strength. I saw my life spiraling the toilet bowl. As in that moment, I experienced a burst of clarity. The Minotaur's murder. His assassin was an androgynous figure in what appeared to be a nude bodysuit. What if that wasn't a bodysuit? Ganymede was the right height, right build. He was comfortable with nudity. And murder, apparently.

I took a not-so-wild leap of logic. "So you're going to kill her like you did the Minotaur?"

"And those snake *putanas*. They live on that corner, they saw me with the Minotaur." He laughed. The sound was slightly crazy, and covered in cold, rancid oil. "They tried to freeze me, but I'm not stupid. I pickpocketed tiny mirrors in the park and wore them on my face."

Mirrored sunglasses. If I survived this, I'd remember that tip.

It came back to me, what had felt wrong last night when I dropped Ganymede here. I never mentioned the half-gorgons. Only that some women had been killed. He was the one that had named them.

"You know what makes me laugh?" Ganymede asked.

"Wigs on cats?"

"Your father drove me to murder them. He even tried to kiss me when he dropped me off at the park. Everyone wants a piece of Ganymede."

"Did King Minos hire you?"

His face reddened. How I'd ever thought him attractive was a mystery. He was ten tons of malice and insanity shoved into a hundred and thirty pound bag.

"Minos? Ha! Minos is as foolish as a sack of satyr heads. He sent the Minotaur to find Ariadne and bring her home. I followed the Minotaur right to her and killed the Minotaur before one of your agents intervened and sent me home. I would have killed her, too, if the snakes hadn't helped her escape." His red face was up close to mine. His sweet-sour breath wafted over me. "Do you know how I wound up pouring nectar and bending over for Zeus?"

"Zeus gave your father a bunch of horses in exchange for your service?"

"There were no horses!" he screamed in my face. Flecks of spit everywhere. "Zeus took me. He saw something he liked and he took it so he could use it. Yes, he made me immortal, but what is immortality if it is your destiny to serve and never be free? You think I want to pour Zeus's nectar and take his cock forever? So I decided to run away. I came to your world. And every time I came here, your agents took me back because Zeus made them."

"There are treaties ..."

"I shit on the treaties! They let people stay all the time. Minos's daughter for one. Why does she get to stay? I hate Zeus and what he has done to me. All I wanted as a boy was to tend to my sheep and find a nice woman to settle down with and have a few men on the side—maybe fellow shepherds. Now instead I live a life of vengeance, making trouble for Zeus's children the way he did for my father. If I kill Minos's brat—Zeus's granddaughter—Minos will seek his own vengeance and break the treaties. Zeus will be furious at him, and I will be pouring his nectar the way I alway do, laughing to myself. For once, I have the power."

He opened his mouth again, then suddenly the passenger side door flew open. Luke was there, his face mottled with fury. He dragged Ganymede out of the Mercedes and out onto the wet pavement. I scrambled out of the car as lightning continued to slash and claw at the darkness.

Luke didn't need my help. He wrestled Ganymede to the ground, slapped handcuffs around his wrists, then he dragged the psycho cupbearer toward Labyrinth's door, loincloth and all.

"Get the door," Luke called out to me.

It took me a second to realize he meant Labyrinth's door. My brain spat out the correct answer and my muscles leaped into gear. I hurried past them and yanked on the door, praying it was unlocked.

Fortune favored the soaking wet and desperate.

Luke hauled Ganymede through, kicking and screaming. Just as we stepped inside, a giant crack of lightning struck the sidewalk, leaving a smoking crater in its wake.

"Oh my God, Virgin Mary!" I yelped.

"Next door," Luke said.

I dodged the flailing cupbearer to open the interior door that led to the corridor. Figuring Luke would also need me to get the door at the end of the corridor, I held that one open for him, too.

He nodded once. "Go home."

The door closed behind them.

CHAPTER 21

THE STORM DIED IMMEDIATELY. As I eased back into Ariadne's car, my whole body shaking, the sky was already showing signs of stars. By the time I parked in the street outside my parents' house, there was no sign that a woman-frying storm had ever put the city in jeopardy. Lights were on. Trees were fine. Streets and lawns were sodden—but hey, we needed the rain.

The adrenalin had worn off. Ganymede was the bad guy, and now the Minotaur, Ariadne, and Stella were all safe. Even Zeus was happy that he had his favorite captive back. None of it sat right with me, though. Ganymede was a murderer, but he was also a victim of Zeus and the world in which they existed. The cupbearer was right, no one should be forced into slavery, sexual or otherwise.

I kicked off the platform shoes and carried them in my hand.

"Where are your shoes?" Yiayia called out from the porch.

I held up my hands.

She grunted. "Put them back on or people will think we are poor."

"I am poor," I told her.

It was nearly eleven o'clock when I dropped my bag on the coffee table and dumped my shoes and wig on my bedroom floor. I peeled off Ariadne's blouse and my flowing skirt, and tossed both into the dirty laundry before wrapping myself in my summer robe. It was black satin and skimmed my thighs, and made me feel like a bit of a ho. Tonight I didn't want to feel like no ho. I swapped out the satin for my cozy winter robe and kicked the A/C up a notch so I didn't sweat in the fuzzy fabric.

Luke had bought two bottles of wine to dinner last night. We'd finished the retsina but the mavrodaphne sat untouched on the counter. I popped the cork and poured a glass. The sweet red wine doubled as dessert.

My feelings for Luke tied themselves in knots. We had a complicated history, preceded by a simple history, and followed by no history. We hadn't been part of each other's lives for years. Circumstances had thrown us together this week, and I wasn't sure what to make of it. One thing was certain, I was glad he'd showed up to save me from Ganymede.

I left the light on in the kitchen and made my way to the bathroom with my wineglass in hand. A day like today called for something gentler than a shower. I sat on the edge of the tub and poured Mr. Bubble under the faucet—original bubble gum scent, because at heart I was still a kid. I lit candles, a gift from Lena. One called *Not Today, Satan*. The other, *Just Pooping*.

While the tub was filling up with bubbles, I went back to the living room for a book. After wine, bath, and a good story, I'd be relaxed in no time. Greek mythology would be a weird, distant memory. Tomorrow—Tuesday—I'd get up and do what I did best: search for a new job. Yes, Luke had mentioned that Daedalus would be falling all over himself to reinstate me, but I didn't believe it. What would he want with an agent who couldn't subdue one homicidal cupbearer? Luke was the only reason I was scanning my bookshelves, trying to find the perfect comfort read instead of dead in the parking lot outside the Labyrinth Agency. I possessed no real survival skills of my own.

I selected an old favorite—*The Other Boleyn Girl*—and carried it back to the bathroom with me. My hands were on the robe's belt when the hairs on the back of my neck stood up. I shuddered. Someone had just marched over my grave.

Something was wrong.

Slowly, quietly, I set aside the book and turned off the faucet. I tightened my robe as though it were armor that would protect me from a home intruder. I glanced around for a weapon.

Hairspray. Heavy hold. Strong enough to grip hair in a windstorm and freeze flies in their tracks. If someone was there, maybe I could temporarily blind them and make a getaway.

Wait. What was I thinking? Was I thinking? My family was downstairs. All I had to do ...

Nothing. That's what I could do.

The bathroom window was small and placed where there was no balcony or overhang to catch me. It would be a long but fast fall down into Mom's rosebushes. Best case scenario, I'd break a lot of bones and still be in traction come Christmas. I could scream, but by the time help came it would be too late.

"Where is she?"

Slowly, hairspray in hand, I turned. The voice—male,

harsh, pompous—emanated from the shadows pooling in my hallway. The kitchen light was the only other light in the house, and neither it nor the flicking candle light touched the hall.

"Get out. I'm armed."

The shadow moved. "Armed with what? Not your wits, surely. From what I can discern, you have none."

"I do, too," I said.

(If I survived, the perfect comeback would pop into my head at a random moment, years from now.)

"Where is my daughter? I know you know her. Do not deny it. I saw you earlier, dressed in her garb." He spat. On my floor. Gross. "As if *you* could be a princess of Crete."

Fear radiated through me. My intestines turned watery. "Minos."

"*King* Minos, you peasant."

"We don't have kings in this country. Not sure about peasants. The traditional farming kind don't really exist here. Mostly we have the uncouth, mouth-breathing peasants."

Like King Minos. He might consider himself royalty, seeing as how he did have a four-letter title stuck in front of his name, but his manners were low class and sinking by the second.

"Such insolence, and from a woman. Were we in my world, I would send you into the labyrinth and let my Minotaur maul you."

"The Minotaur? Big half-man, half-bull? Loves to dance? Has problems with finding shirts to fit, but may be in the market for a nice poncho with a stretchy neckline? We're practically pals."

Minos—king—emerged from the shadows. Not exactly what I expected given the myriad tales of his abuse of power and general assholish behavior. In my mind I'd pictured a bear of a man. Real life Minos was a skinny-fat shrimp, probably from enjoying a lifetime of pandering servants, who made sure he never had to wipe his own backside. His beard was made of soft, dark ringlets that merged at some point with his hair. His eyes were angry and his nose was the kind of triangle that gave Pythagoras a happy feeling in his underpants. King Minos's eyebrows were violent slashes that dipped toward his nose. He wore a chiton that left one bony shoulder bare. The other side was fastened with a set of gold teeth. He held a dagger in one hand. A mean looking thing with squiggly sides. Probably there was name for that style. The word *kris* came to mind, but I wasn't confident that was Greek.

"I know Daedalus," he said. "Did he tell you that?"

"He might have mentioned it."

"The labyrinth is *mine*. It belongs to *me*. He was only its architect. He built it for me so I could hide that bull bastard away from the eyes of the world, hoping everyone would forget—"

"That you made sweet monkey love to a cow? It's okay. Studies have shown that about forty to fifty percent of males in rural communities have had relations with at least one farm animal."

"It was one time! One, okay? Anyway, it doesn't change that fact that Daedalus betrayed me—and used my own daughter to do so! Do you know what will happen if our treaties fail?"

"No. Also, I don't work for Daedalus anymore. Didn't anybody tell you that part?"

He wafted his dagger hand through the air as if dismissing a fart.

"If the treaties fail, Daedalus will have no choice but to

shutter the labyrinth. Our worlds will no longer be connected. All our citizens will be forced to return home."

"Including Ariadne," I said.

"And the labyrinth will be returned to me. The fastest way to violate the treaty is an assassination of an ordinary citizen from your world." He may have grinned an evil grin, but it was lost in all that Scarlet O'Hara beard hair he had going on. "Since you are here and I am here, let us get this done."

I took a step backward. There was nowhere to go except the tub. He advanced on me with the wiggly-sided dagger. That was bound to make a mess. At least we were in the bathroom. Easier to get blood out of tile than wood floors.

"Wait!" I held up one hand, not caring that I was insulting him in Greek. Maybe the *moutsa* didn't go back that far, historically speaking. Not that his feelings were a priority. "How did you get through the labyrinth without tripping Daedalus's security."

"You forget: *he* built the labyrinth for *me.* I know plenty of its secrets, its hidden entrances and exits. New ones form and vanish all the time. My labyrinth is a living organism."

"Aren't entrances and exits the same thing?"

"You know nothing."

"I know doors generally work both ways."

"Not in my dungeons."

Maybe it was like a supermarket that way.

I gulped. The hard, cold lump in my throat refused to budge. "So this is all about breaking the treaty so you get your labyrinth back and your daughter home?"

"Nothing matters to Greeks more than family."

"What about Ganymede?"

"What about that little *pousti*?"

"He killed the Minotaur to get back at Zeus—"

His eyes rolled up at the ceiling. "He has been trying to do that forever. When it is not me, it is one of Zeus's other children."

"I'm not saying he has a point, but he kind of has a point. Zeus shouldn't have abducted him and forced him to be a servant slash—"

"Catamite?"

"Have you tried being someone your daughter wants to spend time with? Be a nice father, maybe she'll come visit."

"She betrayed me!"

"By helping out a cute guy who happened to be a hero? Big deal. Women—especially young women—make those kinds of mistakes all the time. Can't you just be glad she was trying to be a nice, helpful person?"

"Theseus killed my Minotaur!"

"And your Minotaur came back from the dead like it always does in your crazy, fictional and yet weirdly real world where not much makes sense."

"Ariadne made a mockery of me! All the other worlds associate my name with that one story. What of my accomplishments? My world bows down to King Minos, son of Zeus. They bring tributes from all over to win my favor so that I do not slaughter them. Those are the stories that should be told. I am kind of a big deal."

"But what happens when Zeus discovers you're the reason the treaty is broken? He doesn't strike me as the calmest, most reasonable guy."

He scratched his chin with the dagger's sharp point. "That is a problem. I will figure something out. If I do this right, no one will ever know I was here."

"Won't the body be a giveaway?"

The body. My body.

"I have a plan to make it look as though someone else is

to blame for your death. Do you think a man like me does his own dirty work?"

I shivered. "Who's your flunky this time?"

"Ariadne is not my only child, but she is the most disobedient. All I have to do is crook my finger and her half-brother will come running to do my biding."

The enormity of what he was saying struck me like a city bus. "You mean the Minotaur."

"What is the point of fucking a cow if you cannot reap the benefits of the resulting offspring? He has always been my most malleable child. So eager to please me, and quite insane. He will tear your limbs off your body and suck the marrow from your bones—after he is done with the meat, of course. By then I will be back in my palace, eating grapes from the hand of a virgin. Male or female, I don't care."

So this was it. I was destined to be the Minotaur's dinner, no matter that we'd worked side by side all day. While it was true that the Minotaur was on Team Ariadne, there was no doubt he was depressed and desperate for approval. The man-bull would go along with his father's wishes just for that brief "atta man-bull." And all because Minos was a petty little weasel and a lousy father.

Spots danced in front of my eyes. Each time I blinked, they skittered away and formed new patterns. Small hammers tapped on my temples. I couldn't think straight with my head spinning and the clanking in my skull.

"Don't die before the Minotaur gets here. He likes his meat squirming."

I shook my head. "I just need to sit."

My life flashed before me. Not all of it. The embarrassing bits, mostly. Marrying Chaz after he proposed to me outside the Abercrombie & Fitch at the Washington Square Mall because his mother said women adored public proposals. Farting during story time in my first grade class. I was known as Fart Girl for the rest of the school year. And now this. Some stupid how, I'd come to the bathroom without my phone. I couldn't even yell for help because my family were two solid concrete floors down.

Damn this sturdy, soundproof house and the summertime heat that meant windows were closed and air conditioners were drowning ambient noise.

With watery legs, I sat on the edge of the tub and tried to breathe. I didn't want to die. I had to act, even if I failed. At least I'd die trying, right? Right.

Minos moved into the bathroom. He knew I was weak and pathetically mortal. But so was he. He could die. Yes, he'd be back. But he could still die. The way I saw it, he was smaller than me. It was just the title of king that made him seem bigger.

I refreshed my grip on the hairspray. I bowed my head.

"Hey, Minos?"

"King, you nothing of a woman."

I mumbled, "Who does your hair, weirdo?"

"Eh?" He moved closer.

I lunged forward, pressing down on the hairspray's button. Spray misted out of the nozzle at high velocity, directly into his eyes.

Minos screeched. He threw his body forward, dagger swinging wildly. The vicious edge caught me as I ducked under his arm. Liquid gushed down my neck, blazing hot. I made a gurgling sounds. Heat leeched out of my body as it registered that he'd stabbed me. All that moisture was blood. For something that was supposed to be inside me, it sure was making a quick getaway.

If I folded now, I was done for.

Well, screw that guy. I didn't give a rat's ass if he was king of his world—if I was going to exit stage left, I was taking him out with me. Kick and screaming, preferably.

Driven by fury, desperation, and an abundance of spite, I wheeled around so that I was facing him again. He was slashing and poking at the air, temporarily blinded by the spray.

I rushed at him.

He staggered backwards. His mouth made an O of surprise, partially obscured by his curly face locks. The tub's lip struck his shins. His knees buckled. He fell backwards, creating his own personal sized tsunami.

I didn't want to do it, but I did it anyway because it was me or him. I jumped on King Minos and held him under. He rose up. I pushed.

"Oh, *kaka*," he said. "Not again."

I held him there until he quit kicking, snot bubbling down my chin, tears rolling down my face. The pain in my neck was hot like the coals when Dad was grilling lamb on a spit.

My bubbles turned pink, the color of gum.

Minos's hair and beard floated to the surface as I faded out.

CHAPTER 22

"She's awake," Rod the snake said. He was eyeballing my head, probably comparing it to the size of his mouth, wondering if he could make me fit.

Asclepius showed up in my field of vision next. "The Minotaur got to you just in time."

For the next few minutes, the god of medicine and his talking snake retold the tale of my rescue. The Minotaur, summoned by Minos, arrived to do his loony dad's bidding and discovered me bleeding out in the tub and called for Asclepius. King Minos was consumed by the harpies, who'd complained that a king should taste better. Ultimately the king returned to the primordial mythology goop, from which he'd eventually emerge to rule Crete again.

I worried about that. What if he came back for revenge?

Wouldn't happen, Asclepius assured me. (Did I feel assured? I did not.) He had spoken to his dad, Apollo, and Apollo was going to speak with his dad, Zeus, and Zeus would ensure Minos couldn't jeopardize the treaty between our worlds again.

Rod made me tell the part where I drowned Minos

several times, each time cackling harder than the last. ("That's how he always gets it!" he said. "Someone always drowns him. Ya gotta love fate!")

Ganymede had also confessed to his spate of spite murders. Zeus apparently issued his cupbearer a ticket to Tartarus. Asclepius said he'd probably be out in about a hundred years on good behavior. If there was one thing Ganymede was good at it was sucking up to people and non-people.

Daedalus reinstated me without bothering to dispense the good news himself. He had Nikki swing by and have me sign paperwork that granted me cool things like health insurance and a 401k. Reinstatement came with a new assignment. A cynocephaly—dog-headed being—was stuck at a local pet shelter, caught by an overzealous do-gooder. My job was to apply to adopt the cynocephaly. If that didn't work out, I was to bust them out, method at my discretion. Nikki also saw to it that I got paid for the Minotaur case and Ganymede's adventures in Salem. Plus a bonus because Daedalus admitted to sending the robot birds after me. He'd wanted to scare me away from the agency. Apparently I was supposed to feel better because the birds wouldn't have harmed me permanently. The money helped win my forgiveness.

My coffers were filling up. The knots that lived in my shoulders untied some. If this kept up, soon I'd be able to fight Chaz for custody of Chunky. My little snookums would no longer be subjected to the cat shows he despised.

King Minos's wavy-edged dagger left no visible signs of damage except for a small and delicate tattoo of a green snake where the blade bit me. ("Like it? I did it myself," Rod told me.) Whatever magic Asclepius possessed, it extended to healing mortal women in this world. *If* we were in my world. My understanding of the labyrinth and the space it occupied was iffy at best. But at least I could go home to my family without them panicking that my new job might kill me.

Nikki walked with me back to the office. "Your ride is waiting."

"I didn't call for one, did I?"

"There was a volunteer."

My first and only thought was "Please let it be someone human with an actual driver's license."

"Sibyl's prophecy wasn't completely wrong," I told Nikki. "Minos is a dick. There were birds. Ganymede lost his loin-cloth, thanks to those birds. I'd give her a three out of five figs."

"Tell her next time you see her."

"You mean she'll be back?"

"For sure. She shows up regularly. It's the 1980s reruns that keep her interested in our world."

I pushed my way outside. Luke Remis was leaning against the grill of a gleaming new Jeep. The man looked good, and from the way he was grinning, I knew he was aware he gave great exterior. His arms were folded. His legs crossed at the ankle. Between now and the last time I'd seen him, earlier this evening, dragging Ganymede into the labyrinth, he had showered, shaved, and found clean clothes. The same outfit he'd adopted at fourteen: faded jeans, white t-shirt, leather jacket. Borderline irresistible.

Yet here I was, resisting. My self-control impressed the heck out of me.

"You."

"Get in," Luke said.

"Not gonna offer me candy first?"

"There's a Snickers in the console."

"Really?"

"Only one way to find out."

Okay, he had me. I couldn't turn down a free ride/Snickers combo.

When he realized I was on the verge of acquiescing, he pushed away from the Jeep and opened the passenger door. He raised his eyebrows at me.

I climbed in and glanced in the backseat to make sure no crazed mythological figures were playing stowaway. The backseat was empty, except for Luke's laptop and duffel bag.

The Jeep listed slightly as he angled into the driver's seat.

My head tilted toward his luggage. "Going somewhere?"

"Not sure if you remember, but I don't have a house right now."

"Doesn't your grandmother have a spare room that she keeps as a shrine to your awesomeness?"

"You think I'm awesome, huh?"

"I think you better pony up that Snickers bar."

He popped open the console and handed over the candy. Because I was experiencing a burst of benevolence, I snapped it in half and presented him with his very own piece. We ate in silence until the chocolate vanished.

"Yeah, she does," he admitted. "But I don't want to stay with her." He grimaced. "She treats me like I'm still a kid."

"You'll always be her Loukaki. Ickle bickle, little Luke."

His grimace devolved into a wince. He started up the Jeep. The air-conditioned air perked me up, although physically I already felt spectacular. It was as if Asclepius had given me a tune-up as part of the package. I could only blame the night's trauma and my lucky comeback for the insanity that popped out of my mouth next.

"As it just so happens, I've got a spare room. The bed is a princess bed, but you *are* a pretty princess."

He flashed me a grin. "You asking me to live with you?"

"No—I'm giving you a place to stay temporarily, until you make other arrangements and/or your house is inhabitable again."

"You feeling guilty?"

"Little bit."

"You did burn down my house."

"Technically the horse did it."

He reached over and took my hand in his. "You could have been killed."

"I'm pretty spry. I set the horse on fire and ran."

"Talking about Minos, cupcake. I was busy dealing with Ganymede, otherwise I would have been there."

"It's okay."

Luke curled his arm around my shoulders and pulled us close until our foreheads touched. "Why did we stop being friends?"

"Because I got boobs, then later we started boning. Then you lied to me, and then you flipped out at my wedding." He went to speak. I shushed him. "Okay, yes, I realize now that you weren't lying about the rock, but deep down inside, I'm still that person who believed you lied. The me that knows you were telling the truth is a new layer, over the old suspicious ones. I'm an onion, same as Shrek. I'm not saying we can't be friends again. But it's going to take time. Let me grow a couple more layers."

"I can deal with that."

He pulled away and backed out of the parking slot. Traffic was light. Once or twice he dodged a homeless person who decided it was safe to sit on the curb with their legs stuck straight in the street.

"What happened with Ganymede?"

"It wasn't pretty," Luke said. "I took him back to his boss."

"I can't help feeling sorry for him, in a way. What Zeus did to him was monstrous."

"They're not like us, the gods. They might be part of a pantheon, but they don't have a pantheon of feelings. They're bad at guilt and nuance. Zeus saw something he wanted and took it. He doesn't know or care that it was wrong. But Ganymede had options, too."

"To kill or not to kill," I said.

"Yeah. He chose to perpetuate the misery instead of ending the cycle. Zeus cast him into Tartarus. Could be a bad idea. The place isn't nearly as secure as it sounds. And it's a good place for evil to gather allies."

"What about Ariadne and Stella? Are they okay?"

"Safe. Ariadne will be back to running the bakery tomorrow. The Minotaur is staying with them for a while. Daedalus gave them the okay."

Somehow, knowing a giant man-bull beast was watching over the king's daughter and granddaughter made me feel better.

Luke pulled up outside my parents' house. One of these days, I'd move out and find my own place, but not tonight. Tonight this was home, despite the fact that King Minos had tried to murder me here.

Yiayia and Grandpa were on the porch, sniping at each other. They stopped to gawk at us as we trudged up the driveway.

Grandpa gave Luke an I-own-all-the-guns eyebrow raise. "You two been on a date?"

"Work thing," I said. "So don't get excited. Shouldn't you be asleep? It's the middle of the night."

"Still waiting on the prune juice to kick in," Grandpa said. "Can't speak for the old bat.

Yiayia didn't pony up an excuse for being up this late. Instead, she crossed herself. She squinted at me. Then she pivoted and rushed into the house, arms flapping.

"*Panayia*, *Christos*, and *Theos*! Come and see! Penny got a tattoo!"

Obviously this was dire enough that she had to wake my parents. Now I'd never hear the end of it.

The tiny snake on my neck triggered a memory. "Do you have any other snakes besides that one over your liver?" I asked Luke.

That coaxed a smirk out of him. He leaned forward until his body heat mingled with mine. "A few. Want to know where?"

"Nope. I'm assessing the damage level of my new job."

"And?"

"In the past five seconds I just set a new career goal."

Mom bustled out in her nightgown. "A tattoo!" she cried. "Now nobody will marry you! Again." Her discerning gaze zeroed in on Luke.

He shrugged. "Penny wouldn't have me."

Mom gave me *the* look. "Penny is a *kolopetha*."

I was not a butt child, thank you very much. Anyway, everyone knew that butt sex was a lousy way to get pregnant.

"Luke is staying in my spare room for a while," I announced, eager to shift the conversation away from marriage, tattoos, and my inability to be a Good Greek Girl.

Mom gave him the pointed index finger. "You sleep in your room, yes?"

"Of course," Luke said.

She glared at us both in Greek mother, crossed herself, and hurried back into the house.

We headed around the side to the stairs that led to the second and third floors. Inside her place, Yiayia was turning lights off. I could hear the hum of her television as she played an old episode of *Greece's Top Hoplite*.

"What's the new career goal?"

"I'll tell you if you tell me."

"Tell you what?"

"What did Hera turn you into?"

The smile sprawled across his face, lazy and slow. "Cupcake, you'll never know."

Thank you so much for reading the first book in the **PENNY POST** series. I'm quite fond of the characters, so you'll be seeing them again soon.

Want to be notified when my next book is released? Sign up for my mailing list: http://eepurl.com/ZSeuL. Or like my Facebook page at: https://www.facebook.com/alexkingbooks.

All my best,

Alex A. King

ALSO BY ALEX A. KING

GLOSSARY

Ade (ah-thay): An expression of pleasure or anger. A bit like "c'mon" or "go on".

Ade gamisou (*a-they ga-mee-soo*): Go make sweet monkey love to yourself.

Ai sto dialo (*eye-sto-thya-lo*): Go to the devil.

A-pah-pah! (a-pa-pa): A sound Greeks make when they disapprove of something.

Archidia (ar-hee-thee-ah): Testicles.

Booboona (boo-boo-nah): A moron.

Despinida (des-pe-nee-tha): Miss. As in "Miss Jackson, if you're nasty."

Faka: (fah-kah): Mousetrap.

Ftero: (Fff-teh-ro): Feather.

Gamo (*ga-mo*): Fuck.

Gamos (ga-moss): A wedding.

Gamo tin putana (ga-mo teen pu-tah-nah): Make sweet monkey love to a woman of purchasable affections.

Gamo ton kerato (ga-mo ton ke-rah-toh): Make sweet monkey love to a horn. Why? I don't know.

Hezo (he-zo): The act of pooping on something.

Hondros (hon-dross): Fat.
   Kaka (ka-ka): Poop

Kalamari (kal-a-ma-ree): Calamari. Squid.

Kalo ste (kah-lo-stay): Welcome! Good to see you!

Katsika (Ka-tsee-kah) : A nanny goat.

Klasimo (Kla-see-mo): A fart

Klania (kla-nee-ah): Also a fart

Kolos (ko-loss): Butt

Kolotripa (ko-lo-tree-pah): The hole in a butt. You know the one. (Hopefully it's just one, otherwise please consult a physician.)

Kota (ko-tah): Hen.

Kotsoboles (kot-so-bo-lez): Gossip

Koulouraki (koo-loo-ra-kee): a Greek cookie. Harder and slightly less sweet than its American and British counterparts.

Koumbara/koumbaros (koom-bah-rah/koom-bah-ross):

Kyria (kee-ree-ah): Mrs. A married woman.

Kyrios (kee-ree-oss): A man, married or not.

Lambada (lam-ba-tha): A long, skinny, decorative candle used at midnight service on Easter Saturday.

Loukaniko (loo-kah-nee-koh): Sausage.

Loukoumada (loo-koo-mah-tha): Fried balls of dough, drowning in syrup.

Maimou: (my-moo): Monkey.

Malakas (mah-lah-kas): A person who touches themselves so much that their brain turns to mush. Can be an insult or a term of endearment.

Malakies (mah-lah-kee-ez): Nonsense or bullshit.

Malakismeni (mah-lah-kiz-men-ee): Crazy from an excess of masturbation.

Mana mou (mah-nah moo): My mother. Or rather, mother my.

Mati (Ma-tee): An eye. Could be the evil eye, could be a regular eye.

Mezedes (meh-zeh-thes): Appetizers.

Mouni (moo-knee): Vagina, pussy, twat.

Mounoskeela - (moo-knee-skee-lah): Vagina bitch. It really loses something in translation.

Moutsa (moot-sa): An obscene hand gesture. Open palm, facing someone. Can mean that they're a *malakas*, or that you're rubbing poop in their face.

Nanos (Nah-nos): A derogatory term for little person/dwarf.

Ouro (ou-row): Pee.

Panayia mou (pah-nah-yee-ah moo): My Virgin Mary. Or rather, Virgin Mary my.

Papou (pah-poo): Grandfather

Parakalo (pa-ra-ka-low): Doubles as "please" and "you're welcome".

Paralia (pa-ra-lee-ah): The beach or waterfront.
    Periptero (pe-rip-te-ro): A small, boxy newsstand.

Philotimo (fee-lo-tee-mo): A combination of love and generosity towards other. Does not apply if you disagree with their politics or sports.

Po-po (po-po): An exclamation of sorts. A cross between "For crying out loud" and "I can't believe this person is so boneheaded".

Poutsa (put-sa): Penis, wiener, ding-dong, dick.

Propapou (pro-pah-pooh): Great-grandfather.

Proyiayia (pro-ya-ya): Great-grandmother.

Putana (puh-tah-nah): Person who dispenses nookie for a negotiable fee.

Revithia (re-vee-thee-ah): Chickpea soup/stew.

Servietta (ser-vee-eh-tah): Feminine hygiene product.

Skata (ska-tah): Shit.

Skata na fas (ska-tah nah faass): Consume a meal of shit.

Skatoula (ska-too-lah): Little shit.

Skeela (skee-lah): Female dog.

Taverna (ta-ver-nah): A small restaurant that sells Greek food.

Thea (thee-ah): Aunt.

Theo (thee-oh): Uncle.

Tiropita (tee-ro-pee-tah): Cheese pie - typically feta. Can include feta with softer cheese like cottage cheese or ricotta.

Tzatziki (za-zee-kee): A sauce made with yogurt, cucumbers, dill, and all the garlic.

Vaskania (vas-kah-nee-ah): A prayer to remove the evil eye.

Vlakas (vlah-kas): A stupid person

Vre/re: Kind of like "hey, you idiot", but not quite. Informal and can be mildly negative but also indicative of familiarity.

Vromoskeelos (vro-mo-slee-los): Dirty dog.

Vromoskeela (vro-mo-skee-lah): Dirty female dog.

Xematiase (kse-mat-ya-say): Removing the evil eye.

Yiayia (yah-yah): Grandmother.

Yia sas (Ya-sas): Howdy, y'all

Yiftes (yiff-tez): A common derogatory term for the Roma people.

AUTHOR'S NOTE

Traditional Greek naming conventions mean women frequently lose the "s" on the end of their last names, which is why Luke is Luke Remis, while his grandmother uses Remi. It's not me experiencing low blood caffeine, I swear.

Presently, there is a liquor store across the street from Waterfront Park. As far as I know, its owners and staff are perfectly lovely people who would absolutely notice the bodies of mythological creatures piled up in their store. And I'm sure their customers aren't delusional drunk drivers. *Crosses fingers*

The Wicked Sweet Bakery is also real. I have no connection to the establishment except as my daughter's purchaser of donuts. (I'm a massively lame person who can't eat any dairy products.) She tells me they're amazing and I believe her. If you're in the Salem, Oregon area, you should definitely go there.

—Alex

Printed in Great Britain
by Amazon

20032226R10180